DIFFICULT LOVES

BOOKS BY ITALO CALVINO

The Baron in the Trees

The Nonexistent Knight and the Cloven Viscount

Cosmicomics

t zero

The Watcher and Other Stories

Invisible Cities

The Castle of Crossed Destinies

Italian Folktales

If on a winter's night a traveler

Marcovaldo, or The seasons in the city

Difficult Loves

Mr. Palomar

The Uses of Literature

Six Memos for the Next Millennium

Under the Jaguar Sun

Italo Calvino

DIFFICULT LOVES

Translated from the Italian by
WILLIAM WEAVER
and
ARCHIBALD COLQUHOUN and PEGGY WRIGHT

A Harvest Book
A Helen and Kurt Wolff Book
Harcourt Brace & Company
San Diego New York London

This is a translation of *Gli Amori Difficili*

Library of Congress Cataloging-in-Publication Data
Calvino, Italo.
Difficult loves.
Translation of: Gli amori difficili.
"A Helen and Kurt Wolff book."
I. Title.
PQ4809.A45A813 1984 853'.914 84-685
ISBN 0-15-626055-7 (Harvest: pbk.)

Designed by Dalia Hartman
Printed in the United States of America

First Harvest edition 1985

G H I J K

CONTENTS

NOTE

"Riviera Stories," "Wartime Stories," and "Postwar Stories" were written between 1945 and 1949 and collected in the volume *Ultimo viene il corvo* (Turin: Einaudi, 1949). The remaining stories were written during the 1950s and collected in the volume *I racconti* (Turin: Einaudi, 1958).

The stories on pp. 3, 16, 22, 31, 71, 79, 87, 95, 102, 112, 131, 141, 155, and 164 were translated by Archibald Colquhoun and Peggy Wright for the volume *Adam, One Afternoon and Other Stories* (London: Collins, 1957; London: Secker & Warburg, 1983). The remaining stories were translated for the present volume by William Weaver.

RIVIERA STORIES

ADAM, ONE AFTERNOON

THE NEW gardener's boy had long hair kept in place by a piece of cloth tied around his head with a little bow. He was walking along the path with his watering can filled to the brim and his other arm stretched out to balance the load. Slowly, carefully, he watered the nasturtiums as if pouring out coffee and milk, until the earth at the foot of each plant dissolved into a soft black patch; when it was large and moist enough he lifted the watering can and passed on to the next plant. Maria-nunziata was watching him from the kitchen window, and thinking what a nice calm job gardening must be. He was a young man, she noticed, though he still wore shorts and that long hair made him look like a girl. She stopped washing the dishes and tapped on the window.

"Hey, boy," she called.

The gardener's boy raised his head, saw Maria-nunziata, and smiled. She laughed back at him, partly because she had never seen a boy with such long hair and a bow like that on his head. The gardener's boy beckoned to her with one hand, and Maria-nunziata went on laughing at the funny gesture he'd made, and began gesturing back to explain that she had the dishes to wash. But the boy beckoned again, and pointed at the pots of dahlias with his other hand. Why was he pointing at those dahlias? Maria-nunziata opened the window and stuck her head out.

"What's up?" she asked, and began laughing again.

"D'you want to see something nice?"

"What's that?"

"Something nice. Come and see. Quickly."

"Tell me what."

"I'll give it to you. I'll give you something very nice."

"But I've got the dishes to wash, and the signora'll come along and not find me."

"Do you want it or don't you? Come on, now."

"Wait a second," said Maria-nunziata, and shut the window.

When she came out through the kitchen door the gardener's boy was still there, watering the nasturtiums.

"Hello," said Maria-nunziata.

Maria-nunziata seemed taller than she was because of her high-heeled shoes, which were awful to work in, but she loved wearing them. Her little face looked like a child's amid its mass of black curls, and her legs were thin and childlike, too, though her body, under the folds of her apron, was already round and ripe. She was always laughing: either at what others or she herself said.

"Hello," said the gardener's boy. The skin on his face, neck, and chest was dark brown, perhaps because he was always half naked, as now.

"What's your name?" asked Maria-nunziata.

"Libereso," said the gardener's boy.

Maria-nunziata laughed and repeated: "Libereso . . . Libereso . . . what a funny name, Libereso."

"It's a name in Esperanto," he said. "In Esperanto it means 'liberty.' "

"Esperanto," said Maria-nunziata. "Are you Esperanto?"

"Esperanto's a language," explained Libereso. "My father speaks Esperanto."

"I'm Calabrian," exclaimed Maria-nunziata.

"What's your name?"

"Maria-nunziata," she said and laughed.

"Why are you always laughing?"

"Why are you called Esperanto?"

"Not Esperanto, Libereso."

"Why?"

"Why are you called Maria-nunziata?"

"It is the Madonna's name. I'm named after the Madonna, and my brother after Saint Joseph."

"Senjosef?"

Maria-nunziata burst out laughing: "Senjosef! Saint Joseph, not Senjosef, Libereso!"

"My brother," said Libereso, "is named 'Germinal' and my sister 'Omnia.' "

"That nice thing you mentioned," said Maria-nunziata, "show it to me."

"Come on, then," said Libereso. He put down the watering can and took her by the hand.

Maria-nunziata hesitated. "Tell me what it is first."

"You'll see," he said, "but you must promise me to take care of it."

"Will you give it to me?"

'Yes, I'll give it to you." He had led her to a corner of the garden wall. There the dahlias standing in pots were as tall as the two of them.

"It's there."

"What is?"

"Wait."

Maria-nunziata peeped over his shoulder. Libereso bent down to move a pot, lifted another by the wall, and pointed to the ground.

"There," he said.

"What is it?" asked Maria-nunziata. She could not see anything; the corner was in shadow, full of wet leaves and garden mold.

"Look, it's moving," said the boy. Then she saw something that looked like a moving stone or leaf, something wet, with eyes and feet; a toad.

"*Mammamia!*"

Maria-nunziata went skipping away among the dahlias in her high-heeled shoes. Libereso squatted down by the toad and laughed, showing the white teeth in the middle of his brown face.

"Are you frightened? It's only a toad! Why are you frightened?"

"A toad!" gasped Maria-nunziata.

"Of course it's a toad. Come here," said Libereso.

She pointed at it with a trembling finger. "Kill it."

He put out his hands, as if to protect it. "I don't want to It's so nice."

"A nice toad?"

"All toads are nice. They eat the worms."

"Oh!" said Maria-nunziata, but she did not come any nearer. She was chewing the edge of her apron and trying to watch out of the corners of her eyes.

"Look how pretty it is," said Libereso and put a hand on it.

Maria-nunziata approached, no longer laughing, and looked on, open-mouthed. "No! No! Don't touch it!"

With one finger Libereso was stroking the toad's gray-green back, which was covered with slimy warts.

"Are you mad? Don't you know they burn when you touch them, and make your hand swell up?"

The boy showed her his big brown hands, the palms covered with a layer of yellow calluses.

"Oh, it won't hurt me," he said. "And it's so pretty."

Now he'd taken the toad by the scruff of the neck like a cat and put it in the palm of his hand. Maria-nunziata, still chewing the edge of her apron, came nearer and crouched down beside him.

"*Mammamia!*" she exclaimed.

They were both crouching down behind the dahlias, and Maria-nunziata's rosy knees were grazing the brown, scratched ones of Libereso. Libereso cupped his other hand over the back of the toad, and caught it every now and again as it tried to slip out.

"You stroke it, Maria-nunziata," he said.

The girl hid her hands in her apron.

"No," she said firmly.

"What?" he said. "You don't want it?"

Maria-nunziata lowered her eyes, glanced at the toad, and lowered them again quickly.

"No," she said.

"But it's yours. I'm giving it to you."

Maria-nunziata's eyes clouded over. It was sad to refuse a present—no one ever gave her presents—but the toad really did revolt her.

"You can take it home if you like. It'll keep you company."

"No," she said.

Libereso put the toad back on the ground, and it quickly hopped away and squatted under the leaves.

"Good-bye, Libereso."

"Wait a minute."

"But I must go and finish washing the dishes. The signora doesn't like me to come out in the garden."

"Wait. I want to give you something. Something really nice. Come with me."

She began following him along the gravel paths. What a strange boy this Libereso was, with that long hair, and picking up toads in his hands.

"How old are you, Libereso?"

"Fifteen. And you?"

"Fourteen."

"Now, or on your next birthday?"

"On my next birthday. Assumption Day."

"Has that passed yet?"

"What, don't you know when Assumption Day is?" She began laughing.

"No."

"Assumption Day, when there's the procession. Don't you go to the procession?"

"Me? No."

"Back home there are lovely processions. It's not like here, back home. There are big fields full of bergamots, nothing but bergamots, and everyone picks bergamots from morning till night. I've got fourteen brothers and sisters and they all pick bergamots; five died when they were babies, and then my mother got tetanus, and we were in a train for a week to go to Uncle Carmelo's, and eight of us all slept in a garage there. Tell me, why do you have such long hair?"

They had stopped.

"Because it grows like that. You've got long hair, too."

"I'm a girl. If you wear long hair, you're like a girl."

"I'm not like a girl. You don't tell a boy from a girl by the hair."

"Not by the hair?"

"No, not by the hair."

"Why not by the hair?"

"Would you like me to give you something nice?"

"Oh, yes."

Libereso began moving among the arum lilies, budding white trumpets silhouetted against the sky. Libereso looked into each, groped around with two fingers, and then hid something in his fist. Maria-nunziata had not gone into the flower bed, and was watching him, with silent laughter. What was he up to now? When Libereso had looked into all the lilies, he came up to her, holding one hand over the other.

"Open your hands," he said. Maria-nunziata cupped her hands but was afraid to put them under his.

"What have you got in there?"

"Something very nice. You'll see."

"Show me first."

Libereso opened his hands and let her look inside. His palm was full of multicolored rose chafers, red and black and even purple ones, but the green were the prettiest. They were buzzing and slithering over one another and waving little black legs in the air. Maria-nunziata hid her hands under her apron.

"Here," said Libereso. "Don't you like them?"

"Yes," said Maria-nunziata uncertainly, still keeping her hands under her apron.

"When you hold them tight they tickle; would you like to feel?"

Maria-nunziata held out her hands timidly, and Libereso poured a cascade of rose chafers of every color into them.

"Don't be frightened; they won't bite you."

"*Mammamia!*" It hadn't occurred to her that they might bite her. She opened her hands and the rose chafers spread their wings and the beautiful colors vanished and there was nothing to be seen but a swarm of black insects flying about and settling.

"What a pity. I try to give you a present and you don't want it."

"I must go wash the dishes. The signora will be cross if she can't find me."

"Don't you want a present?"

"What are you going to give me now?"

"Come and see."

He took her hand again and led her through the flower beds.

"I must get back to the kitchen soon, Libereso. There's a chicken to pluck, too."

"Pooh!"

"Why pooh?"

"We don't eat the flesh of dead birds or animals."

"Why, are you always in Lent?"

"What do you mean?"

"Well, what do you eat, then?"

"Oh, all sorts of things, artichokes, lettuce, tomatoes. My father doesn't like us to eat the flesh of dead animals. Or coffee or sugar, either."

"What d'you do with your sugar ration, then?"

"Sell it on the black market."

They had reached some climbing plants, starred all over with red flowers.

"What lovely flowers," said Maria-nunziata. "D'you ever pick them?"

"What for?"

"To take to the Madonna. Flowers are for the Madonna."

"Mesembryanthemum."

"What's that?"

"This plant's called Mesembryanthemum in Latin. All flowers have Latin names."

"The Mass is in Latin, too."

'I wouldn't know about that."

Libereso was now peering closely between the winding branches on the wall.

"There it is," he said.

"What is?"

It was a lizard, green with black markings, basking in the sun.

"I'll catch it."

"No."

But he inched toward the lizard, very slowly, with both hands open; a jump, and he'd caught it. He laughed happily, showing his white teeth. "Look out, it's escaping!" First a stunned-looking head, then a tail, slithered out between his closed fingers. Maria-nunziata was laughing, too, but every time she saw the lizard she skipped back and pulled her skirt tight about her knees.

"So you really don't want me to give you anything at all?" said Libereso, rather sadly, and very carefully he put the lizard back on the wall; off it shot. Maria-nunziata kept her eyes lowered.

"Come on," said Libereso, and took her hand again.

"I'd like to have a lipstick and paint my lips red on Sundays to go out dancing. And a black veil to put on my head afterward for Benediction."

"On Sundays," said Libereso, "I go out to the woods with my brother, and we fill two sacks with pine cones. Then, in the evening, my father reads out loud from Kropotkin. My father has hair down to his shoulders and a beard right down to his chest. And he wears shorts in summer and winter. And I do drawings for the Anarchist Federation windows. The figures in top hats are businessmen, those in caps are generals, and those in round hats are priests; then I paint them in water colors."

They came to a pond with round water-lily leaves floating on it.

"Quiet, now," commanded Libereso.

Under the water a frog could be seen swimming up with sharp little strokes of its green legs. It suddenly surfaced, jumped onto a water-lily leaf, and sat down in the middle.

"There," cried Libereso and put out a hand to catch it, but Maria-nunziata let out a cry—"Ugh!"—and the frog jumped back into the water. Libereso began searching for it, his nose almost touching the surface.

"There it is."

He thrust in a hand and pulled it out in his closed fist.

"Two of them together," he cried. "Look. Two of them, on top of each other."

"Why?" asked Maria-nunziata.

"Male and female stuck together," said Libereso. "Look what they're doing." And he tried to put the frogs into Maria-nunziata's hand. Maria-nunziata wasn't sure whether she was frightened because they were frogs, or because they were male and female stuck together.

"Leave them alone," she said. "You mustn't touch them."

"Male and female," repeated Libereso. "They're making tadpoles." A cloud passed over the sun. Suddenly Maria-nunziata began to feel anxious.

"It's late. The signora must be looking for me."

But she did not go. Instead they went on wandering around, though the sun did not come out again. And then he found a snake, a tiny little snake, behind a hedge of bamboo. Libereso wound it around his arm and stroked its head.

"Once I used to train snakes. I had a dozen of them; one was long and yellow, a water snake, but it shed its skin and escaped. Look at this one opening its mouth; look how its tongue is forked. Stroke it—it won't bite."

But Maria-nunziata was frightened of snakes, too. Then they went to the rock pool. First he showed her the fountains and opened all the jets, which pleased her very much. Then he showed her the goldfish. It was a lonely old goldfish, and its scales were already whitening. At last: Maria-nunziata liked the goldfish. Libereso began to move his hands around in the water to catch it; it was very difficult, but when he'd caught it Maria-nunziata could put it in a bowl and keep it in the kitchen. He managed to catch it, but didn't take it out of the water in case it suffocated.

"Put your hands down here; stroke it," said Libereso. "You can feel it breathing; it has fins like paper and scales that prickle. Not much, though."

But Maria-nunziata did not want to stroke the fish, either.

In the petunia bed the earth was very soft, and Libereso dug about with his fingers and pulled out some long, soft worms.

But Maria-nunziata ran away with little shrieks.

"Put your hand here," said Libereso, pointing to the trunk of an old peach tree. Maria-nunziata did not understand why, but she put her hand there; then she screamed and ran to dip it in the pool. For when she had pulled her hand away it was covered with ants. The peach tree was a mass of them, tiny black "Argentine" ants.

"Look," said Libereso and put a hand on the trunk. The ants could be seen crawling over his hand, but he didn't brush them off.

"Why?" asked Maria-nunziata. "Why are you letting yourself get covered with ants?"

His hand was now quite black, and they were crawling up his wrist.

"Take your hand away," moaned Maria-nunziata. "You'll get them all over you."

The ants were crawling up his naked arm, and had already reached his elbow.

Now his whole arm was covered with a veil of moving black dots; they reach his armpit but he did not brush them off.

"Get rid of them, Libereso. Put your arm in water!"

Libereso laughed, while some ants now even crawled from his neck onto his face.

"Libereso! I'll do whatever you like! I'll accept all those presents you gave me."

She threw her arms around his neck and started to brush off the ants.

Smiling his brown-and-white smile, Libereso took his hand away from the tree and began nonchalantly dusting his arm. But he was obviously touched.

"Very well, then, I'll give you a really big present, I've decided. The biggest present I can."

"What's that?"

"A hedgehog."

"*Mammamia!* The signora! The signora's calling me!"

Maria-nunziata had just finished washing the dishes when she heard a pebble beat against the window. Underneath stood Libereso with a large basket.

"Maria-nunziata, let me in. I want to give you a surprise."

"No, you can't come up. What have you got there?"

But at that moment the signora rang the bell, and Maria-nunziata vanished.

When she returned to the kitchen, Libereso was no longer to be seen. Neither inside the kitchen nor underneath the window. Maria-nunziata went up to the sink. Then she saw the surprise

On every plate she had left to dry there was a crouching frog, a snake was coiled up inside a saucepan, there was a soup bowl full of lizards, and slimy snails were making iridescent streaks all over the glasses. In the basin full of water swam the lonely old goldfish.

Maria-nunziata stepped back, but between her feet she saw a great big toad. And behind it were five little toads in a line, taking little hops toward her across the black-and-white-tiled floor.

THE ENCHANTED GARDEN

GIOVANNINO AND Serenella were strolling along the railroad tracks. Below was a scaly sea of somber, clear blue; above, a sky lightly streaked with white clouds. The railroad tracks were shimmering and burning hot. It was fun going along the tracks, there were so many games to play—he balancing on one rail and holding her hand while she walked along on the other, or else both jumping from one sleeper to the next without ever letting their feet touch the stones in between. Giovannino and Serenella had been out looking for crabs, and now they had decided to explore the railroad tracks as far as the tunnel. He liked playing with Serenella, for she did not behave as all the other little girls did, forever getting frightened or bursting into tears at every joke. Whenever Giovannino said, "Let's go there," or "Let's do this," Serenella followed without a word.

Ping! They both gave a start and looked up. A telephone wire had snapped off the top of the pole. It sounded like an iron stork shutting its beak in a hurry. They stood with their noses in the air and watched. What a pity not to have seen it! Now it would never happen again.

"There's a train coming," said Giovannino.

Serenella did not move from the rail. "Where from?" she asked.

Giovannino looked around in a knowledgeable way. He pointed at the black hole of the tunnel, which showed clear one moment, then misty the next, through the invisible heat haze rising from the stony track.

"From there," he said. It was as though they already heard a snort from the darkness of the tunnel, and saw the train suddenly appear, belching out fire and smoke, the wheels mercilessly eating up the rails as it hurtled toward them.

"Where shall we go, Giovannino?"

There were big gray aloes down by the sea, surrounded by dense, impenetrable nettles, while up the hillside ran a rambling hedge with thick leaves but no flowers. There was still no sign of the train; perhaps it was coasting, with the engine cut off, and would jump out at them all of a sudden. But Giovannino had now found an opening in the hedge. "This way," he called.

The fence under the rambling hedge was an old bent rail. At one point it twisted about on the ground like the corner of a sheet of paper. Giovannino had slipped into the hole and already half vanished.

"Give me a hand, Giovannino."

They found themselves in the corner of a garden, on all fours in a flower bed, with their hair full of dry leaves and moss. Everything was quiet; not a leaf was stirring.

"Come on," said Giovannino, and Serenella nodded in reply.

There were big old flesh-colored eucalyptus trees and winding gravel paths. Giovannino and Serenella tiptoed along the paths, taking care not to crunch the gravel. Suppose the owners appeared now?

Everything was so beautiful: sharp bends in the path and high, curling eucalyptus leaves and patches of sky. But there was always the worrying thought that it was not their garden, and that they might be chased away any moment. Yet not a sound could be heard. A flight of chattering sparrows rose from a clump of arbutus at a turn in the path. Then all was silent again. Perhaps it was an abandoned garden?

But the shade of the big trees came to an end, and they found themselves under the open sky facing flower beds filled with neat rows of petunias and convolvulus, and paths and balustrades and rows of box trees. And up at the end of the garden was a large villa with flashing windowpanes and yellow-and-orange curtains.

And it was all quite deserted. The two children crept forward, treading carefully over the gravel: perhaps the windows would suddenly be flung open, and angry ladies and gentlemen appear on the terraces to unleash great dogs down the paths. Now they found a wheelbarrow standing near a ditch. Giovannino picked it up by the handles and began pushing it along: it creaked like a whistle at every turn. Serenella seated herself in it and they moved slowly forward, Giovannino pushing the barrow with her on top, along the flower beds and fountains.

Every now and then Serenella would point to a flower and say in a low voice, "That one," and Giovannino would put the barrow down, pluck it, and give it to her. Soon she had a lovely bouquet.

Eventually the gravel ended and they reached an open space paved in bricks and mortar. In the middle of this space was a big empty rectangle: a swimming pool. They crept up to the edge; it was lined with blue tiles and filled to the brim with clear water. How lovely it would be to swim in!

"Shall we go for a dip?" Giovannino asked Serenella. The idea must have been quite dangerous if he asked her instead of just saying, "In we go!" But the water was so clear and blue, and Serenella was never afraid. She jumped off the barrow and put her bunch of flowers in it. They were already in bathing suits, since they'd been out for crabs before. Giovannino plunged in—not from the diving board, because the splash would have made too much noise, but from the edge of the pool. Down and down he went with his eyes wide open, seeing only the blue from the tiles and his pink hands like goldfish; it was not the same as under the sea, full of shapeless green-black shadows. A pink form appeared above him: Serenella! He took her hand and they swam up to the surface, a bit anxiously. No, there was no one watching them at all. But it was not so nice as they'd thought it would be; they always had that uncomfortable feeling that they had no right to any of this, and might be chased out at any moment.

They scrambled out of the water, and there beside the swimming pool they found a Ping-Pong table. Instantly Giovannino picked up the paddle and hit the ball, and Serenella, on the other side, was quick to return his shot. And so they went on playing, though giving only light taps at the ball, in case someone in the villa heard them. Then Giovannino, in trying to parry a shot that had bounced high, sent the ball sailing away through the air and smack against a gong hanging in a pergola. There was a long, somber boom. The two children crouched down behind a clump of ranunculus. At once two menservants in white coats appeared, carrying big trays; when they had put the trays down on a round table under an orange-and-yellow-striped umbrella, off they went.

Giovannino and Serenella crept up to the table. There was tea, milk, and sponge cake. They had only to sit down and help themselves. They poured out two cups of tea and cut two slices of cake. But somehow they did not feel at all at ease, and sat perched on the edge of their chairs, their knees shaking. And they could not really enjoy the tea and cake, for nothing seemed to have any taste. Everything in the garden was like that: lovely but impossible to enjoy properly, with that worrying feeling inside that they were only there through an odd stroke of luck, and the fear that they'd soon have to give an account of themselves.

Very quietly they tiptoed up to the villa. Between the slits of a Venetian blind they saw a beautiful shady room, with collections of butterflies hanging on the walls. And in the room was a pale little boy. Lucky boy, he must be the owner of this villa and garden. He was stretched out on a chaise longue, turning the pages of a large book filled with figures. He had big white hands and wore pajamas buttoned up to the neck, though it was summer.

As the two children went on peeping through the slits, the pounding of their hearts gradually subsided. Why, the little rich boy seemed to be sitting there and turning the pages and glancing around with more anxiety and worry than their own. Then he got up and tiptoed around, as if he were afraid that at any moment someone would come and turn him out, as if he felt that that book, that chaise longue, and those butterflies framed on the wall, the garden and games and tea trays, the swimming pool and paths, were only granted to him by some enormous mistake, as if he were incapable of enjoying them and felt the bitterness of the mistake as his own fault.

The pale boy was wandering about his shady room furtively, touching with his white fingers the edges of the cases studded with butterflies; then he stopped to listen. The pounding of Giovannino and Serenella's hearts, which had died down, now got harder than ever. Perhaps it was the fear of a spell that hung over this villa and garden and over all these lovely, comfortable things, the residue of some injustice committed long ago.

Clouds darkened the sun. Very quietly Giovannino and Serenella crept away. They went back along the same paths they had come, stepping fast but never at a run. And they went through the hedge again on all fours. Between the aloes they found a path leading down to the small, stony beach, with banks of seaweed along the shore. Then they invented a wonderful new game: a seaweed fight. They threw great handfuls of it in each other's faces till late in the afternoon. And Serenella never once cried.

A GOATHERD AT LUNCHEON

IT WAS, as usual, a mistake of my father's. He had had a boy sent down from a village in the mountains to look after our goats. And the day the boy arrived, my father insisted on asking him to eat with us.

My father does not understand the things that divide people, the difference between a dining room like ours, with its inlaid furniture, dark-patterned carpets, and majolica plates and those homes of theirs, with smoky stone walls, beaten-earth floors, and newspapers black with flies draped over the mantelpieces. My father always goes about among them with that jolly, ceremonious air of his, and if they invite him to eat when he is out shooting, as they all do, he insists on eating off the same dirty dish; then in the evening they all come to him to settle their disputes. We, his own sons, don't take much part, though. Perhaps my brother, with that air of silent complicity he has, may occasionally be given some rough confidence; but I'm too well aware of the difficulties of communication between human beings, and sense at every minute the gulfs that separate the classes, the abysses that politeness opens up under me.

When the boy came in, I was reading the paper. My father began fussing over him. What was the point? He'd only get all the more confused. But he didn't. I raised my eyes and there he was in the middle of the room, with his heavy hands and his chin on his chest, though looking straight ahead of him, stubbornly. He was a goatherd boy of about my own age, with compact, wooden-looking hair and high features—forehead, nose, cheeks. He wore a dark military shirt with its top button straining over his Adam's apple, and a crumpled old suit out of which his big knobbly hands and great boots, lifting slowly on the gleaming floor, seemed to overflow.

"This is my son Quinto," said my father. "He's at high school."

I got up and put on a smile; my outstretched hand met his and we immediately moved apart without looking each other in the face. My father had already begun saying things about me that no one could want to hear—how long I still had at school, how I'd once killed a squirrel when we were out shooting in the area the goatherd came from; and I kept on shrugging my shoulders as if to say, "Me? No, really!" The goatherd stood there mute and still, showing no sign of following; every now and again he gave a quick glance toward one of the walls or curtains, like an animal looking for an opening in a cage.

Then my father changed the subject and began walking around the room talking about certain varieties of vegetables grown up in those valleys. He kept asking the boy questions, while the goatherd, with his chin on his chest and his mouth half shut, kept on saying he did not know. Hidden behind the newspaper, I waited for the food to be served. But my father, having made his guest sit down, brought him a cu-

cumber from the kitchen and began cutting it up in small pieces in his soup plate, for him to eat as an hors d'oeuvre, my father told him.

Now my mother came in, tall, dressed in black with lace trimmings, her smooth white hair rigidly parted. "Ah, here's our little goatherd boy," she said. "Have you had a good trip?" The boy did not get up or reply, but just raised his eyes to my mother in a look full of uncomprehending distrust. I felt wholeheartedly on his side; disapproving of the tone of affectionate superiority my mother was using, I even found myself preferring my father's manner, his rather servile affability, to her aristocratic condescension. And then I hated that possessive *tu* by which my mother addressed the boy; if she'd been using dialect like my father it might have been all right, but she was talking Italian to the poor goatherd, an Italian cold as a marble wall.

To protect him I tried to turn the conversation away from him, so I read aloud an item of news from the paper, something that could only interest my parents, about a vein of mineral ore discovered in a part of Africa where certain friends of ours lived. I had deliberately chosen an item that could have no conceivable connection with our guest and was full of names unknown to him; I did this not to make his isolation weigh on him more, but so as to dig a moat around him, as it were, give him a breathing space, and distract my parents' besieging attentions for a moment. Perhaps he, too, misinterpreted my move. Anyway, it had the opposite effect. My father went rambling on with a story about Africa, confusing the boy with a tangle of strange names of places, peoples, and animals.

Just as the soup was being served, my grandmother appeared in her wheel chair, pushed by my poor sister, Cristina. They had to shout loudly in her ear to tell her what was happening. My mother, indeed, made a formal introduction: "This is Giovannino, who is going to look after our goats. My mother. My daughter, Cristina."

I blushed with shame at hearing him called Giovannino, little Giovannino; how different that name must have sounded in the rough dialect of the mountains; certainly it was the first time he heard himself called it in that way.

My grandmother nodded with matriarchal calm: "Fine, Giovannino, let's hope you don't let any goats escape, eh!" My sister, Cristina, who treats all our rare visitors as people of great distinction, now muttered "Delighted" in a terrified way, half hidden behind the back of the wheel chair, and she held her hand out to the youth, who shook it heavily.

The goatherd was sitting on the edge of his chair, but with his shoulders back and his hands spread on the tablecloth, looking at my grandmother as if fascinated. The old woman was sunk in her big armchair, with mittens half covering bloodless fingers that made vague movements in the air, a tiny face under its network of wrinkles, spectacles turned toward him as she tried to make out some shape in the confused mass of shadows and colors transmitted by her eyes, and spoke an Italian that sounded as if she were reading out of a book. It must all have seemed so different to him from the other old women he had met that perhaps he thought he was face to face with a new species of human being.

My poor sister, Cristina, had not moved from her corner. As usual when she saw a new face, she now advanced into the middle of the room, her hands joined under the little shawl drawn over her deformed shoulders, her head streaked with premature gray, her face marked with the boredom of her reclusive life. Raising her clear eyes toward the windows, she said, "There's a little boat on the sea, I saw it. And two sailors who kept rowing and rowing. And then it passed behind the roof of a house and no one saw it any more."

I wanted our guest to realize my sister's unfortunate state at once, so that he would take no more notice of her. I jumped up and, with a forced animation that was quite out of place, exclaimed, "But how can you have seen men in a boat from our windows? We're too far away."

My sister went on looking out of the window—not at the sea, but at the sky. "Two men in a boat. Rowing and rowing. And there was a flag, too, the tricolor flag."

Then I realized that as the goatherd listened to my sister he did not seem so uneasy and out of place as he seemed to be with the rest of us. Perhaps he had finally found something that came into his experience, a point of contact between our world and his. And I remembered the idiots who are often to be met in mountain villages, who spend their hours sitting on thresholds amid clouds of flies, and sadden the village nights with their wails. Perhaps this family misfortune of ours, which he understood because it was well known to his own people, brought him closer to us than my father's eccentric jollity, the women's maternal and protective airs, and my own awkward detachment.

My brother arrived late as usual, when we already had spoons in our hands. The instant he came in he took in everything at a glance; before my father had explained and introduced him as "My son Marco, who's studying to be a notary," he had already sat down to eat, without blinking an eyelid, without looking at anyone. His cold spectacles were so impenetrable they seemed black, his depressing little beard stood out spruce and stiff. He gave the impression of having greeted everyone and excused himself for being late, and even perhaps of having smiled at the guest, instead of which he had not opened his mouth or wrinkled his smooth forehead with a single line. Now I knew that the goatherd had a powerful ally on his side, an ally who would protect him and make every retreat possible for him in the atmosphere heavy with awkwardness which only he, Marco, knew how to create.

The goatherd was eating, bent over his bowl of soup, slurping it noisily about in his mouth. Now we three males were with him in leaving obvious manners to the women: my father from natural expansive noisiness, my brother from imperious determination, I from ill grace. I was pleased with this new alliance, this rebellion of us four against the women. Certainly the women disapproved of us all at that moment, and avoided saying so only in order not to humiliate the family in front of the guest, and vice versa. But did the goatherd realize this? Definitely not.

My mother now went into the attack, with a very sweet, "And how old are you, Giovannino?"

The number the boy gave rang out like a shout. He repeated it slowly. "What's that?" said our grandmother and repeated it wrongly. "No, this," and everyone began shouting it in her ear. Only my brother was silent. "A year older than Quinto," my mother now discovered; and this had to be repeated all over again to my grandmother. These were the things I could not bear, which shamed me to the bottom of my heart, for my sake and his; this comparing of him and me, he who had to look after goats to make a living and stank of ram and was strong enough to fell an oak, and I who spent my life on a sofa by the radio reading opera librettos, who would soon be going to the university and disliked flannel next to my skin because it made my back prickle. This injustice, these things lacking in me to be him and lacking in him to be me, gave me a sharp feeling of our being, he and I, two incomplete creatures hiding, diffident and ashamed, behind that soup bowl

It was then that our grandmother asked, "And have you already done your military service?" This question was ridiculous; his class had not yet been called, he had scarcely passed his first check-up. "A soldier of the pope," said my father, one of those jokes of his that no one understood and which he had to repeat twice. "They've made me 'returnable,'" said the goatherd. "Oh," said our grandmother, "refused"; and her voice expressed disapproval and regret. Even if he is, I thought, why make so much of it? "No. 'Returnable.'" "And what does that mean, 'returnable'?" This had to be explained. "Soldier of the pope, ha ha! Soldier of the pope," my father laughed. "Oh, I hope you aren't ill," said my mother. "Ill on the day of the medical," said the goatherd, and luckily my grandmother did not hear.

My brother raised his head from his plate then and through his spectacles gave the guest almost a direct glance, a glance of complicity, while his little beard moved slightly at the corners of his lips in a hint of a smile, as if to say, "Let the others be; I understand you and know all about these things." It was with these unexpected signals of complicity that Marco attracted sympathy; from now on the goatherd would always turn to him and answer every question with a glance in his direction. And yet I guessed that at the root of this apparent shy humanity of my brother, Marco, there lay both the servility of our father and the aristocratic superiority of our mother. And I thought that by allying himself with him the goatherd would not be any less alone.

At this point I thought of something to say that might perhaps interest him, and I explained that I had had my military service deferred until the end of my studies. But now I had brought out the tremendous difference between us two: the impossibility of a common link even about things that seemed everyone's fate, like military service.

Just then my sister came out with one of her remarks: "And will you go into the cavalry, sir, excuse me?" This would have passed unobserved if my grandmother had not taken up the subject. "Ah, the cavalry nowadays . . ." The goatherd muttered something about "*alpini.*" We realized, my brother and I, that we had at that moment an ally in our mother, who certainly found this subject silly. But why did she not intervene, then, to change the conversation? Luckily my father had stopped repeating, "Ah, a soldier of the pope," and now asked if mushrooms were growing in the woods.

We went on thus for the whole length of the meal, with us three poor boys fighting our war against a cruel, torturing world without being able to recognize one another as allies, full of mutual fears. My brother ended by making a grand gesture, after the fruit: he took out a pack of cigarettes and offered one to our guest. They lit up without asking if they were disturbing anyone; and this was the fullest moment of solidarity created during that meal. I was excluded because my parents had forbidden me to smoke till I left school. My brother was satisfied now; he got up, inhaled once or twice, looking down at us, then turned around and went out as silently as he had come.

My father lit his pipe and turned on the radio for the news. The goatherd was looking at the instrument, his hands open on his knees and his eyes staring and reddening with tears. Certainly those eyes were still seeing his village high above the fields, the lines of mountains, and the thick chestnut woods. My father did not let us listen to the radio—he was criticizing the United Nations—and I took advantage of this to leave the dining room.

That whole afternoon and evening we were persecuted by the memory of the goatherd. We had supper in silence by the dim light of the chandelier and could not free ourselves of the thought of him alone in the hut on our land. Now he must have finished the soup in the can in which he had heated it up, and was lying on the straw almost in the dark, while down below the goats could be heard moving about and bumping one another and munching grass. The goatherd would go outside and there would be a slight mist over toward the sea and damp air and a little spring gurgling gently in the silence. The goatherd would head for it along paths covered with wild ivy, and drink, though he was not thirsty. Fireflies could be seen appearing and vanishing in what seemed like a great compact swarm. But he would move his arm in the air without touching them.

THE HOUSE OF THE BEEHIVES

It is difficult to see from far away, and even if someone had already been here once he could not remember the way back; there was a path here at one time, but I made brambles grow over it and wiped out every trace. It's well chosen, this home of mine, lost in this bank of broom, with a single story that can't be seen from the valley, and covered in a chalky whitewash with windows picked out in red.

There's some land around I could have worked and haven't; a patch for vegetables where snails munch the lettuce is enough for me, and a bit of terraced earth to dig up with a pitchfork and grow potatoes, all purple and budding. I only need to work to feed myself, for I've got nothing to share with anyone.

And I don't cut back the brambles, either the ones now clambering over the roof of the house or those already creeping like a slow avalanche over the cultivated ground; I should like them to bury everything, myself included. Lizards have made their nests in the cracks of the walls, ants have scooped out porous cities under the bricks of the floor; I look forward every day to seeing if a new crack has opened, and think of the cities of the human race being smothered and swallowed up by weeds.

Above my home are a few strips of rough meadow where I let my goats roam. At dawn, dogs sometimes pass by, on the scent of hares; I chase them off with stones. I hate dogs, with their servile fidelity to man; I hate all domestic animals, their pretense of having sympathy with human beings just so they can lick the remains off greasy plates. Goats are the only animals I can stand, for they don't expect intimacy or give any.

I don't need chained dogs to guard me. Or even hedges or padlocks, those horrible contraptions of humans. My field is studded with beehives, and a flight of bees is like a thorny hedge that only I can cross. At night the bees sleep in the bean husks, but no man ever comes near my house; people are afraid of me and they are right; not because certain tales they tell about me are true—lies, I say, just the sort of thing they would tell—but they are right to be afraid of me, I want them to be.

When I go over the crest in the morning, I can see the valley dropping away beneath and the sea high all around me and the world. And I see the houses of the human race perched on the edge of the sea, shipwrecked in their false neighborliness; I see the tawny, chalky city, the glittering of its windows, and the smoke of its fires. One day brambles and grass will cover its squares, and the sea will come up and mold the ruins into rocks.

Only the bees are with me now; they buzz around my hands without stinging me when I take the honey from the hives, and settle on me like a living beard; friendly bees, ancient race without a history. For years I've been living on this bank of broom with goats and bees; once I used to make a mark on the wall at the passing of each year; now the brambles choke everything. Why should I live with men and work for them? I loathe their sweaty hands, their savage rites, their dances and churches, their women's acid saliva. But those stories aren't true, believe me, they've always told stories about me, the lying swine.

I don't give anything and I don't owe anything; if it rains at night I cook and eat the big snails slithering down the banks in the morning; the earth in the woods is scattered with soft, damp toadstools. The woods give me everything else I need: sticks and pine cones to burn, and chestnuts; and I snare hares and thrushes, too, for don't think I love wild animals or have an idyllic adoration of nature—one of man's absurd hypocrisies. I know that in this world we must devour one another and that the survival of the fittest holds; I kill only the animals I want to eat, with traps, not with guns, so as not to need dogs or other men to fetch them.

Sometimes I meet men in the woods, if I'm not warned in time by the dull thuds of their axes cutting down trees one by one. I pretend not to see them. On Sundays the poor come to gather fuel in the woods, which they strip like the speckled heads of aloes; the trunks are hauled away on ropes and form rough tracks, which gather the rain during storms and provoke landfalls. May everything go to similar ruin in the cities of the human race; may I, as I walk along one day, see chimney tops emerging from the earth, meet parts of streets falling off into ravines, and stumble on strips of railroad track in the middle of the forest.

But you must wonder if I don't ever feel this solitude of mine weighing on me, if some evening, one of those long twilights, I haven't gone down, without any definite idea in my head, toward the houses of the human race. I did go, one warm twilight, toward those walls surrounding the gardens below, and climbed down over the medlar trees; but when I heard women laughing and a distant child calling, back I came up here. That was the last time; now I'm up here alone. Well, I get frightened of making a mistake every now and again, as you do. And so, like you, I go on as I was before.

You're afraid of me, of course, and you're right. Not because of that affair, though. That, whether it ever happened or not, was so many years ago it doesn't matter now, anyway.

That woman, that dark woman who came up here to scythe —I had only been up here a short time then and was still full of human emotions—well, I saw her working high on the slope and she hailed me and I didn't reply and passed by. Yes, I was still full of human emotions then, and of an old resentment, too; and because of that old resentment—not against her, I don't even remember her face—I went up behind her without her hearing me.

Now, the tale as people tell it is obviously false, for it was late and there wasn't a soul in the valley and when I put my hands around her throat no one heard her. But I would have to tell you my story from the beginning for you to understand.

Ah, well, let's not mention that evening any more. Here I live, sharing my lettuce with snails that perforate the leaves, and I know all the places where toadstools grow and can tell the good ones from the poisonous; about women and their poisons I don't think any more. Being chaste is nothing but a habit, after all.

She was the last one, that dark woman with the scythe. The sky was full of clouds, I remember, dark clouds scudding along. It must have been under a hurrying sky like that, on slopes cropped by goats, that the first human marriage took place. In contact between human beings there can only, I know, be mutual terror and shame. That's what I wanted, to see the terror and shame, just the terror and shame, in her eyes; that's the only reason I did it to her, believe me.

No one has said a word about it to me, ever; there isn't a word they can say, since the valley was deserted that evening. But every night, when the hills are lost in the dark and I can't follow the meaning of an old book by the light of the lantern, and I sense the town with its human beings and its lights and music down below, I feel the voices of you all accusing me.

But there was no one to see me there in the valley; they say those things because the woman never returned home.

And if dogs passing by always stop to sniff at a certain spot, and bay and scratch the ground with their paws, it's because there's an old moles' lair there—I swear it, just an old moles' lair.

BIG FISH, LITTLE FISH

ZEFFIRINO'S FATHER never wore a proper bathing suit. He would put on rolled-up shorts and an undershirt, a white duck cap on his head; and he never moved from the rocky shore. His passion was limpets, the flat mollusks that cling to the rocks until their terribly hard shell virtually becomes part of the rock itself. Zeffirino's father used a knife to prize them loose. Every Sunday, with his bespectacled stare, he passed in review, one by one, all the rocks along the point. He kept on until his little basket was full of limpets; some he ate as he collected them, sucking the moist, hard flesh as if from a spoon; the others he put in a basket. Every now and then he raised his eyes to glance, somewhat bewildered, over the smooth sea, and call, "Zeffirino! Where are you?"

Zeffirino spent whole afternoons in the water. The two of them went out to the point; his father would leave him there, then go off at once after his shellfish. Stubborn and motionless as they were, the limpets held no attraction for Zeffirino; it was the crabs, first and foremost, that interested him, then polyps, medusas, and so on, through all the varieties of fish. In the summer his pursuit became more difficult and ingenious; and by now there wasn't a boy his age who could handle a spear gun as well as he could. In the water, those stocky kids, all breath and muscle, are the best; and that's how Zeffirino was growing up. Seen on the shore, holding his father's hand, he looked like one of those kids with cropped hair and gaping mouth who have to be slapped to make them move. In the water, however, he outstripped them all; and, even better, underwater.

That day Zeffirino had managed to assemble a complete kit for underwater fishing. He had had the mask since the previ ous year, a present from his grandmother; a cousin whose feet were small had lent him her fins; he took the spear gun from his uncle's house without saying anything, but told his father it had been lent him, too. Actually, he was a careful boy, who knew how to use and take care of things, and he could be trusted if he borrowed something.

The sea was beautiful and clear. Zeffirino answered "Yes, Papà" to all the usual warnings, and went into the water. With the glass mask and the snorkel for breathing, with his legs ending like fish, and with that object in his hand—half gun and half spear and a little bit like a pitchfork, too—he no longer resembled a human being. Instead, once in the sea, though he darted off half submerged, you immediately recognized him as himself: from the kick he gave with the fins, from the way the gun jutted out beneath his arm, from his determination as he proceeded, his head at the surface of the water.

The sea bed was pebbles at first, then rocks, some of them bare and eroded, others bearded with thick, dark seaweed. From every cranny of the rocks, or among the tremulous beards swaying in the current, a big fish might suddenly appear; from behind the glass of the mask Zeffirino cast his eyes around, eagerly, intently.

A sea bed seems beautiful the first time, when you discover it; but, as with all things, the really beautiful part comes later when you learn everything, stroke by stroke. You feel as if you were drinking them in, the aquatic trails: you go on and on and never want to stop. The glass of the mask is an enormous, single eye for swallowing colors and shadows. Now the dark ended, and he was beyond that sea of rock. On the sand of the bottom, fine wrinkles could be discerned, traced by the movement of the sea. The sun's rays penetrated all the way down, winking and flashing, and there was the glint of schools of hook-chasers, those tiny fish that swim in a very straight line, then suddenly, all of them together, make a sharp right turn.

A little puff of sand rose and it was the switching tail of a sea bream, there on the bottom. It wasn't even aware that the spear gun was aimed directly at it. Zeffirino was now swimming totally underwater; and the bream, after a few absent flicks of its striped sides, suddenly sped off at mid-depth. Among rocks bristling with sea urchins, the fish and the fisherman swam to an inlet with porous, almost bare rock. He can't get away from me here, Zeffirino thought; and at that moment the bream vanished. From nooks and hollows a stream of little air bubbles rose, then promptly ceased, to resume somewhere else. The sea anemones glowed, expectant. The bream peered from one lair, vanished into another, and promptly popped out from a distant gap. It skirted a spur of rock, headed downward. Zeffirino saw a patch of luminous green toward the bottom; the fish became lost in that light, and he dived after it.

He passed through a low arch at the foot of the cliff, and found the deep water and the sky above him again. Shadows of pale stone surrounded the bed, and out toward the open sea they descended, a half-submerged breakwater. With a twist of his hips and a thrust of the fins, Zeffirino surfaced to breathe. The snorkel surfaced, he blew out some drops that had infiltrated the mask; but the boy kept his head in the water. He had found the bream again: two bream, in fact! He was already taking aim when he saw a whole squadron of them proceeding calmly to the left, while another school glistened on the right. This was a place rich in fish, like an enclosed pond; and wherever Zeffirino looked he saw a flicker of sharp fins, the glint of scales; his joy and wonder were so great, he forgot to shoot even once.

The thing was not to be in a hurry, to study the best shots, and not to sow panic on all sides. Keeping his head down, Zeffirino moved toward the nearest rock; along its face, in the water, he saw a white hand swaying. The sea was motionless; on the taut and polished surface, concentric circles spread out, as if raindrops were falling. The boy raised his head and looked. Lying prone on the edge of the rock shelf, a fat woman in a bathing suit was taking the sun. And she was crying. Her tears ran down her cheeks one after another and dropped into the sea.

Zeffirino pushed his mask up on his forehead and said, "Excuse me."

The fat woman said, "Make yourself at home, kid." And she went on crying. "Fish as much as you like."

"This place is full of fish," he explained. "Did you see how many there are?"

The fat woman kept her head raised, her eyes staring

straight ahead, filled with tears. "I didn't see anything. How could I? I can't stop crying."

As long as it was a matter of sea and fish, Zeffirino was the smartest; but in the presence of people, he resumed his gaping, stammering air. "I'm sorry, signora. . . ." He would have liked to get back to his bream, but a fat, crying woman was such an unusual sight that he stayed there, spellbound, gaping at her in spite of himself.

"I'm not a signora, kid," the fat woman said with her noble, somewhat nasal voice. "Call me 'signorina.' Signorina De Magistris. And what's your name?"

"Zeffirino."

"Well, fine, Zeffirino. How's the fishing—or the shooting? What do you call it?"

"I don't know what they call it. So far I haven't caught anything. But this is a good place."

"Be careful with that gun, though. I don't mean for my sake, poor me. I mean for you. Take care you don't hurt yourself."

Zeffirino assured her she needn't worry. He sat down on the rock beside her and watched her cry for a while. There were moments when it looked as if she might stop, and she sniffed with her reddened nose, raising and shaking her head. But meanwhile, at the corners of her eyes and under her lids, a bubble of tears seemed to swell until her eyes promptly brimmed over.

Zeffirino didn't know quite what to think. Seeing a lady cry was a thing that made your heart ache. But how could anyone be sad in this enclosure of sea crammed with every variety of fish to fill the heart with desire and joy? And how could you dive into that greenness and pursue fish when there was a grown-up person nearby dissolved in tears? At the same moment, in the same place, two yearnings existed, opposed and unreconcilable, but Zeffirino could neither conceive of them both together, nor surrender to the one or to the other.

"Signorina?" he asked.

"Yes?"

"Why are you crying?"

"Because I'm unlucky in love."

"Ah!"

"You can't understand; you're still a kid."

"You want to try swimming with my mask?"

"Thank you very much. Is it nice?"

"It's the nicest thing in the world."

Signorina De Magistris got up and fastened the straps of her suit at the back. Zeffirino gave her the mask and carefully explained how to put it on. She shook her head a little, half joking and half embarrassed, with the mask over her face; but behind it you could see her eyes, which didn't stop crying for a moment. She stepped into the water awkwardly, like a seal, and began paddling, holding her face down.

The gun under his arm, Zeffirino also went in swimming.

"When you see a fish, tell me," he shouted to the signorina. In the water he didn't fool around; and the privilege of coming out fishing with him was one he granted rarely.

But the signorina raised her head and shook it. The glass had clouded over and her features were no longer visible. She took off the mask. "I can't see anything," she said. "My tears make the glass cloud over. I can't. I'm sorry." And she stood there crying in the water.

"This is bad," Zeffirino said. He hadn't brought along a

half of a potato, which you can rub on the glass to clear it again; but he did the best he could with some spit, then put the mask on himself. "Watch me," he said to the fat lady. And they proceeded together through that sea, he all fins, his head down, she swimming on her side, one arm extended and the other bent, her head bitterly erect and inconsolable.

She was a poor swimmer, Signorina De Magistris, always on her side, making clumsy, stabbing strokes. And beneath her, for yards, the fish raced through the sea, starfish and squid navigated, anemones yawned. Now Zeffirino's gaze saw landscapes approaching that would dazzle anyone. The water was deep, and the sandy bed was dotted with little stones among which skeins of seaweed swayed in the barely perceptible motion of the sea—though, observed from above, the rocks themselves seem to sway on the uniform expanse of sand, in the midst of the still water dense with seaweed.

All of a sudden, the signorina saw him disappear, head down, his behind surfacing for a moment, then the fins; and then his pale shadow was underwater, dropping toward the bottom. It was the moment when the bass realized the danger: the trident spear, already fired, caught him obliquely, and its central prong drove through his tail and transfixed him. The bass raised its prickly fins and lunged, slapping the water; the other prongs of the spear hadn't hooked him, and he still hoped to escape by sacrificing his tail. But all he achieved was to catch a fin on one of the other prongs; and so he was a goner. Zeffirino was already winding in the line, and the boy's pink and happy shadow fell above the fish.

The spear rose from the water with the bass impaled on it, then the boy's arm, then the masked head, with a gurgle of water from the snorkel. And Zeffirino bared his face: "Isn't he a beauty? Eh, signorina?" The bass was big, silvery and black. But the woman continued crying.

Zeffirino climbed up on the tip of a rock. With some effort, Signorina De Magistris followed him. To keep the fish fresh, the boy picked a little natural basin, full of water. They crouched down beside it. Zeffirino gazed at the iridescent colors of the bass, stroked its scales, and invited the signorina to do the same.

"You see how beautiful he is? You see how prickly?" When it looked as if a shaft of interest was piercing the fat lady's gloom, he said, "I'll just go off for a moment to see if I can catch another." And, fully equipped, he dived in.

The woman stayed behind with the fish. And she discovered that never had a fish been more unhappy. Now she ran her fingers over its ring-shaped mouth, along its fins, its tail. She saw a thousand tiny holes in its handsome silver body: sea lice, minuscule parasites of fish, had long since taken possession of the bass and were gnawing their way into its flesh.

Unaware of this, Zeffirino was already emerging again with a gilded umbra on the spear; and he held it out to Signorina De Magistris. The two had already divided their tasks: the woman took the fish off the prongs and put it in the pool, and Zeffirino stuck his head back into the water to go catch something else. But each time he first looked to see if the signorina had stopped crying: if the sight of a bass or an umbra wouldn't make her stop, what could possibly console her?

Gilded streaks marked the sides of the umbra. Two fins, parallel, ran down its back. And in the space between these fins, the signorina saw a deep, narrow wound, antedating those of the spear gun. A gull's beak must have pecked the fish's back with such force it was hard to figure out why it hadn't killed the fish. She wondered how long the umbra had been swimming around bearing that pain.

Faster than Zeffirino's spear, down toward a school of tiny, hesitant spicara, the sea bream plunged. He barely had time to gulp down one of the little fish before the spear stuck in his throat. Zeffirino had never fired such a good shot.

"A champion fish!" he cried, taking off his mask. "I was following the little ones! He swallowed one, and then I . . ." And he described the scene, stammering with emotion. It was impossible to catch a bigger, more beautiful fish; Zeffirino would have liked the signorina finally to share his contentment. She looked at the fat, silvery body, the throat that had just swallowed the little greenish fish, only to be ripped by the teeth of the spear: such was life throughout the sea.

In addition, Zeffirino caught a little gray fish and a red fish, a yellow-striped bream, a plump gilthead, and a flat bogue; even a mustached, spiky gurnard. But in all of them, besides the wounds of the spear, Signorina De Magistris discovered the bites of the lice that had gnawed them, or the stain of some unknown affliction, or a hook stuck for ages in the throat. This inlet the boy had discovered, where all sorts of fish gathered, was perhaps a refuge for animals sentenced to a long agony, a marine lazaretto, an arena of desperate duels.

Now Zeffirino was venturing along the rocks: octopus! He had come upon a colony squatting at the foot of a boulder. On the spear one big purplish octopus now emerged, a liquid like watered ink dripping from its wounds; and a strange uneasiness overcame Signorina De Magistris. To keep the octopus they found a more secluded basin, and Zeffirino wanted never to leave it, to stay and admire the gray-pink skin that slowly changed hues. It was late, too, and the boy was beginning to get a bit of gooseflesh, his swim had lasted so long. But Zeffirino was hardly one to renounce a whole family of octopus, now discovered.

The signorina observed the octopus, its slimy flesh, the mouths of the suckers, the reddish and almost liquid eye. Alone among the whole catch, the polyp seemed to be without blemish or torment. The tentacles of an almost human pink, so limp and sinuous and full of secret armpits, prompted thoughts of health and life, and some lazy contractions caused them to twist still, with a slight opening of the suckers. In mid-air, the hand of Signorina De Magistris sketched a caress over the coils of the octopus; her fingers moved to imitate its contraction, closer and closer, and finally touched the coils lightly.

Evening was falling; a wave began to slap the sea. The tentacles vibrated in the air like whips, and suddenly, with all its strength, the octopus was clinging to the arm of Signorina De Magistris. Standing on the rock, as if fleeing from her own imprisoned arm, she let out a cry that sounded like: It's the octopus! The octopus is torturing me!

Zeffirino, who at that very moment had managed to flush a squid, stuck his head out of the water and saw the fat woman with the octopus, which stretched out one tentacle from her arm to catch her by the throat. He also heard the end of the scream: it was a high, constant scream, but—so it seemed to the boy—without tears.

A man armed with a knife rushed up and started aiming blows at the octopus's eye. He decapitated it almost with one stroke. This was Zeffirino's father, who had filled his basket with limpets and was searching along the rocks for his son. Hearing the cry, narrowing his bespectacled gaze, he had seen the woman and run to help her, with the blade he used for his limpets. The tentacles immediately relaxed; Signorina De Magistris fainted.

When she came to, she found the octopus cut into pieces, and Zeffirino and his father made her a present of it, so she could fry it. It was evening, and Zeffirino put on his shirt. His father with precise gestures, explained to her the secret of a good octopus fry. Zeffirino looked at her and several times thought she was about to start up again; but no, not a single tear came from her.

A SHIP LOADED WITH CRABS

The boys from Piazza dei Dolori had their first swim of the summer on an April Sunday, when the blue sky was brand new and the sun was young, carefree. They went running down the steep narrow alleys, waving their patched jersey trunks, some already in clogs clattering over the paving stones, most of them without socks, to spare themselves the nuisance, afterward, of putting them back on wet feet. They ran to the pier, jumping over the nets spread out on the ground and lifted by the callused feet of the fishermen, squatting to mend them. Along the rocks of the breakwater, the kids stripped, excited by that sharp smell of old, rotting seaweed and by the flight of the gulls trying to fill the sky, which was too big. Hiding clothes and shoes in the hollows of the rocks, and setting the baby crabs to flight, they began to jump from rock to rock, barefoot and half naked, waiting for one of their number to make up his mind and dive in first.

The water was calm but not clear, a dense blue with harsh green glints. Gian Maria, known as Mariassa, climbed to the top of a high rock and blew his nose against his thumb, a boxer's gesture he had.

"Come on," he said. He pressed his hands together, held them out in front of himself, and plunged headlong. He surfaced a few yards farther out, spouting water, then playing dead.

"Cold?" they asked him.

"Boiling," he yelled and started making furious strokes to keep from freezing.

"Hey, gang! Follow me!" said Cicin, who considered himself the chief, though nobody ever paid any attention to him.

They all dived in: Pier Lingera made a somersault, Bombolo took a belly-whopper, then Paulò, Carruba, and, last of all, Menin, who was scared to death of the water and jumped in feet first, pinching his nose with his fingers.

Once in the water, Pier Lingera, who was the strongest, ducked the others one by one; then they all ganged up and ducked Pier Lingera.

Gian Maria alias Mariassa suggested, "The ship! Let's go on the ship!"

A vessel still lay in the harbor, sunk by the Germans during the war to block access. Actually, there were two ships, one above the other; the visible one rested on a second, completely submerged.

"Yeah, let's!" the others said.

"Can we climb up on it?" Menin asked. "It's mined."

"Balls. Mined!" Carruba said. "The Arenella guys climb on it whenever they like, and play war."

They started swimming toward the ship.

"Gang! Follow me!" said Cicin, who wanted to be the leader. But the others swam faster and left him behind, except for Menin, who swam frog-style and was always the last.

They reached the ship, whose flanks rose from the water,

black with old tar, bare, and moldy, the stripped superstructures profiled against the fresh blue sky. A beard of stinking seaweed rose to cover the ship from the keel; the old paint was peeling in great flakes. The boys swam all around it, then paused a while below the poop, to look at the almost erased name: *Abukir, Egypt.* The anchor chain, stretched obliquely, swayed now and then with the jabs of the tide, its enormous rusted links creaking.

"Let's stay here," Bombolo said.

"Come on," Pier Lingera said, already gripping the chain with his hands and feet. He scrambled up like a monkey, and the others followed him.

Halfway up, Bombolo slipped and hit the water with his belly; Menin couldn't make it, so two of the others had to pull him up.

On board, they began wandering around that dismantled ship in silence, looking for the wheel of the helm, the siren, the hatches, the lifeboats, all the things there were supposed to be on a ship. But this ship was as barren as a raft, covered only with whitish gull dung. There were five of them, five gulls, perched on a railing; when they heard the barefoot steps of the band, they took flight, one after the other, in a great flapping of wings.

"Hey!" Paulò cried, and threw after the last gull a rivet he had picked up.

"Gang! Let's go to the engine room!" Cicin said. It would surely be more fun to play among the machines or in the hold.

"Can we go down to the other ship, underneath?" Carruba asked. That would have been great: to be down there, all sealed off, with the sea around them and over them, like being in a submarine.

"The one underneath is mined!" Menin said.

"You're mined!" they said to him.

They started down a companionway. After a few steps, they hesitated: at their feet the black water began, rustling in the enclosed space. Standing still and mute, the boys from Piazza dei Dolori looked at it; in the depths of that water there was the black glint of colonies of sea urchins, slowly unfolding their spines. And the walls on every side were encrusted with limpets, their shells dripping green algae; the iron of the walls seemed eroded. And there were crabs teeming at the edges of the water, thousands of crabs of every shape and every age, which scuttled on their curved, spoked legs, and opened their claws, and thrust forward their sightless eyes. The sea slapped dully in the space of the iron walls, licking those flat crab bellies. Perhaps the entire hold of the ship was full of groping crabs, and one day the ship would move on the crabs' legs and walk through the sea.

The boys came up on deck again, at the prow. Then they saw the little girl. They hadn't seen her before, though it was as if she had always been there. She was a little girl of about six, fat, with long curly hair. She was all sunburned, wearing only little white pants. There was no telling where she had come from. She didn't even look at them, totally concerned with a medusa that was lying on its back on the wooden deck, the flabby festoons of its tentacles spread out. With a stick the little girl was trying to turn it upright.

The Piazza dei Dolori boys stopped all around her, gaping. Mariassa was the first to step forward. He sniffed.

"Who're you?" he said.

The girl raised the pale-blue eyes in her dark, plump face; then she resumed working the stick as a lever under the medusa.

"She must be one of the Arenella gang," Carruba said; he knew them.

The Arenella boys let some girls come with them to swim or play ball, and even to make war with reed weapons.

"You," Mariassa said, "are our prisoner."

"Gang!" Cicin said. "Take her alive!"

The little girl went on poking at the jellyfish.

"Battle stations!" Paulò yelled, as he happened to look around. "The Arenella gang!"

While they had been involved with the girl, the Arenella boys, who spent their whole day in the sea, had come swimming underwater and silently climbed the anchor chain; now they appeared over the railings. They were short, stocky kids, light as cats, with shaved heads and dark skin. Their trunks weren't black and long and floppy like those of the Dolori boys, but consisted of a single length of white canvas.

The battle began; the Piazza dei Dolori boys were thin, all nerves, except for Bombolo, who was a fatty; but they had a fanatical fury when they swung their fists, hardened by endless brawls in the little streets of the old city against the gangs from San Siro and the Giardinetti. At first the Arenella kids had the advantage, because of the surprise element; but then the Dolori gang perched on the ladders and there was no dislodging them. They wanted to avoid, at all cost, being forced to the railing, where it would be easy to dump them into the drink. Finally Pier Lingera, who was the strongest of the bunch and also the oldest and who hung out with them only because he had been kept back in school, managed to force one of the Arenella boys to the edge and push him into the sea.

Then the Dolori gang took the offensive, and the Arenella kids, who felt more at home in the water and, being sensible, had no notions about honor in their heads, one by one eluded their enemies and dived in.

"Come and get us in the water. We dare you!" they yelled.

"Gang! Follow me!" yelled Cicin, who was about to dive.

"Are you crazy?" Mariassa held him back. "In the water they'd win hands down!" And he started shouting insults at the fugitives.

The Arenella boys began to splash water up from below; they splashed so hard there wasn't a place on the ship that wasn't wet. Finally they got tired of that and swam out to sea, heads down and arms arched, surfacing every now and then to breathe, in little spurts.

The Piazza dei Dolori boys had remained masters of the field. They went to the prow; the little girl was still there. She had succeeded in turning over the medusa and was now trying to lift it on the stick.

"They left us a hostage!" Mariassa said.

"Hey, gang! A hostage!" Cicin was all excited.

"You cowards!" Carruba shouted behind the other bunch. "Leaving your women in the enemies' hands!"

They had a highly developed sense of honor around Piazza dei Dolori.

"Come with us," Mariassa said, and started to put a hand on her shoulder.

The girl motioned him to keep still; she had almost succeeded in lifting the medusa. As Mariassa bent over to look, the girl pulled up the stick, with the medusa balanced on it, pulled it up, up, and slammed it into Mariassa's face.

"Bitch!" Mariassa yelled, spitting and putting his hands to his face.

The little girl looked at them all and laughed. Then she

turned, went straight to the top of the prow, raised her arms, joining her fingertips, did a swan dive, and swam off without looking back. The Piazza dei Dolori boys hadn't moved.

"Say," Mariassa asked, touching one cheek, "is it true that medusas make your skin burn?"

"Wait and find out," Pier Lingera said. "But the best thing would be to dive in right away."

"Let's go," Mariassa said, starting off with the others.

Then he stopped. "From now on we have to have a woman in our gang, too! Menin! Bring your sister!"

"My sister's a dummy," Menin said.

"That doesn't matter," Mariassa said. "Come on!" And he gave Menin a shove, pushing him into the water because he didn't know how to dive. Then they all dived in.

MAN IN THE WASTELAND

Early in the morning you can see Corsica: it looks like a ship laden with mountains, suspended out there on the horizon. If we lived in another country it would have inspired legends, but not here: Corsica is a poor land, poorer than ours; nobody has ever gone there and nobody has ever given it any thought. If you see Corsica in the morning it means the air is clear and still and there's no rain in the offing.

On one of those mornings, at dawn, my father and I were climbing up the dry, stony gullies of Colla Bella, with the dog on a chain. My father had encased his chest and back in scarves, coats, a hunting jacket, vests, knapsacks, canteens, cartridge belts; from all this, a white goatee emerged; on his legs he wore an old pair of scratched-up, leather puttees. I had on a threadbare, too-tight jerkin that left my wrists and waist exposed, and trousers, also tight and threadbare; and I took long strides like my father, but with my hands dug into my pockets and my long neck pulled down between my shoulders. Both of us carried old hunting guns, a fine make but neglected and streaked with rust. The dog was a harrier, ears drooping till they swept the ground, a short bristling coat on its bones that seemed to scrape the skin. Behind him he dragged a chain that might have served for a bear.

"You stay here with the dog," my father said. "From here you can keep an eye on both trails. I'll go to the other, and when I get there I'll give you a whistle. Then you turn the dog loose. Watch out: a hare can slip past in a second."

My father continued up the stony track, and I crouched down on the ground with the dog, whimpering because he wanted to follow. Colla Bella is a height rising from the pale shore, all barren terrain, weeds hard to crop, crumbling walls of ancient embankments. Farther down, the black haze of the olive groves begins; farther up, the tawny woods, made patchy by fires, like the backs of mangy old dogs. Everything lazed in the gray of the dawn as in a half-opening of still-sleepy eyelids. At sea no outlines could be distinguished; the water was striped by shafts of mist for all its breadth.

My father's whistle came. Released from the chain, the dog set off in great zigzags up the stony bed, snapping the air with yelps. Then, silent, it began to sniff the ground and ran off, still sniffing diligently, its tail erect, a rhomboid white spot under it that seemed illuminated.

I kept the gun aimed, resting on my knees, and my eyes aimed, resting on the intersection of the trails, because a hare can slip past in a second. Dawn was revealing colors, one by one. First the red of the wild arum berries, the reddish slashes on the pine trees. Then green, the hundred, the thousand greens of the fields, bushes, woods, which a short time before had been uniform: now, instead, a new green appeared every moment, distinct from the others. Then the blue: the loud blue of the sea which deafened everything and made the sky turn wan and timid. Corsica vanished, engulfed by the light, but the border between sea and sky did not become firm: it remained that ambiguous, confused zone frightening to look at because it does not exist.

All of a sudden houses, roofs, streets were born at the foot of the hills, along the sea. Every morning the city was born like this from the realm of shadows, all at once, tawny with tiles, sparkling with glass, lime-white with stucco. The light every morning described it in the smallest details, narrowed its every doorway, enumerated all its houses. Then the light moved up along the hills, revealing more and more particulars: new terraces, new houses. It arrived at Colla Bella, yellow and barren and deserted; and it discovered a house up there as well, isolated, the highest house before the woods, within range of my gun, the house of Baciccin the Blissful.

In shadow, the house of Baciccin the Blissful seemed a heap of stones; around it there was a dirt terrace, caked, gray, like the surface of the moon, from which rose scrawny plants, as if he cultivated poles. There were some wires stretched, for laundry, it seemed; but they were his vineyard of consumptive, skeletal vines. Only a slender fig tree seemed to have the strength to support its leaves, writhing under the weight, at the edge of the terrace.

Baciccin came out; he was so thin that, to be seen, he had to stand in profile; otherwise all you saw was his mustache, gray and bristling. He was wearing a woolen Balaclava helmet and a homespun suit. He saw me waiting and came over.

"Hare, hare," he said.

"Hare. As usual," I answered.

"Shot at one this big last week on that track. Close as here to there. Missed."

"Bad luck."

"Bad luck, bad luck. I'm not one for hare anyway. I'd rather stand under a pine tree and wait for thrush. In one morning you can get five or six shots."

"So you shoot your dinner, Baciccin."

"That's right. But then I miss them all."

"It happens. It's the cartridges."

"The cartridges, the cartridges."

"The ones they sell are no good. Make your own."

"That's right. I do make my own. Maybe I make them wrong."

"Ah, you have to have the knack."

"That's right, that's right."

Meanwhile he had assumed a position, his arms folded, in the center of the crossing and was not going to move. The hare would never go by if he stood in the way like that. I'll tell him to move, I thought; but I didn't tell him, and I sat there waiting all the same.

"No rain, no rain," Baciccin said.

"Corsica: did you see it this morning?"

"Corsica. All dry, Corsica."

"A bad year, Baciccin."

"Bad year. Planted beans. Did they grow?"

"Did they grow?"

"Did they grow? No."

"They sold you bad seed, Baciccin."

"Bad seed, bad year. Eight artichoke plants."

"Damn."

"Tell me what I got from them."

"You tell."

"All died."

"Damn."

Costanzina, the daughter of Baciccin the Blissful, came from the house. She could have been sixteen: olive-shaped face, eyes, mouth, nostrils, shaped like an olive; and braids down her back. She must have had olive-shaped breasts, too: all the same style; like a statuette, wild as a she-goat, wool socks up to her knees.

"Costanzina," I called.

"Oh!"

But she did not come closer; she was afraid of frightening the hares.

"Hasn't barked yet, hasn't flushed it," Baciccin said.

We pricked up our ears.

"He hasn't barked. No use going away yet," and he went off.

Costanzina sat down beside me. Baciccin the Blissful had started wandering around his bleak terrace, pruning the scraggy vines; every now and then he would stop and come back to talk.

"What's new around Colla Bella, Tancina?" I asked.

The girl began to recount, dutifully: "Last night I saw the hares over there, jumping in the moonlight. They went 'hee! hee!' Yesterday a mushroom sprouted behind the oak. Poisonous, red with white spots. I killed it with a stone. A big, yellow snake came down the path at noon. She lives in that bush. Don't throw stones at her; she's harmless."

"Do you like living on Colla Bella, Tancina?"

"Not in the evening. The mist comes up at four o'clock, and the city disappears. Then, at night, you can hear the owl cry."

"Scared of owls?"

"No. Scared of bombs, planes."

Baciccin came over. "The war? How's the war going?"

"The war's been over a good while, Baciccin."

"Fine. What's taken the war's place, then? Anyway, I don't believe it's over. Whenever they used to say that, it would start up again—every time, in some different way. Am I right?"

"Yes, you're right. . . . Which do you like best, Tancina: Colla Bella or the city?" I asked.

"In the city there's the shooting gallery," she answered, "trams, people shoving, movies, ice cream, the beach with umbrellas on it."

"This girl," Baciccin said, "isn't all that crazy about going to the city; the other one liked it so much she never came back."

"Where is she now?"

"Hmph."

"Hmph. We need rain."

"That's the truth. Need rain. Corsica, this morning. Am I right?"

"You're right, yes."

In the distance there was an explosion of yelps.

"Dog's flushed a hare," I said.

Baciccin came and stood in the trail, his arms folded.

"He's hunting. A good hunter," he said. "I had a dog, a bitch name of Cililla. She'd trail a hare for three days. Once she flushed him at the top of the wood and chased him two yards in front of my gun. I fired twice. Missed."

"You can't get a hit every time."

"Can't. Well, she went on after that hare for two hours. . . ."

They heard two shots, but then the yelping began again, coming closer.

". . . two hours later," Baciccin resumed, "she brought the hare back to me, like before. I missed it again, goddamnit."

All of a sudden a hare appeared, darting along the trail. It came almost to Baciccin's legs, then swerved into the bushes and disappeared. I hadn't even had time to take aim.

"Damnation!" I yelled.

"What's wrong?" Baciccin asked.

"Nothing," I said.

Costanzina hadn't seen it, either; she had gone back into the house.

"Well," Baciccin went on, "you know that bitch kept chasing that hare and bringing it back to me over and over until I hit it? What a dog!"

"Where is she now?"

"Ran off."

"Well, you can't win every time."

My father came back with the panting dog. He was cursing.

"Missed by a fraction of an inch. This close. A big one. Did you see him?"

"Not a thing," Baciccin said.

I slung the gun over my shoulder and we started on our way down.

LAZY SONS

AT DAWN my brother and I are asleep, faces buried in the pillows, and already our father's hobnail tread can be heard as he moves around the rooms. When he gets up, our father makes a lot of noise, deliberately perhaps; and he sees to it that he has to go up and down the steps, in his cleated boots, at least twenty times, never for any reason. Maybe this is his whole life, a waste of energy, a great useless exertion; and maybe he does it as a protest against the two of us—we get him so angry.

My mother doesn't make any noise, but she is already up, too, in the big kitchen, poking the fire, peeling things with those hands that become blacker and more scarred all the time, polishing glasses and furniture, jabbing at the laundry. This, too, is a protest against us, her doing housework always in silence and managing it all without any maids.

"Sell the house, and we'll spend the money," I say with a shrug when they start pestering me about how things can't go on like this. But my mother continues toiling silently, day and night, till there's no telling when she sleeps; and meanwhile the cracks in the ceilings widen and lines of ants trace the walls, and weeds and brambles keep growing higher in the rank garden. Soon nothing will be left of our house but a ruin covered with vines. In the morning, however, mother doesn't come and tell me to get up because she knows it's no use anyway, and that silent attention to the house crumbling around her is her way of persecuting us.

My father, on the contrary, is already flinging open our window at six o'clock, in hunting jacket and puttees, and yelling at us: "I'm going to take a stick to you two! Bums! Everybody works in this house but the pair of you! Pietro! get up if you don't want me to hang you! And make that gallows bird of a brother, Andrea, get up, too!"

In our sleep, we have already heard him approaching; digging our heads into the pillows, we don't even roll over. We protest now and then with grunts when he doesn't let up. But he soon goes away; he knows it's all useless, this is all a play he puts on, a ritual ceremony, a refusal to admit defeat.

We grope our way back into sleep: most times, my brother hasn't even waked up, he's become so used to this and he doesn't give a damn. Egotistic and insensitive, that's my brother: sometimes he makes me mad. I act the same way he does, but at least I understand that it's not right, and I'm the first to be discontent. Still I keep on, though with anger.

"Dog," I say to my brother Andrea, "you dog, you're killing your father and mother." He doesn't answer: he knows I'm a hypocrite and a clown, and nobody's a bigger do-nothing than me.

Ten, maybe twenty minutes later, my father's at the door again, in a stew. Now he uses a different method: kindly, almost indifferent invitations, a pathetic farce. He says: "Well, who's coming to San Cosimo with me? The vines have to be tied."

San Cosimo is our farm. Everything is drying up and there's no manpower or money to keep it running.

"The potatoes have to be dug. Are you coming, Andrea? Well? Are you coming? I'm speaking to you, Andrea. We have to water the beans. Are you coming?"

Andrea raises his mouth from the pillow. "No," he says, and goes back to sleep.

"Why not?" My father continues his farce. "It was all settled. Pietro? Are you coming, Pietro?"

Then he explodes again and calms down again and talks about the things to be done at San Cosimo, as if it were understood that we're going. That dog, I think of my brother, that dog, he could get up and give the poor old man some satisfaction, at least this once. But I myself feel no urge to get up, and I make an effort to be immersed again in my sleep, by now disturbed.

"Well, hurry up. I'll wait for you," our father says and goes off as if we were now in agreement. We hear him pacing and fuming downstairs, preparing the fertilizer, the sulphate, the seeds to be taken up there; every day he sets out and comes back laden like a mule.

We are thinking he's already gone when he yells again, from the foot of the stairs: "Pietro! Andrea! For God's sake, aren't you ready yet?"

This is his final outburst; then we hear his hobnailed footsteps behind the house, the gate slams, and he goes off along the path, hawking and spitting.

Now we could have a good long sleep, but I can't manage to doze off; I think of my father, burdened, climbing up the track spitting, and afterward at work, in a rage with the tenants who steal from him and let everything go to rack and ruin. And he looks at the plants and the fields, where the insects gnaw and burrow all over, and at the yellowing leaves and the thick weeds, all the work of his life that is falling to pieces like the sustaining walls of the terrace that crumble more with every rain; and he curses his sons.

Dog, I say, thinking of my brother, you dog. Then I prick up my ears and from below I can hear something clatter to the floor, a falling broomstick. My mother is alone in that enormous kitchen, and daylight is just brightening the windowpanes, and she is slaving for people who turn their backs on her. As I am thinking this, I fall asleep.

It's not yet ten o'clock when Mother starts yelling from the stairs, "Pietro! Andrea! It's ten already!" She sounds very angry, as if she were irritated by something extraordinary; but it's the same every morning. "Awright . . ." we yell back. And, awake by now, we stay in bed another half-hour, to become used to the idea of getting up.

Then I start saying, "Come on, Andrea, wake up. Let's get up, all right? Andrea, come on, start getting out of bed." Andrea grunts.

Finally, with a lot of huffing and stretching, we're on our feet. Andrea walks around in his pajamas with an old man's movements, his hair all disheveled and his eyes half blind, and he's already licking a paper to roll a smoke. He smokes at the window, then begins to wash and shave.

Meanwhile he has started grumbling, and little by little the grumbling gives way to singing. My brother has a baritone voice, and though in company he is always mournful and never sings, when he's alone, shaving or taking a bath, he strikes up one of those cadenced tunes of his in a grim voice. He doesn't know any songs, so he always comes forth with a Carducci poem he learned as a child: "On Verona's castle strikes the noonday sun. . . ."

I'm getting dressed on the other side of the room, and I act as chorus, joylessly, but with a kind of violence: "And the green Adige flows murmuring into the open country. . . ."

My brother continues his chant to the end, not overlooking a single stanza, as he washes his head and brushes his shoes. "Black as an old raven, and with eyes of coal. . . ."

The more he sings, the more I'm filled with anger, and I also start singing fiercely: "Ill-luck is mine, and an evil beast has bitten me. . . ."

This is the only time we make noise. Afterward we're quiet for the whole day.

We go downstairs and warm up some milk, then dip bread into it and eat noisily. Mother hovers over us and talks, complaining, but without insistence, about all the things that have to be done, the chores that could be performed. "Yes, yes," we answer, forgetting immediately.

As a rule I don't go out in the morning. I stay home, dawdling in the halls with my hands in my pockets, or I arrange my library. I haven't bought any new books for some time: it would take money; besides, I've lost interest in too many things, and if I started reading again I'd want to read everything, and I don't feel up to it. But I keep arranging the few books I have on the shelf: Italian, French, English; or else by subject—history, philosophy, fiction—or else I put all the bound volumes together, with the fine editions and the shabby books elsewhere.

My brother, on the contrary, goes to the Caffè Imperia and watches the billiards game. He himself doesn't play, because he doesn't know how: he stays there for hours and hours, looking at the players, following the balls in fancy triple shots, smoking, never getting excited, never betting since he has no money. Sometimes they let him keep score, but often his mind wanders and he makes mistakes. He transacts a little deal or two, enough to pay for his smokes. Six months ago he filed an application with the Aqueduct Administration for a job that would support him, but he hasn't followed it up; for the present he gets enough to eat, anyway.

At dinner my brother arrives late, and both of us eat in silence. My parents are always arguing about expenses and income and debts and about how to manage with two sons who aren't earning anything; and our father says, "Look at your friend Costanzo, look at your friend Augusto." Our friends aren't like us: they've formed a partnership, buying and selling the timber rights to some woods, and they're always out and about on business, dealing and bargaining, sometimes with our father, too; they earn piles of money and soon will own their own truck. They're crooks and our father knows it; still, he would like us to be like them rather than the way we are. "Your friend Costanzo earned such-and-such an amount on that deal," he says. "See if you can go in with them, too." But our friends hang around with us in their free time, and they never suggest deals to us; they know we're lazy and good-for-nothing.

In the afternoon, my brother goes back to sleep: there's no figuring out how he manages to sleep so much, but he does. I go to the movies: I go every day; if they're showing a film I've already seen, then I don't have to make any effort to follow the story.

After supper, stretched out on the sofa, I read some long, translated novels people lend me; often, as I read, I lose the thread of the plot and can never make heads or tails of it. My brother gets up as soon as he's eaten and leaves, to watch the billiards game.

My parents go straight to bed because they get up early in the morning: "Go to your room; you're wasting electricity here," they say to me as they climb the stairs. "I'm going," I say and remain lying there.

I'm already in bed and have been sleeping for a while when my brother comes back, around two. He turns on the light, stirs around the room, and has a last smoke. He tells me what's going on in the city, expresses kindly opinions of people. This is the hour when he is really awake and glad to talk. He opens the window to let the smoke out; we look at the hill with the lighted road and the dark, clear sky. I sit up in bed and, carefree, we chat for a long time about trivial things, until we're sleepy again.

WARTIME STORIES

FEAR ON THE FOOTPATH

AT A quarter past nine, just as the moon was rising, he reached the Colla Bracca meadow; at ten he was already at the juncture of the two trees; by half past twelve he'd be at the fountain; he might reach Vendetta's camp by one—ten hours of walking at a normal speed, but six hours at the most for Binda, the courier of the first battalion, the fastest courier in the partisan brigade.

He went hard at it, did Binda, flinging himself headlong down short cuts, never making a mistake at crossroads that all looked alike, recognizing stones and bushes in the dark. His firm chest kept the same rhythm of breathing; his legs went like pistons. "Hurry up, Binda!" his comrades would say as they saw him from a distance climbing up toward their camp. They tried to read in his face whether the news and orders he was bringing were good or bad; but Binda's face was shut like a fist, a narrow mountaineer's face with hairy lips on a short bony body more like a boy's than a youth's, with muscles like stones.

His was a tough and solitary job, being woken at all hours, sent out even to Serpe's camp or Pelle's, having to march in the dark valleys at night, accompanied only by a French tommy gun, light as a little wooden rifle, hanging on his shoulder; and when he reached a detachment he had to move on to another or return with the answer; he would wake up the cook and grope around in the cold pots, then leave again with a panful of chestnuts still sticking in his gullet. But it was the natural job for him, because he never got lost in the woods and knew all the paths, from having led goats about them or gone there for wood or hay since he was a child; and he never went lame or rubbed the skin off his feet scrambling about the rocks, as so many partisans did who'd come up from the towns or the navy.

Glimpses caught as he went along—a chestnut tree with a hollow trunk, blue lichen on a stone, the bare space around a charcoal pit—linked themselves in his mind to his remotest memories—an escaped goat, a polecat driven from its lair, the raised skirt of a girl. And now the war in these parts was like a continuation of his normal life; work, play, hunting, all turned into war: the smell of gunpowder at the Loreto bridge, escapes down the bushy slopes, minefields sown with death.

The war twisted closely around and around in those valleys like a dog trying to bite its tail; partisans elbow to elbow with *bersaglieri* and Fascist militia; each side alternating between mountain and valley, making wide turns around the crests so as not to run into one another and find themselves fired on; and always someone killed, either on hill or valley. Binda's village, San Faustino, was down among fields, three groups of houses on each side of the valley. His girl, Regina, hung out sheets from her window on days when there were roundups. Binda's village was a short halt on his way up and down; a sip of milk, a clean vest ready washed by his mother; then off he had to hurry, in case the Fascists suddenly arrived, for there hadn't been enough partisans killed at San Faustino.

All winter it was a game of hide and seek; the *bersaglieri* at Baiardo, the Militia at Molini, the Germans at Briga, and in the middle of them the partisans squeezed into two corners of the valley, avoiding the round-ups by moving from one to the other during the night. That very night a German column was marching on Briga, had perhaps already reached Carmo, and the Militia were getting ready to reinforce Molini. The partisan detachments were sleeping in stalls around half-spent braziers; Binda marched along in the dark woods, with their salvation in his legs, for the order he carried was: "Evacuate the valleys at once. Entire battalion and heavy machine guns to be on Mount Pellegrino by dawn."

Binda felt anxiety fluttering in his lungs like bats' wings; he longed to grasp the slope two miles away, pull himself up it, whisper the order like a breath of wind into the grass and hear it flowing off through his mustache and nostrils, till it reached Vendetta, Serpe, Gueriglia; then scoop himself out a hole in the chestnut leaves and bury himself in it, he and Regina, first removing the cones that might prick Regina's legs; but the more leaves he scooped out the more cones he found—it was impossible to make a place for Regina's legs there, her big soft legs with their smooth thin skin.

The dry leaves and the chestnut cones rustled, almost gurgled, under Binda's feet; the squirrels, with round, glittering eyes, ran to hide at the tops of the trees. "Be quick, Binda!" the commander, Fegato, had said to him when giving him the message. Sleep rose from the heart of the night, there was a velvety feel on the inside of his eyelids; Binda would have liked to lose the path, plunge into a sea of dry leaves and swim in them until they submerged him. "Be quick, Binda!"

He was now walking on a narrow path along the upper slopes of the Tumena valley, which was still covered with ice.

The widest valley in the area, it had high sides wide apart; the one opposite him was glimmering in the dark, the one on which he was walking had bare slopes scattered with an occasional bush from which, in daytime, groups of partridges rose fluttering. Binda felt he saw a distant light, down in lower Tumena, moving ahead of him. It zigzagged every now and again as if going around a curve, vanished, and reappeared a little farther on in an unexpected spot. Who on earth could it be at that hour? Sometimes it seemed to Binda that the light was much farther away, on the other side of the valley, sometimes that it had stopped, and sometimes that it was behind him. Who could be carrying so many different lights along all the paths of lower Tumena—perhaps in front of him, too, in higher Tumena—winking on and off like that? The Germans!

Following on Binda's tracks was an animal roused from deep back in his childhood; it was coming after him, would soon catch up with him: the animal of fear. Those lights were the Germans searching Tumena, bush by bush, in battalions. Impossible, Binda knew, although it would be almost pleasant to believe it, to abandon himself to the blandishments of that animal from childhood, which was following him so closely. Time was drumming, gulping in Binda's throat. Perhaps it was too late now to arrive before the Germans and save his comrades. Already Binda could see Vendetta's hut at Castagna burned out, the bleeding bodies of his comrades, the heads of some of them hanging by their long hair on branches of larch trees. "Be quick, Binda!"

He was amazed at where he was, for he seemed to have gone such a little way in such a long time; perhaps he had slowed down or even stopped without realizing it. He did not change his pace, however; he knew well that it was always regular and sure, that he mustn't trust the animal that came to visit him on these night missions, wetting his temples with its invisible fingers slimy with saliva. Binda was a healthy lad, with good nerves, cool in every eventuality; and he held on to all his power to act even though he was carrying that animal around with him like a monkey tethered to his neck.

The surface of the Colla Bracca meadow looked soft in the moonlight. "Mines!" thought Binda. There were no mines up there, Binda knew; they were a long way off, on the other slope of the mountain. But now Binda began thinking that the mines might have moved underground from one part of the mountain to the other, following his steps like enormous underground spiders. The earth above mines produces strange funguses, disastrous to knock over; everything would go up in a second, but each second would become as long as a century and the world would have stopped as if by magic.

Now Binda was going down through the wood. Drowsiness and darkness drew gloomy masks on the tree trunks and bushes. There were Germans all around. They must have seen him pass the Colla Bracca meadow in the moonlight, they were following him, waiting for him at the entrance to the wood. An owl hooted nearby: it was a whistle, a signal for the Germans to close in around him. There, another whistle; he was surrounded! An animal moved behind a bush of heather; perhaps it was a hare, perhaps a fox, perhaps a German lying in the thickets keeping him covered. There was a German in every thicket, a German perched at the top of every tree, with the squirrels. The stones were pullulating with helmets, rifles were sprouting among the branches, the roots of the trees ended in human feet. Binda was walking between a double row of hidden Germans, who were looking at him with glistening eyes from among the leaves; the farther he walked the deeper he penetrated their ranks. At the third, the fourth, the sixth hoot of the owl all the Germans would jump to their feet around him, their guns pointed, their chests crossed by Sten-gun straps.

One named Gund, in the middle of them, with a terrible white smile under his helmet, would stretch out huge hands to seize him. Binda was afraid to turn around in case he saw Gund looming above his shoulders, Sten gun at the ready, hands open in the air. Or perhaps Gund would appear on the path ahead, pointing a finger at him, or come up and begin walking silently along beside him.

Suddenly he thought he must have missed the way; yet he recognized the path, the stones, the trees, the smell of musk. But they were stones, trees, musk from another place, far away, from a thousand different faraway places. After these stone steps there should be a short drop, not a bramble bush. After that slope a bush of broom, not of holly; the side of the path should be dry, not full of water and frogs. The frogs were in another valley, near the Germans; at the turn of the path there was a German ambush waiting and he'd suddenly fall into their hands, find himself facing the big German named Gund who is deep down in all of us, and who opens his enormous hands above us all, yet never succeeds in catching us.

To drive away Gund he must think of Regina, scoop a niche for Regina in the snow but the snow is hard and frozen —Regina can't sit on it in her thin dress; nor can she sit under the pines—there are endless layers of pine needles; the earth beneath is all ant hills, and Gund is already above, lowering his hands to their heads and throats lowering still.

. . . He gave a shriek. No, he must think of Regina, the girl who is in all of us and for whom we all want to scoop a niche deep in the woods—the girl with big hips, dressed only in hair that falls down over her shoulders.

But the pursuit between Binda and Gund is nearing its end; Vendetta's camp is now only fifteen, twenty minutes away. Though Binda's thoughts run ahead, his feet go on placing themselves regularly one in front of the other so he won't lose breath. When he reaches his comrades his fear will have vanished, canceled even from the bottom of his memory as something impossible. He must think of waking up Vendetta and Sciabola, the commissar, to explain Fegato's order to them; then he'll set off again for Serpe's camp.

But would he ever reach the hut? Wasn't he tied by a wire that dragged him farther away the nearer he got? And as he arrived wouldn't he hear *ausch ausch* from Germans sitting around the fire eating up the remaining chestnuts? Binda imagined himself arriving at the hut to find it half burned out and deserted. He would go inside: empty. But in a corner, huge, sitting on his haunches, with his helmet touching the ceiling, would be Gund, with his eyes round and glistening like the squirrels' and his white toothy smile between damp lips. Gund would make a sign to him: "Sit down." And Binda would sit down.

There, a hundred yards off, a light! It was them! Which of them? He longed to turn back, to flee, as if all the danger were up there in the hut. But he walked on quickly, his face hard and closed like a fist. Now the fire suddenly seemed to be getting too near—was it moving to meet him?—now to be getting farther off—was it running away? But it was motionless, a campfire that had not yet gone out, as Binda knew

"Who goes there?"

He did not quiver an eyelash. "Binda," he said.

Sentry: "I'm Civetta. Any news, Binda?"

"Is Vendetta asleep?"

Now he was inside the hut, with sleeping comrades breathing all around him. Comrades, of course; who could ever have thought they'd be anything else?

"Germans down at Briga, Fascists up at Molini. Evacuate. By dawn you're all to be up on the crest of Mount Pellegrino with the heavies."

Vendetta, scarcely awake, was fluttering his eyelids. "God," he said. Then he got up, clapped his hands. "Wake up, everyone, we've got to go out and fight."

Binda was now sucking at a can of boiled chestnuts, spitting out the bits of skin sticking to them. The men divided up into shifts for carrying the ammunition and the tripod of the heavy. He set off. "I'm going on to Serpe's," he said. "Be quick, Binda!" exclaimed his comrades.

HUNGER AT BÉVERA

THE FRONT had stopped there, as it had in '40, except that this time the war did not end and there seemed no chance that things would move. People did not want to do as they had in '40, load a few rags and chickens on to a cart and set off with a mule in front and a goat behind. When they got back in '40 they had found all their drawers overturned on the floor and human excrement in the cooking pots; for Italians, when soldiers, don't bother whether the damage they do is to friends or enemies. So people stayed on, with the French shells hitting their houses day and night and the German shells whistling over their heads.

"One day or another, when they really decide to advance," people said, and had to go on repeating this to each other from September 1944 to April 1945, "they'll put their backs into it, those blessed Allies will."

The valley of Bévera was full of people, peasants and also refugees from Ventimiglia, and they had nothing to eat; there were no reserves of food, and flour had to be fetched from the town. And the road into the town was under shellfire night and day.

By now they were living more in holes than in houses; one day the men of the village collected in a cave to decide what to do.

"What we'll have to do," said the man from the Committee of Liberation, "is take turns going down to Ventimiglia to fetch bread."

"Fine," said another. "So one by one we'll all be blown to bits on the way."

"Or if not, the Germans will get us one by one and off we'll go to Germany," said a third.

And another asked, "What about an animal to transport the stuff? Will anyone offer theirs? No one'll risk it who still has one. Obviously whoever gets through won't come back, any more than animals or bread."

The animals had already been requisitioned, and anyone who'd saved his kept it hidden.

"Well," said the man from the committee, "if we don't get bread here, how are we going to live? Is there anyone who feels like taking a mule down to Ventimiglia? I'm wanted by the Fascists down there or I'd go myself."

He looked around; the men were sitting on the floors of the cave with expressionless eyes, scooping at the tufa with their fingers.

Then old Bisma, who'd been down at the end, looking around with his mouth open and not understanding anything, got up and went out of the cave. The others thought he wanted to urinate: he was old and needed to fairly often.

"Careful, Bisma," they shouted after him. "Do it under cover."

But he did not turn around.

"As far as he's concerned they might not be shelling at all," someone said. "He's deaf and doesn't notice."

Bisma was more than eighty and his back seemed permanently bent under a load of faggots—all the faggots he had hauled throughout his life from woods to stalls. They called him Bisma because of his mustaches, which had once, they said, looked like Bismarck's; now they were a pair of scraggy white tufts that seemed about to fall off at any moment, like all the other parts of his body. Nothing fell off, though, and Bisma dragged himself along, his head swaying, with the expressionless and rather mistrustful look that deaf people have.

He reappeared at the mouth of the cave.

"Eeee!" he was calling.

Then the others saw that he was dragging his mule behind him, and that he'd put on its pack saddle. Bisma's mule seemed older than its master; its neck was flat as a board and hung to the ground, and its movements were cautious, as if the jutting bones were about to break through its skin and appear through the sores, black with flies.

"Where're you taking the mule to, Bisma?" they asked.

He swayed his head from side to side, with his mouth open. He couldn't hear.

"The sacks," he said. "Give them to me."

"Hey," they exclaimed. "How far d'you think you're going to get, you and that old bag of bones?"

"How many pounds?" he asked. "Well? How many pounds?"

They gave him the sacks, indicating the number of pounds on their fingers, and off he set. At every whistle of a shell the men peered out from the threshold of the cave, at the roaa and at that bent figure drawing farther away; both the mule and the man riding on the pack saddle seemed to be swaying and looked as if they might fall down at any minute. The shells were falling ahead of them, raising a thick dust, pitting the track in front of the mule's cautious steps; and when they fell behind Bisma did not even turn around. At every shell fired, at every whistle, the men held their breath. "This one'll get him," they said. Suddenly he vanished altogether, wrapped in dust. The men were silent; when the dust settled they would see a bare road, without even a trace of him. Instead both reappeared like ghosts, the man and the mule, and went hobbling slowly along. Then they got to the last turn in the road and moved out of sight. "He won't make it," said the men, and turned their backs.

But Bisma kept riding along the stony road. The old mule kept putting its hoofs down uncertainly on the surface pitted with flints and new holes; its skin was stretched tight from the burning of the sores under its pack saddle. The explosions made no impression on it; it had suffered so much in its life that nothing could make any impression on it any more. It was walking along with its muzzle bent down, and its eyes, limited by the black blinkers, were noticing all sorts of things: snails, broken by the shelling, spilling an iridescent slime on the stones; ant hills ripped open and the black and white ants hurrying hither and thither with eggs; torn-up grasses showing strange hairy roots like trees.

And the man riding on the pack saddle was trying to keep himself upright on the thin haunches, while all his poor bones were starting in their sockets at the roughness of the road. But he had lived his life with mules, and his ideas were as few and as resigned as theirs; it had always been long and tiring to find his bread, bread for himself and bread for others, and now bread for the whole of Bévera. The world, this silent world which surrounded him, seemed to be trying to speak to him, too, with confused boomings that reached even his sleeping eardrums, and strange disturbances of the earth. He could see banks crumbling, clouds rising from the fields, stones flying, and red flashes appearing and disappearing on the hills; the world was trying to change its old face and show its underbelly of earth and roots. And the silence, the terrible silence of his old age, was ruffled by those distant sounds.

The road at the mule's feet sent out huge sparks, its nostrils and throat filled with earth, a hail of splintered stones hit the man and the mule from the side while the branches of a big olive tree whirled in the air above. Yet the man wouldn't fall unless the mule fell. And the mule held on, its hoofs rooted in the torn-up earth, its knees just not giving way.

In the evening, up at Bévera, someone shouted, "Look! It's Bisma coming back! He's made it!"

Then the men and women and children came out of the houses and caves and saw the mule at the last turn of the road, coming ahead more bent than ever under the weight of sacks, and Bisma behind, on foot, hanging on to its tail so that they couldn't tell whether he was pushing or being pulled.

Bisma had a great welcome from the people of the valley when he got in with the bread. It was distributed in the big cave; the inhabitants passed through one by one while the man from the committee handed out a loaf a head. Near him stood Bisma, munching his loaf with his few teeth and looking around at everyone.

Bisma went to Ventimiglia the next day, too. His mule was the only animal the Germans were sure not to want. He went down every day to fetch bread, and every day he passed unhurt through the shells; he must have made a deal with the devil, they said.

Then the Germans evacuated the left bank of the Bévera River, blew up two bridges and a piece of road, and laid down mines. The inhabitants were given forty-eight hours to leave the village and the area. They left the village but not the area back they went into their holes. But now they were isolated, caught between two fronts, with no way of getting supplies. It meant starvation.

When they heard the village had been evacuated, the Black Brigade came up. They were singing. One of them was carrying a tin of paint and a brush. On the walls he wrote: *They shall not pass. We go straight ahead. The Axis does not give way.*

Meanwhile, the others were wandering around the streets, with Sten guns on their shoulders, glancing at the houses. Then they began breaking in a door or two with their shoulders. At that moment Bisma appeared on his mule. He appeared at the top of a road on a slope, and came down between two rows of houses.

"Hey, where are you going?" said the men of the Black Brigade.

The old man did not seem to see them; the mule went on putting one wobbly leg in front of the other.

"Hey, we're talking to you!" The haggard, impassive old man, perched on that skeleton of a mule, seemed a ghost issued from the stones of the uninhabited and half-ruined village.

"He's deaf," they said.

The old man looked at them, one by one. The Black Brigade men went down a side alley. They reached a little square where the only sounds were water trickling in the fountain and distant guns.

"I know there's stuff in that house," said one of the Black Brigade, pointing. He was only a boy, with a red blotch under his eye. The echo among the houses of the empty square repeated his words one by one. The boy made a nervous gesture. The one with the brush wrote on a ruined wall: *Honor Is*

Struggle. A window that had been left open was banging and making more noise than the guns.

"Wait," said the boy with the red blotch to two others who were pushing at a door. He put the mouth of his Sten gun against the lock and fired a burst. The lock, all burned out, gave way. At that moment Bisma reappeared from the direction opposite to the one where they'd left him. He seemed to be promenading up and down the village on that ruin of a mule.

"Wait till he's passed," said one of the Black Brigade, and they stood in front of the door looking indifferent.

Rome or Death, wrote the man with the brush.

Very slowly, the mule crossed the square; every step seemed to be its last. The man riding it appeared to be on the point of falling asleep.

"Go away," shouted the boy with the blotch. "The village is evacuated."

Bisma did not turn around, intent on piloting his mule across that empty square.

"If we see you again," went on the same boy, "we'll shoot."

We shall win, wrote the man with the brush.

Now only Bisma's decrepit back could be seen above the black legs of the mule, which seemed almost halted.

"Let's go down there," decided the Black Brigade men and they turned under an arch.

"Hey. No time to lose. Let's begin with this house." They opened it up, and the boy with the blotch entered first. The house was empty, with nothing in it but echoes. They wandered around the rooms and came out again.

"I'd like to set fire to the whole village, I would," said the boy with the blotch.

We shall go straight ahead, wrote the other man.

At the end of the little alley Bisma reappeared. He advanced toward them.

"Don't," said the Black Brigade men to the boy with the blotch, who was taking aim.

Duce, wrote the other man.

But the boy with the blotch had fired a burst. They were mown down together, the man and the mule, but they remained on foot. It seemed as if the mule had fallen on its four hoofs and still, black spindly legs, all in one piece. The Black Brigade stood looking on; the boy with the blotch had loosened the sten gun on its holster and was picking his teeth. Then they bowed together, man and mule, and seemed to take another step; instead they fell down in a heap.

That night the people of the village came to take them away. Bisma they buried; the mule they cooked and ate. It was tough meat, but they were hungry.

GOING TO HEADQUARTERS

It was a sparse wood, almost destroyed by fire, gray with charred tree trunks amid the dry reddish needles of the pines. Two men, one armed, the other unarmed, were zigzagging down between the trees.

"To headquarters," the armed man was saying. "To headquarters, that's where we're going. Half an hour's walk at the most."

"And then?"

"Then what?"

"Then will they let me go?" said the unarmed man. He was listening to every syllable of every reply as if searching for a false note.

"Yes, they'll let you go," said the armed man. "I hand them the papers from battalion, they enter them on their list, then you can go home."

The unarmed man shook his head, looking pessimistic.

"Oh, they take a long time, these things do. I know . . " he said, perhaps just to hear the other man repeat, "They'll let you go at once, I tell you."

"I was hoping," the unarmed man went on, "I was hoping to be home this afternoon. Ah, well, patience."

"You'll make it, I tell you," replied the armed man. "Just a few questions, and they'll let you go. They've got to cross off your name from the list of spies."

"Have you got a list of spies?"

"Of course we have. We know 'em all, the spies. And we get 'em, one by one."

"And my name's on it?"

"Yes, your name, too. They must cross it off properly now, or you risk being taken again."

"Then I really should go there myself, so I can explain the whole thing to them."

"We're going there now. They have to look into it properly to check."

"But by now," said the unarmed man, "by now you all know I'm on your side and have never been a spy."

"Exactly. We know all about it now You don't have to worry now."

The unarmed man nodded and looked around. They were in a big clearing, with mangy pines and larches killed by fire and draped with fallen branches. They had left, refound, and lost the path again, and were walking apparently at random among the scattered pines through the wood. The unarmed man did not know this area. Evening was creeping up in thin layers of mist. Down below, the woods were lost in the dark. It worried him, their leaving the path; the other seemed to be walking at random. He tried bearing right, hoping to find the path again; the other also bore right, apparently at random. Then the unarmed man turned wherever the walking was easier, with the armed man following him.

He decided to ask, "But where's the headquarters?"

"We're going toward it," replied the armed man. "You'll soon see it now."

"But what place, what area is it, more or less?"

"Well," he replied, "one can't say headquarters is in any place or area. Headquarters is wherever it is. You understand?"

He understood; he was a person who understood things. But he asked, "Isn't there a path to it?"

The other replied, "A path? You understand. A path always goes somewhere. One doesn't get to headquarters by paths. You understand."

The unarmed man understood; he was a person who understood things, an astute man.

He asked, "D'you often go to headquarters?"

"Often," said the armed man. "Yes, often."

He had a sad face, with a vacant look. Apparently he didn't know those parts very well. Every now and again he seemed lost, yet he went walking on as if it did not matter.

"And why have they told you to take me along today?" asked the unarmed man, scrutinizing him.

"That's my job, to take you along," he replied. "I'm the one who takes people along to headquarters."

"You're their courier, are you?"

"That's right," said the armed man. "Their courier."

"A strange courier"—thought the unarmed man—"who doesn't know the way. But"—he thought—"today he doesn't want to go by the paths in case I realize where the headquarters is, for they don't trust me. A bad sign, their not trusting me yet," the unarmed man couldn't help thinking. But though it was a bad sign, it did mean that they really were bringing him to headquarters and intended to let him go free.

Another bad sign, apart from this, was that the woods were getting thicker and thicker. Then there was the silence and this gloomy armed man.

"Did you take the secretary along to headquarters, too? And the brothers from the mill? And the schoolmistress?" He asked this question all in one breath, without stopping to think, for it was the decisive question, the question that meant everything; the secretary of the commune, the brothers from the mill, the schoolmistress, were all people who had been taken away and never returned, of whom nothing more had ever been heard.

"The secretary was a Fascist," said the armed man. "The brothers from the mill were in the Militia, the schoolmistress worked with the Fascists."

"I just wondered, since they'd never come back."

"What I mean is," insisted the armed man, "they were what they were. You're what you are. There's no comparison."

"Of course," said the other. "There's no comparison. I only asked what had happened to them out of curiosity."

He felt sure of himself, the unarmed man did, enormously sure of himself. He was the astutest man in the village; it was difficult to get the better of him. The others, the secretary and the schoolmistress, had not come back; he would come back. "I big *Kamerad*," he would say to the German sergeant. "Partisan not *kaput* me. I *kaput* all partisans." Perhaps the sergeant might laugh.

But the burned trees seemed interminable and ambiguous and his thoughts were surrounded by darkness and the unknown, like the bare spaces in the middle of these woods.

"I don't know about the secretary and the others. I'm the courier."

"They'll know at headquarters though?" insisted the unarmed man.

"Yes. Ask them at headquarters. They'll know there."

Dusk was falling. He had to walk carefully in the undergrowth, watching where his feet went in case they slipped on rocks hidden under the thick scrub; and watching where his thoughts went, too, as they followed each other in growing disquiet, in case they suddenly plunged headlong into panic.

Surely if they'd thought him a spy they would never have let him go through the woods like this, alone with this man who didn't seem to be taking any notice of him at all; he could have escaped from him any time he wanted. Suppose he tried to escape now—what would the other man do?

As he wound down among the trees the unarmed man began to draw a little way off, to bear left when the other bore right. But the armed man went on walking almost, it seemed, without taking any notice of him; down through the sparse woods they went, now some distance from each other. Sometimes they even lost sight of each other, hidden by trunks and shrubs; then suddenly the unarmed man would turn around and see the other above him.

"If they let me free for a moment, this time they won't get me again," the unarmed man had thought till then. But now he surprised himself thinking, "If I manage to escape, then this time . . ." And already in his mind he saw Germans, columns of Germans, Germans in trucks and armored cars, a sight that meant death for the others and safety for him, who was an astute man, a man no one could get the better of.

Now they were out of the glades and undergrowth and entering thick green woods, untouched by fire; the ground was covered with dry pine needles. The armed man had remained behind; perhaps he had taken another route. Then, very cautiously, his tongue between his teeth, the unarmed man hurried his pace, pushing deeper into the thick woods, flinging himself down slopes, among the pine trees. He was escaping, he suddenly realized. He had a moment of panic; but he realized also that he'd got too far away now and that the other must have noticed he was trying to escape and was sure to be following him. The only thing to do was go on running, for things might be ugly if he came within the other's range again after trying to escape.

He turned at the sound of a footstep above him; a few yards away the armed man was coming toward him with his calm, indifferent pace. His gun was in his hand. He said, "There must be a short cut this way," and gestured the other to go ahead of him.

Everything then went back to the way it was before: an ambiguous world, where things might go completely wrong or completely right; the wood thickening instead of thinning out, this man who'd almost let him escape without a word.

He asked, "Does it go on forever, this wood?"

"Just around the hillside and there we are," said the other. "Bear up, you'll be home by tonight."

"Are they sure to let me go, just like that? I mean, won't they keep me there as a hostage, for instance?"

"We aren't Germans; we don't take hostages. At the most they might take your boots as hostages: we're all nearly barefoot."

The man began to grumble as if his boots were the one thing he was frightened of losing, but at heart he was pleased; every detail of his future, good or bad, helped to restore a slight feeling of confidence.

"Well," said the armed man. "Since you hold by your boots so much, let's do this: you put on mine until we get to headquarters, and since mine are all in pieces they won't take them off you. I'll put on yours, and when I come back with you I'll hand them over again."

Even a child would have realized this was just a trick. The armed man wanted his boots; all right, the unarmed man would give him whatever he wanted; he was a man who understood, and felt pleased at getting off so cheaply. "I great *Kamerad,*" he'd say to the German sergeant. "I give them boots and they let me go." Perhaps the sergeant would let him have a pair of knee boots like the ones German soldiers wore.

"Then you don't hold anyone hostage? Not even the secretary and the others?"

"The secretary had three of our comrades taken; the brothers from the mill went on round-ups with the Militia; the schoolmistress went to bed with the men of the Tenth Flotilla."*

The unarmed man halted. He said: "You don't by any chance think I'm a spy, too? You haven't by any chance brought me here to kill me?" And he bared a few teeth as if in a smile.

"If we thought you a spy," said the armed man, "I wouldn't do this." He snapped back the safety catch of the gun. "And this." He put it to his shoulder and made a motion as if about to fire at him.

"There," thought the spy. "He's not firing."

But the other never lowered his gun; he pressed the trigger instead.

"In salvos, it fires in salvos," the spy just had time to think.

* Tenth Motor Torpedo Boat Flotilla (Decima Mas); Fascist Marines.

And when he felt the bullets hitting him like fiery fists that never stopped, the thought still crossed his mind, "He thinks he's killed me, but I'm alive."

He fell face downward and the last shot caught him with a vision of stockinged feet and his boots being pulled off.

So he remained, a corpse in the depth of the woods, his mouth full of pine needles. Two hours later he was already black with ants.

THE CROW COMES LAST

THE CURRENT was a network of light transparent ripples with the water flowing in the middle. Every now and again silver wings seemed to flutter on the surface, a trout's back glittering before it zigzagged down.

"It's full of trout," said one of the men.

"If we throw a grenade in, they'll all come to the surface with their bellies in the air," said the other; he took a grenade from his belt and began to unscrew the cap.

Then a boy who was watching stepped forward, a mountaineer with an apple face. "Give it to me," he said and took the rifle from one of the men. "What does he want?" said the man and tried to take the rifle away. But the boy was aiming the gun at the water as if looking for a target. "If you fire into the water you'll frighten the fish, that's all," the man tried to say, but he didn't even finish. A trout had surfaced with a flash, and the boy had fired a shot at it as if expecting it at that very spot. And the trout was now floating with its white belly in the air. "O-o-oh!" said the men. The boy reloaded the gun and swung it around; the air was bright and tight; the pine needles on the other bank and the ripples on the current showed up clearly. Something darted to the surface; another trout. He fired; it was floating, dead. The men looked at the trout and then at him. "He's a good shot, this kid," they said.

The boy swung the muzzle of the gun around again. It was strange, thinking it over, to be so surrounded by air, separated from other things by yards of air. When he aimed the gun, on the other hand, the air was a straight invisible line drawn tight from the mouth of the rifle to the target, to the hawk flying up there in the sky with wings that did not seem to move. When he pressed the trigger, the air was still as empty and transparent as before, but up there, at the other end of the line, the hawk was folding its wings and dropping like a stone. From the open bolt floated the good smell of gunpowder.

They gave him some more cartridges when he asked for them. Lots of men were looking on now from the bank behind him. Why, he thought, could he see the pine cones at the tops of the trees on the other bank and not touch them? Why was there this empty distance between things and himself? Why were the pine cones—which seemed part of him, inside his eyes—so far away instead? Surely it was an illusion when he aimed the gun into the empty distance and touched the trigger and at the same second a pine cone dropped in smithereens? The sense of emptiness felt like a caress—emptiness inside the rifle barrel continuing through the air and filling out when he shot; the pine cone up there, a squirrel, a white stone, a butterfly. "He never misses once, this kid," said the men, and none of them felt like laughing.

"You come with us," said the commander. "If you give me a rifle," replied the boy. "Well, of course." So he went.

He left with two cheeses and a haversack full of apples The village was a blotch of slate, straw, and cow dung at the bottom of the valley. It was fine to leave, because there were new things to be seen at every turn, trees with cones, birds flying from branches, lichen on stones, all at those false distances, the distances that could be filled by a shot swallowing the air in between. He must not fire, though, they told him: these parts had to be passed in silence, and the cartridges were needed for the war. But at a certain point a hare, frightened by their steps, ran across the path amid waves and shouts from the men. Just as it was vanishing into the thickets, a bullet from the boy stopped it. "Good shot," even the commander said, "but we're not out hunting here. You mustn't fire again even if you see a pheasant." Not an hour passed before more shots rang out from the file of men. "That boy again!" cried the commander furiously and went up to him. The boy was laughing all over his pink-and-white apple face. "Partridges," he said, showing them. "They rose from a thicket." "Partridges or grasshoppers, I told you. Give me that rifle. And if you make me angry again, you go back home." The boy grumbled a bit; it wasn't much fun walking along unarmed; but if he stayed with them there was always a chance of getting the rifle back.

That night they slept in a shepherd's hut. The boy woke up as the first light was showing in the sky, while the others were asleep. He took their best rifle, filled his haversack with cartridges, and took off. The early-morning air was mild and bright. Not far from the hut was a mulberry tree. It was the hour when the jays arrived. There was one; he fired, ran to fetch it, and put it in his haversack. Without moving from the spot he tried another target; a squirrel! Terrified by the shot, it was running to hide at the top of a chestnut tree. Now it was dead, a big squirrel with a gray tail, which shed tufts of hair when touched. From under the chestnut tree he saw a toadstool, red with white spots, poisonous, in a meadow lower down. He pulverized it with a shot, then went to see if he had really hit it. It was a lovely game going like this from one target to another; perhaps he could go around the world doing it. He saw a big snail on a stone and aimed at its shell; when he got to the place he found only the splintered stone and a little iridescent slime.

So he gradually got farther and farther away from the hut, down among unknown fields. From the stone he saw a lizard on a wall, from the wall a puddle and a frog, from the puddle a signpost on the road with a zigzag on it and below it . . . below it were men in uniform coming up with arms at the ready. When they saw that boy with a rifle smiling all over his pink-and-white apple face, they shouted and aimed their guns at him. But the boy had already picked out some gilt buttons on the chest of one of them and fired at a button. He heard the men's shouts and the bullets whistling singly or in bursts over his head; but he was now lying stretched on the ground behind a heap of stones at the roadside, under cover. It was a long heap, and he could move about, peep over at some unexpected point, see the gleam on the barrels of the soldiers' weapons, the gray and glittering parts of their uniforms, shoot at a stripe, a badge. Then he'd drop back to the ground and slide quickly over to another side to fire. After a bit he heard bursts from behind him firing over his head and hitting the soldiers; these were his comrades coming to reinforce him with machine guns. "If that boy hadn't woken us with his shots . . ." they were saying.

Covered by his comrades' fire, the boy could take better aim. Suddenly a bullet grazed one of his cheeks. He turned; a soldier had reached the road above him. He flung himself into a hole under cover, but had fired meanwhile and hit not the soldier but the rifle, by the bolt. He heard the soldier trying to reload, then fling the gun on the ground. The boy looked out then and fired at the soldier, who'd taken to his heels; the bullet tore off a shoulder strap.

He followed. Every now and again the soldier vanished in the wood, then reappeared. The boy nipped off the top of his helmet, then a strap on his belt. Meanwhile they had reached a remote valley where the sound of battle didn't reach. Suddenly the soldier found there were no more woods in front of him, only a glade, with thick bushy slopes. The boy was just coming out of the wood now; in the middle of the glade was a big rock; the soldier just had time to crouch down behind it, with his head between his knees. There for the moment he felt safe; he had some hand grenades with him and the boy could get no nearer, but could only keep the rock covered in case the soldier tried to escape. If only, thought the soldier, he could make a run for the bushes and slide down the thickly covered slope. But that bare space had to be crossed —how long would the boy stay there? And would he never lower that gun?

The soldier decided to make a test; he put his helmet on the point of his bayonet and hoisted it slightly above the rock. A shot rang out and the helmet rolled to the ground, pierced through.

The soldier did not lose heart; it was obviously easy to aim at the edges of the rock, but if he moved quickly it should be impossible to hit him. At that moment a bird winged quickly across the sky, a pigeon perhaps. One shot and it fell. The soldier dried the sweat on his neck. Another bird passed, a thrush; that fell, too. The soldier swallowed saliva. This must be a place of passage; birds went on flying overhead, all of them different, and the boy went on shooting and bringing them down. An idea came to the soldier: "If he is watching the birds he won't be watching me so much. The second he fires I'll run for it." But perhaps it would be better to make a test first. He took up the helmet again and put it back on the point of his bayonet, ready. Two birds passed together, snipe. The soldier was sorry to waste such a good opportunity for the test, but he did not dare risk it yet. The boy fired at one of the snipe, then the soldier pushed up the helmet, heard the shot and saw the helmet whirl in the air.

Now the soldier felt a taste of lead in his mouth; he scarcely noticed the other bird falling at a new shot. He must not hurry things, anyway; he was safe behind that rock, with his grenades. And why not try and get him with a grenade, while staying under cover? He stretched back on the ground, drew his arm out behind him, taking care not to show himself, gathered up all his strength and threw the grenade. A good effort; it would have gone a long way; but in the middle of its flight a shot exploded it in mid-air. The soldier flung himself on the ground to avoid the shrapnel.

When he raised his head the crow had come. It was wheeling slowly around in the sky above him. Was it a crow? he wondered. Now the boy would be certain to shoot it down. But the shot seemed to be a long time in coming. Perhaps the crow was flying too high? And yet he had hit other birds flying higher and faster. Finally there was a shot; now the crow would fall, but no, it went on flying around in slow impassive turns. A pine cone fell though, from a tree nearby. Was he beginning to shoot at pine cones now? One by one other pine cones were hit and fell with little thuds. At every shot the soldier looked at the crow; was he falling? No, the black bird was making lower and lower turns above him. Surely it was impossible the boy hadn't seen it? Perhaps the crow did not exist? Perhaps it was a hallucination of his? Perhaps when one is about to die one sees every kind of bird pass; when one sees the crow it means one's time has come. He must warn the boy, who was still going on firing at the pine cones. So the soldier got to his feet and pointed at the black bird. "There's a crow!" he shouted in his own language. The bullet hit him in the middle of an eagle with spread wings embroidered on his tunic.

Slowly the crow came circling down.

ONE OF THE THREE IS STILL ALIVE

THREE NAKED men were sitting on a stone. All the men of the village were standing around them and facing a bearded old man.

". . . and they were the highest flames I've ever seen in the mountains," the old man with the beard was saying. "And I said to myself: How can a village burn so high?

"And the smell of smoke was unbearable and I said to myself: How can smoke from our village stink like that?"

The tallest of the three naked men, who was hugging his shoulders because there was a slight wind, gave the oldest a dig in the ribs to get him to explain; he still wanted to understand, and the other was the only one who knew a little of the language. But the oldest of the three did not raise his head from between his hands, and now and again a quiver passed along the vertebrae on his bent back. The fat man was no longer to be counted on; the womanish fat on his body was trembling all over, his eyes were like windowpanes streaked by rain.

"And then they told me that the flames burning our houses came from our own grain, and the stink was from our sons being burned alive; Tancin's son, Gé's son, the son of the customs guard. . . ."

"My son Bastian!" shouted a man with haunted eyes. He was the only one who interrupted, every now and again. The others were standing there silent and serious, with their hands on their rifles.

The third naked man was not of exactly the same nationality as the others; he came from a part where villages and children had been burned at one time. So he knew what people think about those who burn and kill, and should have felt less hopeful than the others. Instead of which there was something, an anguished uncertainty, that prevented him from resigning himself.

"Now, we've only caught these three men," said the old man with the beard.

"Only three!" shouted the haunted-looking man; the others were still silent.

"Maybe among them, too, there are some who aren't really bad, who obey orders against their will, maybe these three are that sort. . . ."

The haunted-looking man glared at the old man.

"Explain," whispered the tallest of the three naked men to the oldest. But the other's whole life now seemed to be running away down the vertebrae on his spine.

"When children have been killed and houses burned one can't make any distinction between those who're bad and not bad. And we're sure of being in the right by condemning these three to death."

"Death," thought the tallest of the three naked men. "I heard that word. What does it mean—'death'?"

But the oldest one took no notice of him, and the fattest

now seemed to be muttering prayers. Suddenly the fattest had remembered he was a Catholic. He had been the only Catholic in the company, and his comrades had often made fun of him. "I'm a Catholic," he began muttering in his own language. It was not clear whether he was begging for salvation on earth or in heaven.

"I say that before killing them we should . . ." exclaimed the haunted-looking man, but the others had got to their feet and were not listening to him.

"To the Witch's Hole," said one with a black mustache. "So there won't be any graves to dig."

They made the three get up. The fattest put his hands over his front. Nothing made them feel more under accusation than being naked.

The peasants led them up along the rocky path, with rifles in their backs. The Witch's Hole was the opening of a vertical cave, a hole that dropped right down into the belly of the mountain, down, down, no one knew where. The three naked men were led up to the edge, and the armed peasants lined up in front of them; then the oldest of them began screaming. He screamed out despairing phrases, perhaps in his own dialect; the other two did not understand him. He was the father of a family, the oldest was, but he was also the least worthy, and his screams had the effect of making the other two feel annoyed with him and calmer in the face of death. The tall one, though, still felt that strange disquiet, as if he were not quite certain of something. The Catholic was holding his joined hands low; it was not clear whether this was to pray or to hide his front.

Hearing the eldest one screaming made the armed peasants lose their calm; they wanted to have done with the business as soon as possible, and began to fire scattered shots without waiting for an order. The tall one saw the Catholic crumple down beside him and roll into the precipice; then the oldest of them fell with his head back and vanished, dragging his last cry down the walls of rock. Between the puffs of gunpowder the tall one saw a peasant struggling with a blocked bolt; then he, too, fell into the darkness.

A cloud of pain in the back like a swarm of stinging bees prevented him from losing consciousness at once; he had fallen through a briar bush. Then tons of emptiness weighed down on his stomach, and he fainted.

Suddenly he seemed to be back on a height, as if the earth had given a great heave; he had stopped. His fingers were wet and he smelled blood. He must be crushed to bits and about to die. But he did not feel himself getting weaker, and all the agonies of the fall were lively and distinct in his mind. He tried to move a hand, the left one; it responded. He groped along the other arm, touched his pulse, his elbow; but the arm did not feel anything; it might have been dead, for it only moved if raised by the other hand. Then he had the sensation of holding the wrist of his right arm in both hands; this was impossible. He realized that he was holding someone else's arm; he had fallen on the dead body of one of the other two. He prodded the fat flesh of the Catholic; that soft cushion had broken his fall. That was why he was alive. That was one reason; also, he remembered now, he had not been hit but had flung himself down beforehand; he could not remember if he had done it intentionally, but that was not important now Then he discovered that he could see; some light filtered down there in the depths, and the tallest of the three naked men could make out his own hands and those sticking out of the heap of flesh beneath him. He turned and looked up; at the top was an aperture full of light—the opening of the Witch's Hole. First it hurt his eyes like a yellow flash; once they got used to it, he could see the blueness of the sky, far away from him, twice as far as the earth's crust.

The sight of the sky plunged him into despair; it would certainly be better to be dead. There he was with his two dead companions at the bottom of a very deep pit, from which he could never get out again. He shouted The streak of sky above became fringed with heads. "One of them's alive!" they said. They threw something down. The naked man watched it dropping like a stone, then hit against the wall, and heard an explosion. There was a niche in the rock behind him, and the naked man squeezed into it; the well was full of dust and pieces of splintered rock. He pulled at the body of the Catholic and held it up in front of the niche; it was starting to fall apart but there was nothing else he could use to shelter himself. He was just in time: another grenade came down, and reached the bottom, raising a spray of blood and stones. The corpse broke up; now the naked man had no defense or hope. In the patch of sky appeared the white beard of the big old man. The others had drawn to one side.

"Hey!" called the big man with the beard.

"Hey!" replied the naked man, from the depths.

And the big man with the beard repeated: "Hey!"

There was nothing else to say between them.

Then the big man with the beard turned around. "Throw him a rope," he said.

The naked man did not understand. He saw some of the heads leaving and the ones remaining making signs at him, signs of assurance, not to worry. The naked man looked at them with his head stuck out of the niche, not daring to expose himself altogether, feeling the same disquiet as when he had been sitting on the stone during the trial. But the peasants were not throwing grenades any more; they were looking down and asking him questions, to which he replied with groans. The rope did not come, and one by one the peasants left the edge. Then the naked man came out of his hiding place and looked at the distance separating him from the top, the walls of sheer naked rock.

At that moment appeared the face of the haunted man. He was looking around and smiling. Then he moved back from the edge of the Witch's Hole, aimed his rifle into it, and fired. The naked man heard the bullet whistle past his ear; the Witch's Hole was a narrow shaft and not quite vertical, so things thrown in rarely reached the bottom, and bullets easily hit a layer of rock and stopped there. He squatted in his refuge, with foam on his lips, like a dog. Now up there all the peasants were back and one was unwinding a long rope down the shaft. The naked man watched the rope coming down but did not move.

"Hey!" the one with the black mustache shouted down. "Catch hold of it and come up."

But the naked man stayed in his niche.

"Come on; up you go," they shouted. "We won't do you any harm."

And they made the rope dance about in front of his eyes. The naked man was frightened.

"We won't do you any harm. We swear it," the men were saying, trying to sound sincere. And they were sincere; they wanted to save him at all costs so as to be able to shoot him all over again; but at that moment they just wanted to save him, and their voices had a tone of affection, of human brotherhood.

The naked man sensed all this, and anyway he had little choice; he put a hand on the rope. But then among the men holding it he saw the head of the man with the haunted eyes, and he dropped the rope and hid himself. They had to begin convincing him, begging him, all over again; finally he decided and began going up. The rope was full of knots and easy to climb; he could also catch hold of jutting bits of rock. As the naked man moved slowly up toward the light, he saw the heads of the peasants at the top becoming clearer and bigger. Then the man with the haunted eyes reappeared all of a sudden and the others did not have time to hold him back; he was holding an automatic gun and began firing it at once. At the first burst the rope broke right above the naked man's hands. He crashed down, knocking against the sides, and fell back on the remains of his companions. Up there, against the sky, he saw the man with the beard waving his arms and shaking his head.

The others were trying to explain, in gestures and shouts, that it was not their fault, that they'd punish that madman, and that they were going to look for another rope and bring him up again. But the naked man had lost hope now; he would never be able to return to the earth's surface; he would never leave the bottom of this shaft, and he would go mad there drinking blood and eating human flesh, without ever being able to die. Up there, against the sky, there were good angels with ropes, and bad angels with grenades and rifles, and a big old man with a white beard who waved his arms but could not save him.

The armed men, seeing him unconvinced by their fair words, decided to finish him off with hand grenades, and began throwing them down. But the naked man had found another hiding place, a narrow horizontal crack in the rock where he could slip in and be safe. At every grenade that fell he crawled deeper into this crack, until he reached a point where he could not see any more light. He went on dragging himself along on his stomach like a snake, with darkness and the damp slimy rock all around him. From being damp the rock surface beneath him was now getting wet, then covered with water; the naked man could feel the cold trickle running under his stomach. It was the passage opened under the earth by the rains coming down through the Witch's Hole: a long narrow cavern, a subterranean drain. Where would it end? Perhaps it would lose itself in blind caves in the belly of the mountain, or perhaps it would funnel the water through narrow little channels that would issue into springs. And his body would rot away there in a drain and infect the waters of the springs, poisoning entire villages.

The air was almost unbreathable; the naked man felt the moment coming when his lungs would no longer be able to hold out. Instead, the flow of water was increasing, getting deeper and quicker; the naked man was now slithering along with his whole body underwater and could clean off the crust of mud and of his own and others' blood. He did not know whether he had moved far or not; the complete darkness and that slithering movement had deprived him of all sense of distance. He was exhausted. Before his eyes luminous shapeless forms were beginning to appear. The farther he advanced, the clearer these shapes became, taking on definite though continuously transforming edges. Supposing it was not just a dazzle inside the retina of his eyes, but a light, a real light, at the end of the cavern? He had only to close his eyes, or look in the opposite direction, to make certain. But anyone who stares at a light has a dazzled feeling at the roots of his eyes even if he shuts his lids or turns his gaze; he could not distinguish between the light outside and the lights in his own eyes, and remained in doubt.

He noticed something else new, by touch: the stalactites. Slimy stalactites were hanging from the roof of the cave and stalagmites coming up from the ground on the verges of the water, where they were not eroded. The naked man began pulling himself along by the stalactites above his head. And as he moved he noticed that his arms, from being folded to grasp the stalactites, were gradually straightening out, which meant that the cave was getting bigger. Soon the man could arch his back and walk on all fours; and the light was becoming less uncertain; he could tell now whether his eyes were open or shut, and he was beginning to make out the shapes of things, the arch of the roof, the droop of the stalactites, the black glitter of the current.

Finally he was walking erect, up the long cave toward the luminous opening, with the water to his waist—still hanging on to the stalactites, though, to keep himself straight. One stalactite seemed bigger than the others, and when the man seized it he felt it opening in his hand and a cold soft wing beating on his face. A bat! It flew off, and the other bats hanging with their heads down woke up and flew away; soon the whole cave was full of silent flying bats, and the man felt the wind from their wings around him and their skin brushing against his forehead and mouth. He walked on in a cloud until he reached the open air.

The cave came out into a torrent. Once again the naked man was on the crust of the earth, under the sky. Was he safe now? He must take care not to make any mistakes. The torrent was running silently over white and black stones. Around it was a wood full of twisted trees; all that grew in the undergrowth was thorns and brambles. He was naked in wild and deserted parts, and the nearest human beings were enemies who would pursue him with pitchforks and guns as soon as they saw him.

The naked man climbed a willow tree. The valley was all woods and shrub-covered slopes, under a gray hump of mountain. But at the end of it, where the torrent turned, there was a slate roof with white smoke coming up. Life, thought the naked man, was a hell, with rare moments recalling some ancient paradise.

ANIMAL WOODS

ON DAYS of Fascist round-ups the woods might have been a fairground. Off the paths, among the bushes and trees, there was a constant passage of families urging along a cow or a calf, and old women leading a goat on a rope, and girls with a goose under one arm. Some of them were even escaping with their rabbits.

Wherever one went, the thicker the chestnut woods, the more one ran into heavy-bellied bulls and tinkling cows, which were finding it difficult to move on those rocky slopes Best off were the goats, but perhaps the happiest were the mules, which just this once could move without carrying a burden and go cropping leaves along the alleys. The pigs went rooting about in the ground, pricking their snouts all over with chestnut husks; the chickens roosted in the trees and frightened the squirrels; the rabbits, which after centuries of cages had forgotten how to dig themselves lairs, took refuge in hollow tree trunks, where they were sometimes bitten by squirrels.

That morning a peasant named Giuà Dei Fichi was gathering fuel in a remote corner of the woods. He knew nothing about what was happening in the village, for he had left the evening before, intending to gather mushrooms in the morning, and had slept in the middle of the woods in a hut used, in autumn, for drying chestnuts.

So as he was chopping a dead tree trunk with a hatchet he was surprised to hear a vague tinkling of bells far and near through the woods. He stopped chopping and heard voices getting closer. "Oo-u," he shouted.

Giuà Dei Fichi was a short, tubby little man, with a face like a full moon, dark of skin and flushed with wine; he wore a green conical hat with a pheasant's feather stuck in it, a shirt with big yellow spots under a homespun jerkin, and a red scarf around his tubby stomach to hold up trousers covered with purple blotches.

"Coo-u!" came the reply, and between the green lichenous rocks appeared a close friend, a peasant with a mustache and a straw hat, dragging behind him a big, white-bearded goat.

"What're you doing here, Giuà?" asked his friend. "The Germans've reached the village and are going around to all the animal stalls!"

"Oh!" shouted Giuà Dei Fichi. "They'll find my cow, Cochineal, and take her off!"

"Hurry up and you may still be in time to hide her," advised his friend. "We saw the column as it was coming up through the valley and we took off at once. But they may not have reached your place yet."

Giuà left his hatchet and basket of mushrooms and rushed off. As he ran through the woods he met rows of ducks that scattered quacking between his feet, and flocks of sheep marching compactly side by side without moving to let him through, and children and old women who shouted, "They've reached the Madonnetta! They're searching the houses above the bridge! I've seen them turning he last corner before the village!" Giuà Dei Fichi speeded up his short legs, and went rolling down the slopes like a ball, and panting up the hills with his heart in his mouth.

On and on he ran till he reached a top of a hill from which opened a view of the village. A great expanse of tender early-morning air, a misty ring of hills, and in the middle the village, knobbly houses all stone and slate, heaped on top of one another. And through the thin air came the sounds of shouts in German and of fists banging against doors.

"Oh dear! The Germans are already in the houses!"

Giuà Dei Fichi was trembling all through his arms and legs; a bit of a tremor he already had from drinking, and more now came over him at the thought of his cow, Cochineal, the one possession he had in the world, about to be taken away from him.

Very quietly, cutting through fields, keeping under cover of vines, Giuà Dei Fichi drew near the village. His little house was one of the last, on the outskirts, in the middle of a green mass of pumpkins, where the village merged into vegetable patches; possibly the Germans might not have reached it yet.

Peeping around each corner, Giuà made his way into the village. He saw an empty street with the usual smells of hay and stalls; those new noises were coming from the middle of the village—inhuman voices and the stamping of iron-clad feet. There his house was—still shut up. The door of the stall on the ground floor was closed, and so was the one to the rooms at the top of the worn outside staircase, with its clumps of basil planted in cooking pots filled with earth. A voice from inside the stall said, "Mooooo." It was Cochineal recognizing the approach of her owner. Giuà blushed with pleasure.

But now from under an arcade resounded a tramp of feet; Giuà hid in a doorway, sucking in his round paunch. It was a German, with the look of a peasant, wrists and neck jutting out of his short tunic, and long, long legs and a big gun as long as himself. He had left the others to try to find something on his own; besides, the look and smells of the village reminded him of things he knew well. So he was walking along sniffing the air and looking around with a yellow, porkish face under the peak of his squashed cap. At that moment Cochineal lowed: "Mooo." She could not understand why her master had not arrived yet. The German quivered in his shrunken clothes and at once made for the stall; Giuà Dei Fichi held his breath.

He saw the German beginning to kick violently at the door; he'd break it in soon, for sure. Then Giuà slipped around the corner behind the house, went to the haystack, and began groping about under the hay. There he'd hidden his old double-barreled shotgun, with a full belt of cartridges. Giuà loaded the gun with a couple of shots, strapped the belt around his tummy, then very quietly, with the gun at the ready, went and hid behind the door of the stall.

The German was coming out, pulling Cochineal along behind him on a rope. She was a fine red cow with black markings (that was why she was called Cochineal), a young, affectionate, punctilious cow; she did not want to be taken away by this man she did not know, and was balking; the German had to pull her along by the halter.

Giuà Dei Fichi looked on, hidden behind a wall. Now, it should be said that Giuà was the worst shot in the village. Never had he succeeded in hitting, even by mistake, a squirrel, let alone a hare. When he shot at sitting thrushes, they didn't even bother to move from the branch. No one wanted to go shooting with him, for he was apt to hit other men's behinds. He couldn't aim: his hands always trembled.

Now he pointed the gun, but his hands were trembling and the barrel of the shotgun waved about in the air. He tried to aim at the German's heart, but what he saw through the sights was the cow's rump. "Oh dear!" thought Giuà. "Suppose I fire at the German and kill Cochineal?" So he didn't dare fire.

The German was moving along very slowly with this cow; she could sense the nearness of her master and was refusing to be dragged. Suddenly he realized that his fellow soldiers had already evacuated the village and were disappearing down the road. The German tried to catch up with them, pulling that stubborn cow after him; and Giuà followed him at a distance, jumping behind bushes and walls and pointing his shotgun every now and again. But he could not manage to keep the weapon steady, and the German and the cow were always too near each other for him to dare fire a shot. Must he let the German take her away?

To reach the column in the distance, the German took a short cut through the woods. Now it was easier for Giuà to trail him by hiding among the tree trunks. And perhaps now the German would begin walking farther away from the cow so that it would be possible to shoot at him.

Once in the woods, Cochineal seemed to lose her reluctance to move, and since the German was apt to get lost among the paths which he could scarcely make out, she even began guiding him and deciding whenever two paths crossed. Before long the German realized he was not on the short cut to the main road but in the middle of a thick woods; both he and the cow were lost, in fact.

Giuà Dei Fichi, his nose scratched by branches, his feet soaked by rivulets he'd stumbled into, was still following along behind, among flapping birds taking to flight and frogs croaking in the mud. It was even more difficult to aim among the trees, with all those obstacles around and that wine-red-and-black rump, which seemed always to be there under his eyes.

The German was already looking in alarm at the thickness of the woods and wondering how he could get out of it, when he heard a rustling in an arbutus bush and out came a fine red pig. At home he'd never seen pigs wandering about in the woods. He loosened the rope on the cow and began following the pig. As soon as Cochineal felt herself free she trotted off into the woods, which was, she sensed, full of friendly creatures.

Now was the moment for Giuà to shoot. The German was fussing around the pig, clutching at it to keep it still, but it slipped away.

Giuà was about to press the trigger when nearby appeared two small children, a little boy and a little girl, wearing woolen caps with pom-poms and long stockings. Big tears were dropping from their eyes. "Aim carefully, Giuà, please," they said. "If you kill the pig we'll have nothing left!" Giuà Dei Fichi felt the gun dancing about in his hands again; he had such a soft heart and was too easily moved, not by having to kill that German but by having to risk the pig that belonged to those two poor little children.

The German was swaying about among the rocks and bushes, gripping the pig, which was wriggling about and grunting, "Ghee . . . ghee . . . ghee. . . ." Suddenly the pig's grunts were answered by a "baaa" and out from a cave trotted a little lamb. The German let the pig go and ran after the lamb. "What strange woods," he thought, "with pigs in bushes and lambs in caves." And he caught the lamb, which was bleating at the top of its voice, by a leg, hitched it up on his shoulder like the Good Shepherd, and started off. Very quietly Giuà Dei Fichi followed. "This time he won't escape. This time he's had it," he said to himself, and was just about to fire when a hand raised the barrel of his gun. It was an old shepherd with a white beard, who was now holding out his clasped hands toward him and saying, "Giuà, don't kill my little lamb; kill the German but don't kill my little lamb. Aim well, just this once, aim well!" But Giuà was completely confused by now, and couldn't even find the trigger.

The German on his way through the woods was making discoveries that left him open-mouthed: chickens perched on trees, guinea pigs peering from hollow trunks. It was a complete Noah's ark. He saw a turkey spreading its tail on the branch of a pine. At once he put up his hand to catch it, but the turkey gave a little skip and went to perch on a branch higher up, still spreading its tail. The German left the lamb and began climbing up the pine. But for every layer of branches he reached, the turkey went up another layer, without looking in the least put out, still preening itself, its hanging wattles aflame.

Giuà moved under the tree; there was a leafy branch on his head, two others on his shoulders, and one tied to the barrel of his gun. But then a plump young woman with a red handkerchief tied around her head came up to him. "Giuà," she said, "listen to me. If you kill the German I'll marry you; if you kill the turkey I'll bump you off." Giuà, still a bachelor though no longer young, and very modest, blushed scarlet; his gun began waving around like a spit.

The German was still climbing and had reached the smallest branches; suddenly one of them broke under him and down he fell. He very nearly fell right on top of Giuà Dei Fichi, who did this once see straight and get away in time. But on the ground Giuà left all the branches that had been hiding him, so the German fell on them and did not hurt himself.

As he fell he saw a hare on the path. But no, it wasn't a hare; it was round and paunchy and did not run away when it heard a noise, but settled down on the ground. It was a rabbit; the German took it by the ears. He walked on, with the rabbit struggling and twisting about in all directions, so that in order not to let it escape he had to keep jumping about with his arm raised. The woods were full of lowing, bleating, and screeching. At every step were new things to be seen: a parrot on a holly branch, three goldfish wriggling in a spring.

Giuà, from astride the high branch of an ancient oak, was following the German's dance with the rabbit. But it was difficult to aim at him because the rabbit was constantly changing position and getting in between. Giuà felt a pull at a corner of his jerkin; it was a little girl with plaits and a freckly face. "Don't kill the rabbit, Giuà, please; I don't mind if you shoot the German, though."

Meanwhile, the German had reached a place covered with gray stones spotted with blue and green lichen. There were only a few bare pines growing there, and nearby opened a precipice. A hen was scratching about in the carpet of pine needles covering the ground. When the German began running after the hen, the rabbit escaped.

It was the thinnest, oldest, and scraggiest hen he had ever seen. It belonged to Girumina, the poorest old woman in the village. Now the German had it in his hands.

Giuà was lying on top of the rocks and had constructed a

pedestal of stones for his shotgun. He had even put up a sort of little fortress, with only a narrow slit for the barrel. Now he could fire without having any scruples: even if he killed that scraggy hen, little harm was done.

But now old Girumina came up to him, wrapped in her ragged black shawls, and began saying persuasively, "Giuà, it's bad enough that a German should take away my hen, the last thing I possess in all the world. But it's much worse that you should be the one to kill it."

Giuà began trembling more than ever before because of the great responsibility weighing on him. But he pulled himself together and pressed the trigger.

The German heard the shot and saw the chicken wriggling in his hands lose its tail. Another shot, and the chicken lost a wing. Was it bewitched, this chicken, that it exploded every now and again and was falling to pieces in his hands? There was another explosion and the chicken was completely featherless, ready for roasting, and yet it still went on flapping its one wing. Seized with terror, the German was holding the chicken away from himself by the neck. Giuà's fourth cartridge cut the neck off right under his hand and left him holding the head, which was still moving. He flung it aside and ran away. But he could not find any more paths. Near him was that rocky precipice. The last tree before the precipice was a carob, and in its branches the German saw a big cat crouching.

By now he was beyond feeling any surprise at seeing domestic animals scattered in the woods, and he put out a hand to stroke the cat. Then he took it by the nape of the neck hoping to please it and hear it purr.

For some time now the woods had been plagued by a savage

wild cat that killed birds and sometimes even got into the henhouses in the village. The German, who was expecting to hear it purr, suddenly saw the cat fling itself at him with its fur on end, and felt its claws slashing into him. In the struggle that followed both man and beast rolled over the edge of the precipice.

So it was that Giuà, a hopeless shot, was fêted as the greatest partisan and huntsman in the village. And poor Girumina was bought a brood of newly hatched chicks at the expense of the community.

MINE FIELD

"MINED" WAS what the old man had said, waving an opened hand before his eyes, as if he were wiping a clouded pane. "All along there, didn't know exactly where. They came and mined it. We were in hiding."

The man in the baggy trousers had glanced for a moment at the slope of the mountain, then at the old man standing erect in the doorway.

"But since the end of the war," he had said then, "there's been time to do something about it. There must be some kind of path. Somebody must know."

You know it well, old man, the younger man had thought, too; because the old man was surely a smuggler and knew the frontier terrain like the bowl of his pipe.

The old man had looked at the patched, baggy trousers, the other man's limp, torn knapsack, the layer of dust covering him from hair to shoes, bearing witness to the miles he must have covered on foot. "Nobody knows just where," the old man had repeated. "The pass. It's a mine field." Then he had made that gesture, as if there were a clouded glass between himself and everything else.

"Hey, I can't be all that unlucky, can I? To go and step right on a mine?" the younger man had asked, with a smile that seemed to set the old man's teeth on edge as an unripe persimmon would.

"Huh," the old man had said then. Only that: Huh.

Now the younger man was trying to remember the tone of that *huh*. Because it could have been a *huh, I should think not*, or a *huh, you never can tell*, or a *huh, nothing more likely*. But the old man had uttered only a *huh* without any special intonation, as blank as his gaze, bleak as this mountain terrain, where even the grass was short and tough as an ill-shaven human beard.

The trees along the slopes could never grow taller than the brush; every now and then there was a twisted, rubbery pine, situated so as to cast as little shade as possible. The man was now walking along the remnants of climbing trails, gnawed away year after year by the encroaching bushes and trodden only by smugglers' footsteps, an animal tread that leaves little imprint.

"Damn this land," the man said. "I can't wait to be on the other side." Luckily he had already taken this route once, before the war, and he could do without a guide. He also knew that the pass was a broad, high gap, and they couldn't mine the whole thing.

So he had only to be careful where he set his feet: a spot with a mine underneath must surely look different somehow from all other spots. Somehow: loose dirt, stones artfully arranged, fresher grass. Over there, for example: you knew immediately there could be no mines. No mines? What about that slab of slate lying askew? That bare patch in the midst of the field? And that tree across the path? But the pass was still far ahead. There couldn't be any mines, not yet. He walked on.

Perhaps he would have preferred to cross the mined zone at night, crawling in the darkness, not to elude the border guards—these places were safe from them—but to elude the fear of the mines, as if the mines were great dozing beasts that could waken at his passing. Marmots, enormous marmots curled up in underground lairs, with one acting as sentry on top of a rock, the way marmots do, to give the alarm with a hiss on seeing him.

At that hiss, the man thought, the mine field blows up, the enormous marmots fall on me and tear me to pieces with their teeth.

But never had a man been chewed by marmots, and never would he be blown up by mines. It was hunger that prompted these thoughts; he knew it. The man knew hunger, the tricks the imagination plays in times of hunger, when everything seen or heard assumes a meaning associated with food and chewing.

The marmots did exist, however. You could hear the hissing —"gheee . . . gheeeee . . ."—from up in the spills of rock. If I could succeed in killing a marmot with a stone, the man thought, and roast it on a stake . . .

He thought of the greasy smell of marmot, but without nausea; hunger gave him an appetite even for marmot fat, anything that could be eaten. For a week he had been lurking around farms, approaching shepherds to beg a loaf of brown bread, a cup of clotted milk.

"If only we had some for ourselves. We don't have anything," they would say, pointing to the bare, smoke-darkened walls, decorated only with a string or two of garlic.

He came within sight of the gap before he was expecting it and felt a twinge of amazement, almost of fear, at once: he wasn't expecting the rhododendrons to be in bloom. He had thought he would find the gap bare, so he could study every stone, every bush before taking a step forward. Instead, he was plunged up to his knees in a sea of rhododendrons, a uniform, impenetrable sea from which only the humps of the gray stones surfaced.

And under it, the mines. "Don't know exactly where," the old man had said. "All along there." And then he had passed those opened hands through the air. The younger man now thought he could see the shadow of those hands fall on the expanse of rhododendrons, spreading out until it covered them.

He had chosen a route along a winding crevasse flanking the broad gap, uncomfortable for walking but also uncomfortable to mine. Farther up, the rhododendrons thinned out, and among the rocks you could hear the "gheee . . . ghee . . ." of the marmots, as unrelenting as the sun on the back of his neck.

Where there are marmots, he thought, heading in that direction, it's a sign there are no mines.

But this reasoning was erroneous: there were anti-personnel mines, devised to kill men; and the weight of a marmot would not be enough to trip them. He had recalled the name of the mines at this moment, "anti-personnel"; and it frightened him.

Personnel, he repeated, human beings.

That name was suddenly enough to frighten him. Certainly, if they mine a pass it was in order to make it completely useless. He had better turn back, question the men of the area more closely, try some other way.

He turned to retrace his steps. But where had he set his

foot before? The rhododendrons stretched out behind him, a vegetable sea, impenetrable, with no trace of his passage. Perhaps he was already in the heart of the mine field, and a misstep could destroy him: he might as well go forward.

This damned land, he thought. Damned right to the end.

If only he had a dog, a big dog, heavy as a man, to send ahead. Instinctively, he clicked his tongue, as if urging a dog to run. I have to be my own dog, he thought.

Maybe a stone would do. There was one near him: big, but he could lift it. It was just right. He grabbed it with both hands and flung it ahead of himself as far as he could throw, uphill. The stone fell not far away and rolled back toward him. He could only try his luck, as he was doing.

He was already in the higher part of the gap, among the treacherous dry, rocky stream beds. The colonies of marmots had heard the man and were in a state of alarm. Their screams pierced the air like cactus spines.

But the man no longer thought of hunting the animals. He had realized that the gap, broad at its mouth, had gradually narrowed and now was only a passage between cliffs and brush. Then the man understood: the mine field could only be here. This was the only spot where a certain number of mines, placed at the correct interval, could block all passing. Instead of terrifying him, this discovery gave him a strange serenity. Very well: he now found himself in the middle of the mine field, that was sure. Now there was nothing to do but continue climbing, at random, and let what would happen, happen. If it was his fate to die that day, he would die; if not, he would walk between one mine and the next and would be saved.

He formulated this thought about fate without any conviction: he did not believe in fate. If he took a step it was because he could not do otherwise; it was because the movement of his muscles, the course of his thoughts led him to take that step. But there was a moment when he could take this step or that one, when his thoughts were in doubt, his muscles taut but without direction. He decided not to think, to let his legs move like a robot's, to set his feet on the stones without looking; but he had the nagging suspicion that it was his volition that decided whether he would turn right or left, place his foot on this stone or that.

He stopped. He felt a strange inner craving, compounded of hunger and fear, which he could not allay. He searched his pockets: he was carrying a little mirror, the memento of a woman. Maybe this was what he wanted: to look at himself in a mirror. In the little piece of murky glass an eye appeared, red and swollen, then a cheek, the beard caked with dust, then his parched, chapped lips, his gums redder than the lips, then the teeth. . . . Still, the man would have liked to see himself in a big mirror, see himself whole. To run that little piece of mirror over his face and see an eye, an ear did not satisfy him.

He went on. I haven't encountered the mine field so far, he thought. By now it must be another fifty paces, forty. . . .

Every time he set his foot down, feeling the ground beneath him hard and steady, he heaved a sigh. One step is taken, another, and another. This slab of marl seemed a trap, but, no, it's firm; this clump of heather isn't concealing anything; this stone . . . the stone sank two inches beneath his weight. "Gheee . . . gheee . . ." went the marmots. Go ahead: the other foot.

The earth became sun, the air became earth, the "gheee" of

the marmots became thunder. The man felt an iron hand grasp him by the hair, at the nape. Not one hand, a hundred hands seized him, each by the hair, and tore him head to foot, the way you tear up a sheet of paper, into hundreds of little pieces.

POSTWAR STORIES

THEFT IN A PASTRY SHOP

When Dritto got to the place where they were to meet, the others had already been waiting some time. There were two of them, Baby and Uora-Uora. The street was so silent that the ticking of the clocks in the houses could be heard. With two jobs to do, they'd have to hurry to get through them by dawn.

"Come on," said Dritto.

"Where to?" they asked.

But Dritto was never one to explain about any job he was going to do.

"Come on now," he replied. And he walked along in silence, through streets empty as dry rivers, with the moon following them along the tramlines, Dritto ahead, gazing around with those restless yellow eyes of his, his nostrils moving as if they were smelling something peculiar.

Baby was called that because he had a big head like a newborn baby and a stumpy body; also perhaps because of his short hair and pretty little face with its small black mustache. All muscle, he moved so softly he might have been a cat; there was no one like him at climbing up walls and squeezing through openings, and Dritto always had good reason to take him along.

"Will it be a good job, Dritto?" asked Baby.

"If we bring it off," answered Dritto—a reply that didn't mean much.

Meanwhile, by a devious route that only he knew, he had led them around a corner into a yard. The other two soon realized that they were going to work on the back of a shop, and Uora-Uora pushed ahead in case he was left as lookout. It always fell to Uora-Uora to be lookout man; he longed to break into houses, search around, and fill his pockets like the others, but he always found himself standing guard on cold streets, in danger from police patrols, his teeth chattering in the cold, and chain-smoking to calm his nerves. Uora-Uora was an emaciated Sicilian, with a sad mulatto face and wrists jutting out of his sleeves. When on a job he always dressed up in his best, God knows why, complete with hat, tie, and raincoat, and if forced to run for it, he'd snatch up the ends of his raincoat as if spreading wings.

"You're lookout, Uora-Uora," said Dritto, dilating his nostrils. Uora-Uora took off quietly; he knew Dritto and the danger signal of those dilating nostrils, which would move quicker and quicker until they suddenly stopped and he whipped out a revolver.

"There," Dritto said to Baby. He pointed to a little window high off the ground, a piece of cardboard in place of a broken pane.

"You climb up, get in, and open for me," he said. "Be sure not to put on the lights: they'll be seen from outside."

Baby pulled himself up on the smooth wall like a monkey,

pushed in the cardboard without a sound, and stuck his head through. It was then that he became aware of the smell; he took a deep breath and up through his nostrils wafted an aroma of freshly baked cakes. It gave him a feeling of shy excitement, of remote tenderness, rather than of actual greed.

Oh, what a lot of cakes there must be in here, he thought. It was years since he had eaten a proper piece of cake, not since before the war perhaps. He decided to search around till he found them. He jumped down into the darkness, kicked against a telephone, got a broomstick up his trouser leg, and then hit the ground. The smell of cakes was stronger than ever, but he couldn't tell where it was coming from.

Yes, there must be a lot of cakes in here, thought Baby.

He reached out a hand, trying to feel his way in the dark, so he could reach the door and open it for Dritto. Quickly he recoiled in horror; he must be face to face with some animal, some soft slimy sea-thing, perhaps. He stood there with his hand in the air, a hand that had suddenly become damp and sticky, as if covered with leprosy. Between the fingers had sprouted something round and soft, an excrescence, maybe a tumor. He strained his eyes in the dark but could see nothing, not even when he put his hand under his nose. But he could smell, even though he could not see; and he burst out laughing. He realized he had touched a tart and was holding a blob of cream and a crystallized cherry.

At once he began licking the hand, and groping around with the other at the same time. It touched something solid but soft, with a thin covering of fine sugar—a doughnut! Still groping, he popped the whole of it into his mouth and gave a little cry of pleasure on discovering it had jam inside. This really was the most wonderful place; whatever way he stretched out his hand in the dark, it found new kinds of cakes.

Suddenly he became aware of an impatient knocking on a door nearby; it was Dritto waiting to be let in. As Baby moved toward the sound, his hands bumped first into a meringue and then into an almond cake. He opened the door and Dritto's flashlight lit up his little face, its mustache already white with cream.

"It's full of cakes here!" exclaimed Baby, as if the other did not know.

"There isn't time for cakes," said Dritto, pushing him aside. "We've got to hurry." And he went ahead, twisting the beam of his flashlight around in the dark. Everywhere it touched it lit up rows of shelves, and on the shelves rows of trays, and on the trays rows of cakes of every conceivable shape and color, tarts filled with cream that glittered like candle wax, piles of sugar-coated buns, and castles of almond cakes.

It was then that a terrible worry came over Baby, the worry of not having time to eat all he wanted, of being forced to make his escape before he had sampled all the different kinds of cakes, of having all this land of milk and honey at his disposal for only a few minutes in his whole life. And the more cakes he discovered, the more his anxiety increased, so that every new corner and every fresh view of the shop that was lit up by Dritto's flashlight seemed to be about to shut him off.

He flung himself at the shelves, choking himself with cakes, cramming two or three inside his mouth at a time, without even tasting them; he seemed to be battling with the cakes, as if they were threatening enemies, strange monsters besieging him, a crisp and sticky siege which he must break through by the force of his jaw. The slit halves of the big sugared buns seemed to be opening yellow throats and eyes at him, the cream horns to be blossoming like flowers of carnivorous plants; for a horrible moment Baby had the feeling that it was he who was being devoured by the cakes.

Dritto pulled him by the arm. "The till," he said. "We've got to open the till."

At the same time, as he passed, he stuffed a piece of multicolored spongecake into his mouth, a cherry off a tart, and then a brioche—hurriedly, as if anxious not to be distracted from the job at hand. He had switched off his flashlight.

"From outside they could see us clearly," he said.

They had now reached the front of the pastry shop, with its showcases and marble countertops. Through the grilled shutters the lights from the street entered in streaks; outside they could see strange shadows on the trees and houses.

Now the moment had come to force the till.

"Hold this," said Dritto, handing the flashlight to Baby with the beam pointing downward so that it could not be seen from outside.

But Baby was holding the flashlight with one hand and groping around with the other. He seized an entire plum cake and, while Dritto was busy at the lock with his tools, began chewing it as if it were a loaf of bread. But he soon tired of it and left it half eaten on the marble slab.

"Get away from there! Look what a filthy mess you're making," hissed Dritto through clenched teeth; in spite of his trade he had a strange respect for tidy work. Then he couldn't resist the temptation, either, and stuffed two cakes, the kind that were half sponge and half chocolate, into his mouth, though without interrupting his work.

Baby, meanwhile, in order to have both hands free, had constructed a kind of lampshade from tray cloths and pieces of nougat. He then espied some large cakes with "Happy Birthday" written on them. He circled them, studying the plan of attack; first he reviewed them with a finger and licked off a bit of chocolate cream, then he buried his face inside and began biting them from the middle, one by one.

But he still felt a kind of frenzy, which he did not know how to satisfy; he could not discover any way of enjoying everything completely. Now he was crouching on all fours over a table laden with tarts; he would have liked to lie down in those tarts, cover himself with them, never have to leave them. But five or ten minutes from now it would be all over; for the rest of his life pastry shops would be out of bounds to him again, forever, like when he was a child squashing his nose against the windowpane. If only, at least, he could stay there three or four hours . . .

"Dritto," he exclaimed, "suppose we hide here till dawn, who'll see us?"

"Don't be a fool," said Dritto, who had now succeeded in forcing the till and was searching around among the notes. "We've got to get out of here before the cops show up."

Just at that moment they heard a rap on the window. In the dim moonlight Uora-Uora could be seen knocking on the blind and making signs to them. The two in the shop gave a jump, but Uora-Uora motioned for them to keep calm and for Baby to come out and take his place, so that he could come in. The other two shook their fists and made faces at him and gestured for him to get away from the front of the shop if he didn't want his brains blown out.

Dritto, however, had found only a few thousand lire in the

till, and was cursing and blaming Baby for not trying to help him. But Baby seemed beside himself; he was biting into doughnuts, picking at raisins, licking syrups, plastering himself all over and leaving sticky marks on the showcases and counters. He found that he no longer had any desire for cakes—in fact a feeling of nausea was beginning to creep up from the pit of his stomach—but he refused to take it seriously, he simply could not give up yet. And the doughnuts began to turn into soggy pieces of spongecake, the tarts to flypaper, the cakes to asphalt. Now he saw only the corpses of cakes lying putrefying on their marble slabs, or felt them disintegrating like turgid glue inside his stomach.

Dritto, meanwhile, was cursing and swearing at the lock on another till, forgetful of cakes and hunger. Suddenly, from the back of the shop appeared Uora-Uora, swearing in his Sicilian dialect, which was quite unintelligible to either of them.

"The cops?" they asked, already pale.

"Change of guard! Change of guard!" Uora-Uora was croaking in his dialect, trying hard to explain how unjust it was to leave him starving out in the cold while they gorged themselves with cakes inside.

"Go back and keep watch, go and keep watch!" shouted Baby angrily, the nausea from having eaten too much making him feel savage and selfish.

Dritto knew that it was only fair to Uora-Uora to make the change, but he also knew that Baby would not be convinced so easily, and without someone on guard they couldn't stay. So he pulled out his revolver and pointed it at Uora-Uora.

"Back to your post right now, Uora-Uora," he said.

Desperately, Uora-Uora thought of getting some supplies

before leaving, and gathered in his big hands a small pile of little almond cakes with nuts.

"And suppose they catch you with your hands full of cakes, you fool, what'll you tell them?" Dritto swore at him. "Leave them all there and get out."

Uora-Uora burst into tears. Baby felt he hated him. He picked up a cake with "Happy Birthday" written on it and flung it in Uora-Uora's face. Uora-Uora could easily have avoided it, but instead he extended his face to get the full force, then burst out laughing, for his face, hat, and tie were all covered in cream cake. Off he went, licking himself right up to his nose and cheeks.

At last Dritto succeeded in forcing the till and was stuffing into his pocket all the notes he could find, cursing because they stuck to his jammy fingers.

"Come on, Baby, time to go," he said.

But Baby could not leave just like that; this was a feast to be talked over for years to come with his cronies and with Tuscan Mary. Tuscan Mary was Baby's girl friend; she had long smooth legs and a face and body that were almost horse-like. Baby liked her because he could curl himself up and wind around her like a cat.

Uora-Uora's second entrance interrupted the course of these thoughts. Dritto quickly pulled out his revolver, but Uora-Uora shouted, "The cops!" and rushed off, flapping the ends of his raincoat. Dritto gathered up the last few notes and was at the door in a couple of leaps, with Baby behind.

Baby was still thinking of Tuscan Mary, and it was then that he remembered he might have taken some cakes for her; he never gave her presents and she might make a scene about it. He went back, snatched up some cream rolls, thrust them under his shirt, then, quickly realizing that he had chosen the most fragile ones, looked around for some more solid things and stuffed those into his bosom, too. At that moment he saw the shadows of policemen moving on the window, waving their arms and pointing at something at the end of the street; one of them aimed a revolver in that direction and fired.

Baby squatted down behind a counter. The shot did not seem to have hit its target; now they were making angry gestures and peering inside the shop. Shortly afterward he heard them finding the little door open, and then coming in. Now the shop was teeming with armed policemen. Baby remained crouching there, but meanwhile he found some candied fruit within arm's reach and chewed at slivers of citron and bergamot to calm his nerves.

The police had now discovered the theft and also found the remains of half-eaten cakes on the shelves. And so, distractedly, they, too, began to nibble little cakes that were lying about—taking care, though, to leave the traces of the thieves. After a few moments, becoming more enthusiastic in their search for evidence, they were all eating away heartily.

Baby was chewing, but the others were chewing even more loudly and drowned out the sound. All of a sudden he felt a thick liquid oozing up from between his skin and his shirt, and a mounting nausea from his stomach. He was so dizzy with candied fruit that it was some time before he realized that the way to the door was free. Later the police described how they had seen a monkey, its nose plastered with cream, swing across the shop, overturning trays and tarts; and how, by the time that they had recovered from their amazement and cleared the tarts from under their feet, he had escaped.

When Baby got to Tuscan Mary's and opened his shirt, he

found his whole chest covered with a strange sticky paste. And they stayed till morning, he and she, lying on the bed, licking and picking at each other till they had finished the last crumb of cake and blob of cream.

DOLLARS AND THE DEMIMONDAINE

IT WAS after supper and Emanuele was flicking a flyswatter against the windowpane. He was thirty-two years old and plump. His wife, Jolanda, was changing her stockings to go out.

Through the window could be seen the rubble patch where the old warehouse used to be; across it opened a view of the sea, between houses sloping downhill; the sea was darkening, and a slow wind was surging up through the streets. Six sailors from the *Shenandoah*, an American torpedo boat anchored outside the port, entered a tavern called The Tub of Diogenes.

"There are six Americans at Felice's," said Emanuele.

"Officers?" asked Jolanda.

"Sailors. Better. Hurry up." He pushed back his hat and twisted around, groping for the sleeve of his jacket.

Jolanda had fastened her garter and was now tucking in the straps of her brassière, which were sticking out in front. "Ready? Let's go."

Because they trafficked in dollars, Emanuele and Jolanda wanted to ask the sailors if they had any to sell; they were a respectable pair, though, for all their trafficking.

On the deserted rubble patch an odd palm tree or two planted to improve the area were rustling in the wind, as if desolate and disconsolate. And in the middle of the patch stood the brightly lit construction called The Tub of Diogenes, put up by an ex-serviceman called Felice, with the Town Council's permission and in spite of protests that it spoiled the neighborhood. It was shaped like a barrel; inside were a bar and tables.

Emanuele turned to Jolanda. "Now, you go in first and start talking to them, and ask them if they'd like to change any dollars. They're more likely to say yes to you at once. Then I'll come in and clinch the deal."

A strategist, Emanuele. Off Jolanda went.

At Felice's the six sailors were lined along the bar from end to end, and all those white trousers and elbows leaning on the marble made it seem as if there were twelve of them. Jolanda approached and saw twelve eyes fixed on her, rotating in rhythm with closed, chewing, grunting mouths. Most of them, in loose white tunics and with those caps perched on their heads, looked overgrown yet badly developed; but there was one near her, over six feet tall, with apple cheeks and a neck like a pyramid, whose uniform molded him as if he were naked; he had round eyes with pupils that turned all around without ever touching the rims. Jolanda hid a strap on her brassière that kept popping out.

From behind the bar, Felice, a chef's hat perched above swollen, sleepy eyes, was busy refilling glasses and seeing that all went well. From his cobbler's face, its chin perpetually dark in spite of shaving, came a grin of greeting. He spoke English, Felice did, and Jolanda whispered, "Felice, will you just ask them if they want to change any dollars?"

Felice, forever grinning and evasive, replied, "Ask 'em

yourself," and told a young waiter with tar-black hair and an onion-shaped face to bring out more trays of pizza and fried potatoes.

Jolanda was now surrounded by those long white chewing figures, exchanging inhuman grunts as they watched her.

"Please," she said in English, gesticulating. "Me to you lire, you to me dollars?"

They went on chewing. The big one with the bull neck smiled; he had the whitest teeth, so white that no gaps showed between.

A broad, short sailor, with a face as dark as a Spaniard's, now came toward her.

"Me to you dollars," he said in Italian, also gesticulating. "You to me bed."

Then he repeated it all in English, and the others gave long muffled laughs, still chewing and keeping their eyes fixed upon her.

Jolanda turned toward Felice. "Felice," she said, "explain to them."

"Whisky and soda," said Felice in his peculiar English, rolling some glasses on the marble top of the bar. His grin would have been nasty if he had not sounded so sleepy.

The giant sailor spoke; his voice rang out like an iron ring on a buoy buffeted by waves. He ordered Jolanda a drink, then took the glass from Felice's hand and held it out to her; it seemed incredible that the fragile stem of the glass didn't break in those huge fingers.

Jolanda did not know what to do. "Me lire, you dollars," she repeated.

But the others had already learned Italian. "You bed," they cried. "Bed, dollars."

At this moment, in came the husband, to see the circle of

restless backs and hear his wife's voice coming from somewhere in the midst of them. He went up to the bar. "Hey, Felice, tell me, will you . . ." he began.

"What can I get you?" asked Felice with his tired grin. His chin, shaved only two hours earlier, was already getting stubbly.

Emanuele tipped his hat back from his sweating forehead and began making little jumps to try to see over the wall of backs.

"My wife—what's she doing?"

Felice climbed on a bench, stuck out his chin, then jumped down.

"She's still in there," he replied.

Emanuele loosened the knot of his tie a little to breathe more freely.

"Tell her to come out," he said.

But Felice was busy scolding the onion-faced boy for leaving dishes without fried potatoes on them.

"Jolanda?" called her husband, and tried to push in between two Americans; he got a dig on the chin and another in the stomach, and was soon out, jumping up and down around the group again. From the thick of it all a rather tremulous little voice replied, "Emanuele?"

He shouted back, "How's it going? . . ."

"It looks," said her voice, as if she were talking on the telephone, "it looks as if they don't want lire. . . ."

He kept his calm, but started drumming on the counter. "They don't?" he cried. "Then come on out."

"Coming," she replied, and tried to make a little dive through that hedge of men. But there was something holding her back; she glanced down and saw a big hand placed against her, a big, strong, gentle hand. Before her was standing the giant with the apple cheeks, his teeth gleaming like the whites of his eyes.

"Please . . ." she begged softly, trying to loosen his hand, and called out to Emanuele, "Just coming . . ." Instead she stayed there in the middle of them.

"Please," she kept on repeating. "Please."

Felice put a glass under Emanuele's nose.

"What can I get you?" he asked, lowering his head in its chef's hat and leaning on the bar, his ten fingers splayed out.

Emanuele was staring into space. "Wait . . . I've got an idea. . . Wait," he said and left.

Outside, the street lamps were already lit. Emanuele ran across the street, went into the Café Lamarmora and looked all around. Only the regulars were there, playing cards. "Come and join us, Manuele," they called out. "What's up, Manuele?" But he had already hurried out; he ran on without stopping till he reached the Paris Bar. There he made a round of the tables, beating a fist against the palm of his hand. Finally he whispered in the bartender's ear. The man said, "Not here yet—later tonight, maybe." Emanuele hurried out. The bartender burst out laughing and went over to tell the cashier.

At Giglio's La Bolognese, the old tart from Bologna had hardly stretched out her legs under the table—her varicose veins were beginning to hurt—when Emanuele arrived, with his cap on the back of his head, panting so hard she could not understand what he wanted.

"Come on," he cried, pulling her by the hand. "Come on, quick, it's urgent."

"Manuelino, kid, what's up with you?" asked La Bolognese,

opening wide eyes surrounded by latticed wrinkles under a black fringe. "After all these years. . . . What *is* up with you, sweetie?"

But he was already pulling her along by the hand, and she was hobbling behind, her swollen legs hampered by the tight petticoat halfway up her thighs.

In front of the movie theater they ran into Mad Maria accosting a corporal.

"Hey, you come along, too. I'll take you to some Americans."

Mad Maria did not need telling twice; she left the corporal with the flick of a finger and started running along beside Emanuele, her red hair flying in the wind and her eyes piercing the darkness with anticipation.

The situation had not changed much in The Tub of Diogenes. There were several empty bottles on Felice's shelf, the gin had all gone, and the pizzas just being finished. The two women bustled in, Emanuele urging them along from behind; when the sailors found them suddenly pushed into their midst, they shouted cries of greeting. Exhausted, Emanuele slumped onto a stool. Felice poured him out a stiff drink. One of the sailors broke away from the group and came and slapped Emanuele on the back, while the others gave friendly glances in his direction. Felice began telling them something about Emanuele.

"Well," asked Emanuele. "How am I doing?"

Felice gave his eternally sleepy grin.

"Oh, you'll need at least six. . . ."

Things were not improving, in fact; Mad Maria was hanging around the neck of a lanky sailor with a face like a fetus, and squirming in her green dress like a snake trying to change its skin; La Bolognese had the short Spaniard buried in her bosom and was cosseting him in a motherly way.

But Jolanda did not appear. That enormous back, always in front, prevented anyone from seeing her. Emanuele made nervous signs to Mad Maria and La Bolognese to keep moving around, but they seemed oblivious of everything.

"Oooh . . ." said Felice, glancing over Emanuele's shoulders.

"What's that for?" Emanuele asked, but the bartender was busy scolding the boy for not drying the glasses quickly enough. Emanuele turned around and saw more sailors arriving. There must have been fifteen of them. The Tub of Diogenes was soon full of drunken sailors. Mad Maria and La Bolognese flung themselves into the middle of the melee—Maria jumping from one sailor's neck to the other, swirling her monkey legs in the air, and the other, with a constant false smile painted in lipstick, gathering the lost ones to her breast like a broody hen.

Once Emanuele caught a sudden glimpse of Jolanda milling about in the midst of it all; then she vanished again. Every now and then Jolanda felt she was going to be trampled underfoot by the crowd around her, but each time she found beside her the giant sailor with the flashing white teeth and eyes, and each time she felt safe without knowing why. Moving gently, the man always kept beside her; his big body in its tight white uniform must have had muscles as smooth as a cat's; his chest rose and fell slowly, as if full of the great air of the sea. Suddenly that voice of his, booming like a buoy, began producing words one by one in a peculiar rhythm; he burst out into song, and they all began swaying and turning as if to a dance band.

Meanwhile, Mad Maria, who knew every corner of the

place, was pushing and kicking her way toward a small door at the back of the bar, arm in arm with a sailor who had a mustache. At first Felice did not want this door to be opened, but the whole mass of them were pushing behind and finally rammed it in.

Emanuele, crouching on top of his stool, was following the scene with misty eyes.

"What's in there, Felice? What's in there?" But Felice did not reply; he was worrying because there was nothing more to eat or drink.

"Go to Valkyria's and ask 'em to lend us something to drink," he said to the onion-faced boy. "Anything, even beer. And cakes. Hurry, now."

While this was happening, Jolanda had been pushed through the little door. Inside was a small room, curtained and clean, containing a bed all made up with a blue coverlet, a wash basin, and so forth. The giant began to turn the others out of the room, calmly and firmly, pushing at them with his big hands, and keeping Jolanda behind his shoulders. But for some reason or other all the sailors wanted to stay in the little room, and for each wave that the giant sailor repulsed another wave returned—lessening each time, though, as some tired and stayed outside. Jolanda was pleased that the giant was doing this, because she was able to breathe more freely and also hide the straps that kept popping out of her brassière.

Emanuele was watching it all: he saw the giant's hands pushing the others out of the door, and his wife vanishing so that she must certainly be inside, and the other sailors returning again and again, in waves, with one or two less in each wave, first ten, then nine, then seven. How many minutes would it take the giant to succeed in shutting the door?

Then Emanuele hurried outside again. He crossed the square in hops, as if in a sack race. There was a line of taxis in the rank with all the drivers asleep. He went from one to another, waking them and explaining what he wanted them to do, furious when they didn't understand. One by one the taxis drove off in different directions. Emanuele went off in a taxi, too, standing on the running board.

The noise woke Baci, the old cabman on top of his box, and he hurried down to see if there was any fare to take. He quickly grasped the situation, like the old hand at the job he was, clambered back on his box, and woke up his old horse. When Baci's cab had gone creaking off, the square was left deserted and silent, save for the noise coming from The Tub of Diogenes in the middle of the rubble patch.

At Iris's the girls were all dancing; they were very young, with budlike mouths and tight jerseys molding their jutting breasts. Emanuele was in too much of a hurry to wait till the dance ended. "Hey, you," he called to a girl dancing with her back pressed against a man whose hands were around her. The man turned toward Emanuele; he was a porter with hair low on his forehead and an open shirt. "What d'you want?" he exclaimed. Another three or four stopped around him: boxers' faces, breathing hard through their noses. "Let's get out," muttered Emanuele's driver, "or there'll be another row here, too."

They went off to the Panther's place: but she didn't want to open up since she already had a client. "Dollars," shouted Emanuele, "dollars." She opened then, wrapped in a dressing gown, looking like an allegorical statue. They dragged her down the stairs and pushed her into the taxi. Then they picked up Babilla walking along the sea front with her dog on a leash, Belbambin at the Traveler's Café with her fox fur around her neck, and Bekuana at the Hotel Pace with her ivory cigarette holder. At the Ninfea they discovered the proprietress had three new girls, who were giggling away and thought they were being taken for a ride in the country. They were all loaded in. Emanuele was sitting in front, rather overcome by the uproar made by all those women crushed in at the back; the tax driver was only worrying if the springs would hold.

Suddenly a figure ran into the middle of the road as if wanting to be run over. He signed for them to stop; it was the onion-faced boy, laden with a crate of beer and a tray of cakes, wanting a lift. The door flew open and with a gasp the boy vanished inside, beer, cakes, and all. Off the taxi started again. Passers-by stopped and stared after this taxi racing along as if it were going to an emergency room, with those screams and high voices coming from inside. Every now and again Emanuele heard a long squeak and said to the driver, "Something's broken—can't you hear that noise?"

The driver shook his head. "It's the boy," he said. Emanuele wiped the sweat from his brow.

When the taxi pulled up in front of the Tub, the boy jumped out first, holding the tray above his head and the crate under his other arm. His hair was standing on end, his eyes were open so wide they took up half his face, and he hopped away like a monkey.

"Felice," he cried, "everything's safe! I didn't let them take a thing! But, oh, if you knew what they did to me, Felice!"

Jolanda was still inside the little room, and the giant was still busy pushing sailors away from the door. But by now there was only one left who insisted on trying to get in; completely drunk, he kept bouncing back on the giant's hands. When the new arrivals made their entry, Felice, wearily surveying the scene from the top of a stool, saw the sea of white caps part and a plumed hat, a shoulder covered in black silk, a fat haunch like a pig's, a breast draped with artificial flowers, swirling up to the surface and vanishing again like bubbles of air.

There was a sound of brakes outside, and four, five, six—an entire line of taxis arrived; from every taxi emerged women. There was the Wriggler, with her ladylike hair style, advancing majestically, screwing up her shortsighted eyes; there was Spanish Carmen, swathed in veils, her face hollow as a skull, twisting her bony hips like a cat; there was old Lame Joan, hobbling on her little Chinese umbrella; there was the Black Girl of Long Alley with her black-woman's hair and furry legs; there was the Mouse, in a dress covered with the designs of cigarette brands; there was Milena the drug addict, in a dress patterned with playing cards; there was Lollypop, with her face covered with spots; and Inés the Femme Fatale, in an all-lace gown.

Wheels could be heard crunching on the gravel: it was Baci's old cab with the horse half dead; when he stopped, a woman jumped out of there, too. She had a full velvet skirt trimmed with bows and lace, a bosom roped in necklaces, a black band around her throat, dangling earrings, a lorgnette, and blond wig topped by a big romantic hat decorated with artificial roses and grapes and clouds of ostrich feathers.

More waves of sailors had arrived at The Tub of Diogenes. One was playing an accordion and another a saxophone, and women were dancing on the tables. Despite Emanuele's efforts, there were still many more sailors than women, yet no one could reach a hand out without touching a bosom or a thigh that seemed to have got lost, since it was impossible to tell who it belonged to; there were legs in mid-air and bosoms knee-high. Velvety hands, creeping claws, sharply pointed red nails, quivering fingertips, were groping at tunics, caressing muscles, tickling arms. And mouths met, almost flying through the air, and clung behind ears like clams; huge lips seemed coated with scarlet almost up to the nostrils. Innumerable legs were squirming everywhere, like the tentacles of some enormous octopus, legs sliding about and colliding with haunches and thighs. Then everything seemed to melt away in the sailors' hands, and they found themselves holding a hat trimmed with bunches of grapes, or a dental plate, or a stocking wrapped around the neck, or a sponge, or a piece of silk trimming.

Jolanda had remained alone in the little room with the giant sailor. The door was locked and she was combing her hair in front of the mirror over the wash basin. The giant went to the window and opened the curtains. Outside could be seen the dark naval area and the mole with a line of lights reflected in the water. Then the giant began singing an American song that went, "The day is over, the night is falling, the skies are blue, the bells are beginning to ring."

Jolanda approached the window, too, and gazed out into the darkness; their hands met on the window sill and remained there motionless beside each other. The big sailor went on singing in his voice of iron, "Children of God, let us sing Hallelujah!"

And Jolanda repeated: "Let us sing Hallelujah, Hallelujah!"

During all this time Emanuele was anxiously moving

around among the sailors without finding a sign of his wife, pushing away the bodies of excited women who every now and then fell into his arms. Suddenly, he was confronted by the group of taxi drivers, who had pushed in to get him to pay the fares shown on their meters. Emanuele's eyes were tearful, but the drivers weren't going to let him off without paying. Now they were joined by old Baci, who was cracking his big coachman's whip and muttering, "If you don't pay up, I'll take her away again!"

Then whistles shrilled and the bar was surrounded by military police. It was the patrol from the *Shenandoah* with rifles and helmets. They turned out all the sailors, one by one. Then the Italian police trucks arrived and loaded up all the women they could lay hands on.

The sailors were lined up outside the bar and marched off toward the port. When the police trucks laden with women passed them on their way, there was a great shout of greetings from both sides. The giant sailor, who was in the leading file, began singing in his resounding voice, "The day is over, the sun is setting, let us sing Hallelujah, Hallelujah!"

Jolanda, squeezed inside a truck between Lollypop and the Wriggler, heard his voice getting farther away and took up the song: "The day is over, the work is done—Hallelujah!"

And they all began singing the song, the sailors and the women, one group going toward the port, the other toward the police station.

At The Tub of Diogenes Felice was beginning to pile up the tables. But Emanuele sat there slumped on a stool, his chin on his chest and his hat on the back of his head. They had been about to arrest him, too, but the American officer in charge of operations had made some inquiries and gestured for him to be left alone. And now he, the officer, had also stayed on, and there were only the two of them left in the bar, Emanuele drooping desolately on his stool and the American standing in front of him with his arms crossed. When he was certain that they were quite alone, the officer shook the plump man by an arm and began talking to him. Felice approached to act as interpreter, a broad grin on his stubbly cobbler's face.

"Tell him that you can get him a girl, too," he said to Emanuele.

Emanuele blinked his eyes, then let his chin fall on his chest again.

"You to me, girl," said the officer. "Me to you, dollars."

"Dollars! . . ." Emanuele mopped his face with his handkerchief. He got up. "Dollars," he repeated. "Dollars."

He and the officer left the bar together. Night clouds were flying high in the sky. From the end of the mole the lighthouse was winking slowly, rhythmically. The air was still full of the song: "Hallelujah!"

"The day is ending, the skies are blue, Hallelujah!" sang Emanuele and the officer, as they strolled along in the middle of the street, arm in arm, in search of a haunt for an all-night spree.

SLEEPING LIKE DOGS

EVERY TIME he opened his eyes he felt the acid yellow light of the big arc lamps in the ticket office glaring down at him; and he would pull up the lapels of his jacket in search of darkness and warmth. When he'd lain down he had not noticed how hard and icy the stone tiles on the floor were; now shafts of cold were infiltrating, coming up under his clothes and through the holes in his shoes, and the scarce flesh on his hips was aching, squashed between bone and stone.

But he'd chosen a good place, quiet and out of people's way, in that corner under the stairs; so much so that after he'd been there a little time four women's legs came high over his head and he heard voices say, "Hey, he's taken our place."

The man lying down heard, though he was not properly awake; a dribble was oozing from a corner of his mouth onto the bent cardboard of the little suitcase that was his pillow, and his hair had settled itself to sleep on its own, following the horizontal line of his body.

"Well," said the same voice from above the dirty knees and the spreading bell of the skirt, "let's put our things down. At least we can get our bed ready."

And one of those feet, a woman's in a boot, prodded his

hips like a sniffling snout. The man pulled himself up on his elbows, blinking his stunned and aching pupils in the yellow light, while his hair, apparently taking no notice, stood straight up on its own. Then back he dropped, as if he wanted to thump his head into the suitcase.

The women had taken the sacks off their heads. A man now came up behind, put down a roll of blankets, and began to arrange them. "Hey, you," said the older of the women to the man lying down, "move up, you can get underneath, too, then." No answer; he was asleep.

"He must be dead tired," said the younger of the two women, who was all bones, with the fleshy parts almost hanging as she bent down to spread the blankets and prop the sacks of flour underneath.

They were three black marketeers, on their way south with full sacks and empty tins; people whose bones had grown hard from sleeping on the floor in railroad stations and traveling in cattle cars; but they had learned to organize themselves and took blankets with them, to put underneath for softness and above for warmth; the sacks and tins acted as pillows.

The older woman tried to slip a corner of blanket under the sleeping man, but had to raise him a bit at a time because he never moved. "He must really be dead tired," said the older woman. "Maybe he's one of those emigrants."

Meanwhile, the man with them, a thin man, had got between two of the blankets and pulled an end over his eyes. "Hey, come down here; aren't you ready?" he said to the back of the younger woman, who was still bending down arranging the sacks as pillows. The younger woman was his wife, but they knew the floors of station waiting rooms almost better than their marriage bed. The two women got underneath the blankets, and the younger one and her husband lay against each other making shivering noises, while the older one was tucking up that poor sleeping wretch. Perhaps the older one was not so old, but she was trodden down by the life she led, always lugging loads of flour and oil on her head up and down in those trains; even her dress was like a sack, and her hair went in all directions.

The head of the sleeping man was slipping off the suitcase, which was too high and wrenched his neck; she tried to arrange him better, but his head nearly fell on the ground; so she propped his head on one of her shoulders and the man shut his lips, swallowed, settled farther down on a softer part, and began snoring again.

They were all just getting off to sleep when a trio from southern Italy arrived, a father with a black mustache and two dark, plump daughters, all three very short; they were carrying wattle baskets and their eyes were gummed with sleep under all that light. The daughters seemed to be wanting to go in one direction and the father in another; so they were quarreling, without looking one another in the face and almost without talking, except for short phrases between clenched teeth and jerky arm movements. When they found the place under the stairs already occupied by those four, they stood looking on, more stunned than ever, until two youths in puttees with coats slung over their shoulders came up to them.

These two at once began trying to persuade the trio of southerners to put all their blankets together and make up one group with the four already there. The two youths were Venetians emigrating to France, and they made the black-market group get up and rearrange all the blankets so that the whole bunch could settle down together. It was obvious that all this was just a maneuver to get near the two girls, already half asleep; but finally they were all settled, including the older of the black-market women, who had not moved because she had that man's head sleeping on her breast. The two Venetians had, of course, got the girls in between them, leaving the father on one side; but their hands also succeeded in reaching the other women by groping about under the blankets and coats.

Someone was already snoring, but the father from southern Italy could not manage to doze off in spite of all the sleep weighing on him. The acid yellow light burrowed right under his lids, under the hand covering his eyes; and the inhuman calls of the loudspeakers—"Slow train . . . platform . . . leaving . . ."—kept him in a state of continual restlessness. He needed to urinate, too, but did not know where to go and was afraid of getting lost in that huge station. Finally he decided to wake one of the men and began shaking him; it was the unfortunate man who had been sleeping there first of all.

"The latrine, friend, the latrine," he said and pulled him by an elbow, sitting up in the middle of that heap of wrapped-up bodies.

The sleeping man suddenly sat up with a start and opened his misty red eyes and rubbery mouth at that face bending over him; a little wrinkled face, like a cat's, with a black mustache.

"The latrine, friend," said the southerner.

The other sat there stunned, glancing around in alarm. They both kept looking at each other open-mouthed, he and the man from southern Italy. The man still half asleep could not understand anything; he found that woman's face on the floor beside him and gazed at it terror-struck. He may have been about to let out a shriek, but then, suddenly, he buried his head in the woman's breast again and dropped back to sleep.

The man from southern Italy got up, overturning two or three bodies, and began moving with uncertain steps along that huge, glaringly bright and cold hall. Through the windows could be seen the limpid darkness of the night and a view of geometric iron girders. He saw a dark little man, even shorter than himself, wearing a flashy crumpled suit, come up to him with a careless air.

"The latrine, friend," the man from southern Italy asked him imploringly.

"Cigarettes, American, Swiss," answered the other, who hadn't understood, showing the corner of a pack.

It was Belmoretto, who spent the whole year hanging around stations and had no home or even a bed on the face of the earth, and who every now and again took a train and changed cities, wherever his uncertain trafficking in cigarettes and chewing tobacco took him. At night he ended up joining with some group sleeping in the station between trains, and so managed to lie down for an hour or two under a blanket; if not he wandered around till morning, unless he happened to run into someone who would take him home and give him a bath and some food and make him sleep with him. Belmoretto came from southern Italy, too; he was very kind to the old man with the black mustache; he took him to the latrine and waited till he had finished, so as to accompany him back. He gave him a cigarette and they smoked together, looking through eyes sandy with sleep at the trains leaving and the mounds of people sleeping on the floor down in the hall below.

"We sleep like dogs," said the old man "Six days and six nights since I've seen a bed."

"A bed," said Belmoretto. "Sometimes I dream of it, a bed. A lovely white bed all to myself."

The old man went back to try to get some sleep. When he raised a blanket to make room for himself, he saw the hand of one of the Venetians on the leg of one of his daughters. He tried to pull the hand away, but the Venetian thought it was his friend trying to have a taste, too, and pushed him. The old man cursed and raised his fist over him. But the others shouted that they could not sleep, and the old man eventually climbed back to his place on his knees and got under the blankets, quietly. He felt cold and curled himself up. A longing to cry came over him. Then, very cautiously, he advanced his hand among the nearest bodies and met two women's knees, which he began to stroke.

The older of the black-market women still had resting on her breast the face of the man who looked as if he had been squashed down by tons of sleep; whenever she touched him there was no reaction, only slight signs here and there of partial reawakening. Now the woman felt a hand, a small hand all lines and calluses, on her knee, and she squeezed her legs around the hand, which stopped and was quiet at once. The old man from southern Italy could not manage to sleep but he felt happier; the soft warmth in which his little hand was wrapped seemed to be diffusing itself all over his body.

At that moment all of them felt a strange creature moving in among them, as if a dog were scooping among the blankets. One of the women screamed. The blankets were hurriedly pulled away so they could find out what it was. And in the middle of them they discovered Belmoretto, who was already snoring, his shoes off, twisted up like a fetus. He was woken by thumps on the back. "Excuse me," he said. "I didn't want to disturb you."

But now they were all awake and cursing, except for the first man, who was dribbling.

"My bones are breaking, my back's freezing," they were saying. "We ought to bust up that light and cut the cord of that loud-speaker."

"I'll show you how to make up a mattress, if you like," said Belmoretto.

"Mattress!" repeated the others. "Mattress!"

But Belmoretto had already cleared a bit of blanket and begun to fold it up into pleats, in the way anyone who's been in prison knows. They told him to stop: there weren't enough blankets and someone would find himself without any at all. Then they discussed how one couldn't sleep without something under one's head and not all of them had anything, as the southerners' baskets weren't any use. So Belmoretto arranged a complete system, by which every man rested his head on the leg of a woman; this was very difficult to do because of the blankets, but finally they were all arranged and a lot of new combinations resulted. A little while later, however, everything was in confusion again, because they could not keep still; then Belmoretto managed to sell everyone a Nazionale cigarette and they all began to smoke and tell one another how many nights it was since they'd slept.

"Three weeks we've been traveling," said the Venetians. "Three times we've tried to pass this ——— frontier and they've turned us back. In France we'll get into the first bed we see and sleep for forty-eight hours on end."

"A bed," said Belmoretto. "With newly washed sheets and

a feather mattress to sink into. A warm narrow bed, to be alone in."

"What about us, then, who've always led this life?" said the black-market man. "When we get home we spend a night in bed and then off we go on the trains again."

"A warm bed with clean sheets," said Belmoretto. "Naked, I'd get in all naked."

"Six nights since we've taken our clothes off," said the old southerner. "Since we've changed underclothes. Six nights we've been sleeping like dogs."

"I'd creep into a house like a thief," said one of the Venetians. "But not to steal. Just to get into a bed and sleep till morning."

"Or to steal a bed and bring it here to sleep in," said the other.

Belmoretto had an idea. "Wait," he said, and off he went.

He wandered around under the arches outside till he met Mad Maria. If Mad Maria spent a night without finding a client she had to go without a meal next day, so she never gave up, even in the small hours, and went on marching up and down those pavements till dawn, with his thick red hair and her muscular calves. Belmoretto was a great friend of hers.

In the encampment at the station they were still talking about sleep and beds and the dogs' lives they led, and waiting for the darkness to clear in the windows. Ten minutes had gone by when Belmoretto came back, with a rolled-up mattress on his shoulders.

"Down you go," he said, rolling it out on the floor. "Half an hour's turn for fifty lire; you can sleep two at a time. Come on, now, what's twenty-five lire a head?"

He had rented a mattress from Mad Maria, who had two

on her bed, and was now subletting it by the half hour. Other sleepy travelers who were waiting to change trains came up, looking interested.

"Down you go," said Belmoretto. "I'll take care of waking you. We'll put a blanket on top of you and then no one'll see you and you can do what you like. Down you go, now."

One of the Venetians tried first, together with one of the girls from southern Italy. The older of the black-market women booked the second shift for herself and that poor sleeping man she was still propping up. Belmoretto had already pulled out a notebook and was jotting down the bookings, pleased as could be.

At dawn he'd take the mattress back to Mad Maria and they'd turn somersaults all over the bed till high noon. Then, at last, they'd fall asleep.

DESIRE IN NOVEMBER

THE COLD hit the city one morning in November, under a deceitful sun in a clear calm sky; it cut like blades down the long straight streets, chasing the cats from the gutters back into kitchens with fires still unlit. People who had got up late and had not opened their windows went out in light overcoats, saying once again, "Winter's late this year," then suddenly shivered as they breathed the icy air. But then they thought of the coal and wood supplies laid in during summer and congratulated themselves on their own foresight.

It was a bad day for the poor, though; now they had to face problems they had so far put aside: heating, clothes. The public gardens were full of lanky young men eying the scraggy plane trees and eluding the keepers as they fingered the saws under their patched coats. A cluster of people were reading a notice about the distribution of winter vests and pants by a charitable organization.

In one of the parishes the poor were told to collect these garments from a local priest, Don Grillo. Don Grillo lived in an old house with dark narrow stairs, onto which the door of his flat opened directly, with only a slip of landing. On these stairs the poor lined up on distribution days, to knock one by one on the closed door, hand their certificates and coupons to an aged and lacrimose housekeeper, and then wait on the stairs again for her to return with the meager bundle. There was a glimpse of a room inside, full of worm-eaten old furniture and a table covered with bundles, at which sat Don Grillo, looking enormous and shouting in his deep resounding voice as he jotted everything down in registers.

Sometimes the line wound down past the corners of the stairs: widows in reduced circumstances who seldom left their attics, beggars with hacking coughs, dusty countrymen stamping about in hobnailed boots, disheveled youths—emigrants from somewhere or other—who wore sandals in winter and raincoats in summer. Sometimes this slow and squalid stream spread right on down past the mezzanine floor and the glass doors of Fabrizia's, the furriers. And the elegant women going to Fabrizia's to have their mink or astrakhan altered had to hug the banisters to avoid brushing against the ragged crew.

On the day that flannel vests and pants were being distributed at Don Grillo's, the line was joined by a porter, a strong old man who had a white beard streaked with blond. He was wearing a military overcoat and nothing underneath at all. Buttoned and muffled up though he was, his shins were bare and ended in a pair of boots without any socks. People would look down and stand open-mouthed; he would laugh back. Under the fringe of white hair falling over his forehead he had two big, merry blue eyes, and a broad, vinous, happy face.

His name was Barbagallo and his clothes had been stolen from the riverbank that summer while he was carrying loads of gravel. Till then he had got along with a few rags and a visit every now and then to prison or workhouse; but after a while he was let out of prison and escaped from the workhouse, to wander around the city and the villages nearby, loitering or doing an odd job as a porter by the hour here and there. Having no clothes was a good excuse for him to beg or to get put back in prison when he had nowhere better to go. The cold that morning had made him decide to lay hands on a suit, so he was going around naked except for that overcoat, terrifying the girls and being stopped by the police at every intersection as he was shuttled from one charity organization to another.

Once he joined the line, no one spoke of anything else; meanwhile, he was elbowing and pushing his way up the stairs, trying out every trick to get ahead.

"Yes, yes, I'm naked! D'you see? Not just my legs! Would you like me to unbutton my coat? Hey, either you let me pass or I *will* unbutton it! Am I cold? Never been better! Like to feel, madam, how warm I am? He's only handing out pants, the priest? What use are they to me? I'll take 'em, and then I'll go and sell 'em!"

Finally he sat down in the line, on a step that was actually the landing in front of Fabrizia's. Ladies were coming and going, showing off their furs for the first time. "Oh," they cried, when they saw the bare legs of the old man sitting down outside.

"Now, don't call the police, signora, they've already stopped me and sent me here to get myself some clothes. And anyway, I'm not showing anything, so don't make such a fuss."

The ladies passed hurriedly by, and Barbagallo felt himself brushed by the soft folds smelling of camphor and lily of the valley. "A fine fur, signora, unquestionably; it must be nice and warm under that!"

As each woman passed, he stretched out his hand and stroked her fur. "Help," they screamed. Then he rubbed his cheek against the furs like a cat.

There was a confabulation inside Fabrizia's; no one dared come out any more. "Should we call the police?" they asked one another. "But they've sent him here to get clothes!" Every now and then they opened the door a crack. "Is he still there?" Once he stuck his bearded head in through the door, without getting up. "Oooh!" They nearly fainted.

Eventually Barbagallo made up his mind to go and parley with them. He got up and rang Fabrizia's bell. Two employees opened the door, one a pale woman who was all knees, the other a girl with black braids. "Call the ladies!" "Go away," said the pale woman. But Barbagallo did not let her shut the door. "Go and call 'em," he said to the other girl. She turned and went away. "Good girl," said Barbagallo. The owner of the shop appeared with her clients. "How much will you give me not to unbutton my coat?" said Barbagallo. "What?" "Come on, now, no nonsense!" And he began to unbutton himself from the neck with one hand, while holding the other out. The ladies hurriedly searched about in their bags for change to give him. One, a matron heavily loaded with jewels, did not seem to be able to find any change and was watching him with her big painted eyes. Barbagallo stopped unbuttoning. "Well, then; how much will you give me if I *do* unbutton?" "Ha ha ha!" exploded the salesgirl with the braids. "Linda!" shouted her mistress. Barbagallo pocketed the money and went out. "So long, Linda," he said.

In the line the rumor was going around that there weren't enough clothes for everyone.

"Me first, because I'm naked!" exclaimed Barbagallo and succeeded in getting to the head.

The housekeeper at the door clasped her hands together on seeing him. "With nothing underneath! What's to be done? Wait, no, don't come in!"

"Let me pass, old girl, or I'll tempt you to sin. Where is His Reverence?"

And he went into the priest's room, among the Sacred Hearts bleeding away in their baroque frames, the towering cupboards and the crucifixes splayed all over the walls like black birds. Don Grillo rose from his desk and burst into a loud laugh:

"Ho ho ho! And who got you up like that? Ho ho ho!"

"Tell me, Father, today is the day for flannel underclothes, but I'm here for trousers. Do you have any?"

The priest had flung himself back in his high-backed armchair and was laughing and laughing, his double chin and stomach in the air. "No, no, ho ho ho, no, I don't have any. . . ."

"I'm not asking for a pair of yours, you know. . . . Well, in that case I'll have to stay here, till you telephone the bishop and have a pair sent over for me."

"That's it, that's it, my son, go to the archbishop's, go to the palace, ho ho ho, I'll give you a note. . . ."

"A note. And what about the flannel underclothes?"

The priest began turning over sets of vests and long pants but could not find a size large enough for Barbagallo When they had found the biggest pair there was, Barbagallo said,

"Now I'll put them on." The housekeeper was just in time to escape onto the landing before he took off his overcoat.

When he was naked, Barbagallo did a few exercises to warm himself up, then began to put on the underclothes. Don Grillo could not stop laughing at seeing that Garibaldi-like figure, squeezed from neck to wrists and down to the ankles into very tight vest and pants, with boots below.

"Oooh!" cried Barbagallo, and sprang back as if he had had a shock.

"What's the matter, what's the matter, my son?"

"It tickles, it tickles me everywhere. . . . What's this vest you've given me, Father? I'm prickling all over!"

"Go on with you, it's new, you know, it's new; you'll soon get used to it."

"Oh, my skin's so delicate since I've got used to being naked. . . . Oooh, how it pricks me!" And he twisted himself around to scratch his back.

"Come on, all you have to do is wash it once and it'll become as soft as silk. . . . Now, go to the address I've given you and they'll see about getting you a suit. Off with you. . . ." And he pushed Barbagallo toward the door, making him put on his overcoat again.

Barbagallo made no further resistance; he was a defeated man. They shut the door behind him. He started downstairs, doubled up, complaining and scratching himself, and all those still waiting in the line asked him, "What've they done to you? Did they hit you? What a scandal! A priest, hitting a poor old man! What lovely pants, though." And they looked at his shins encased in white flannel.

Barbagallo seemed to have aged about ten years; his blue eyes were swollen with tears. On his way downstairs, he passed by the door of the furriers. Suddenly he turned around, stopped his complaining, and knocked.

The salesgirl with the braids peeped out from the door. "But . . ." she said. "Look," said Barbagallo with a smile on his still-tearful face, and pointed to the white pants at his ankles. And the girl exclaimed, "Oh . . ."

He was inside now. "Call your mistress, go on!" The girl went out. Barbagallo leapt into a side room and locked himself in. Signora Fabrizia came, did not see him, and went back, shaking her head. "Why they don't keep madmen shut up, I don't know. . . ."

As soon as the key had turned in the lock, Barbagallo tore off his overcoat, the vest, the boots, and the pants, and breathed freely, naked at last. Seeing himself reflected in a large mirror, he flexed his muscles and did some exercises. There was no heating and it was bitterly cold, but he felt very happy. Then he began to look around.

He had locked himself into Fabrizia's storeroom. Hung on a long clothes rack were all the furs in a row. The old man's eyes shone with joy. Furs! He began to pass his hands along them, from one to the other, as if playing a harp; then he rubbed his shoulder, his face in them. There was gray and sullen mink, astrakhan of voluptuous softness, silver foxes like grassy clouds, gray squirrels and stone martens exquisitely smooth and light, firm brown cozy beavers, good-natured and dignified rabbits, little white-speckled goats with a dry rustle, leopards with a shuddering caress. Barbagallo noticed that his teeth were chattering from the cold. He took a lamb's-wool jacket and tried it on; it fitted him like a glove. He tied a fox fur around his hips, twisting the tawny tail to make a loincloth. Then he slipped into a sable coat that must have been made for an enormous woman, it wrapped him in such big soft folds. He also found a pair of boots lined with beaver, and then a beautiful bearskin hat; he was really comfortable Then a muff, and he was set. He preened himself in front of the mirror for a bit; it was impossible to distinguish what was beard and what was fur.

The clothes rack was still loaded with furs. Barbagallo flung them to the ground one by one until he had a wide soft bed under him to sink into. Then he stretched out and made all the rest of the furs cascade down on top of him like an avalanche. It was so warm that it seemed a pity to fall asleep and not enjoy just lying there, but the old porter could not hold out for long and soon sank into a serene and dreamless sleep.

When he woke up he saw night through the window. All around, silence. Obviously the fur shop was closed, and he wondered how he would ever get out. He listened and thought he heard a cough in the adjoining room. A light filtered through the keyhole.

Decked with mink, silver foxes, antelopes, and a bearskin hat, he got up and slowly opened the door. The girl with the black braids was sewing, bent over a table, by the light of a lamp. Because of the value of the goods in the storeroom, Signora Fabrizia made one of the girls stay and sleep in a bed in the workroom, to give the alarm in case of theft.

"Linda," said Barbagallo. The girl opened her eyes wide; there, standing in the shadow, she saw a gigantic human bear with its arms entwined in an astrakhan muff. "How lovely . . ." she said.

Barbagallo took a few steps up and down, peacocking like a model.

Linda said, "But now I must call the police."

"The police!" Barbagallo was upset. "But I'm not stealing anything. What can I do with these things? Obviously I can't go around the streets like this. I only came in here to take off my vest, which was prickling me."

They arranged that he would stay the night there and leave early in the morning. What was more, Linda knew how to wash flannel so that it would stop tickling him, and she would wash his vest and pants for him.

Barbagallo helped her to wring them out and put up the line, then hang them near the electric fire. Linda had some apples, which they ate.

Then Barbagallo said, "Let's see how you look in these furs." And he made her try them all on, in all variations, with her braids up and with her hair loose, and they exchanged impressions on the softness of the various furs against the skin.

Finally, they constructed a hut entirely of furs, big enough for them both to lie under, and they went inside to sleep.

When Linda awoke he was already up and putting on the vest and pants. The dawn was showing through the window.

"Are they quite dry?"

"A little damp, but I must go."

"Do they still tickle?"

"Not a bit. I'm as comfortable as a pope."

He helped Linda straighten up the storeroom, put on his military overcoat, and said good-bye to her at the door.

Linda stood watching him as he walked away, with the white strip of pants between his overcoat and boots, and his proud tuft of hair in the cold dawn air.

Barbagallo had no intention of asking for a suit at the archbishop's palace; he had got a new idea—going around the squares of the surrounding villages in his vest and pants, giving exhibitions of physical prowess.

TRANSIT BED

THE IMPORTANT thing was not to get himself arrested immediately. Gim flattened himself in the recess of a doorway; the police seemed to run straight past, but then, all at once, he heard their steps come back, turn into the alley. He darted off, in agile leaps.

"Stop or we'll shoot, Gim!"

Sure, sure, go ahead and shoot! he thought, and he was already out of their range, his feet thrusting him from the edge of the pebbled steps, down the slanting streets of the old city. Above the fountain, he jumped over the railing of the stairs; then he was under the archway, which amplified the pounding of his steps.

The whole circuit that came into his mind had to be rejected: Lola no, Nilde no, Renée no. Those guys would soon be all over the place, knocking at doors. It was a mild night, the clouds so pale they wouldn't have looked out of place in the daytime, above the arches set high over the alleyways.

On reaching the broad streets of the new city, Mario Albanesi, alias Gim Bolero, slowed his pace a little, tucked behind his ears the strings of hair that fell from his temples.

Not a step could be heard. Determined and discreet, he crossed over, reached Armanda's doorway, and climbed to her apartment. At this time of night she surely didn't have anybody with her; she would be sleeping. Gim knocked hard.

"Who's there?" a man's voice asked, irritated, after a moment. "At this time of night people get their sleep. . . ." It was Lilin.

"Open up a minute, Armanda. It's me, it's Gim," he said, not loud, but firmly.

Armanda rolled over in bed. "Oh, Gim boy, just a minute, I'll open the door. . . . Uh, it's Gim." She grabbed the cord at the head of the bed that opened the front door and pulled.

The door clicked, obedient; Gim went along the corridor, hands in his pockets; he entered the bedroom. In Armanda's huge bed, her body, in great mounds under the sheet, seemed to take up all the space. On the pillow, her face, without makeup under the black bangs, hung slack, baggy, and wrinkled. Beyond, as if in a fold of the blanket, on the far side of the bed, her husband, Lilin, was lying; he seemed to want to bury his little bluish face in the pillow, to recover his interrupted sleep.

Lilin has to wait till the last customer has gone before he can get into bed and sleep off the weariness that accumulates during his lazy days. There is nothing in the world that Lilin knows how to do or wants to do; if he has his smokes, he's content. Armanda can't say Lilin costs her much, except for the packs of tobacco he consumes in the course of a day. He goes out with his pack in the morning, sits for a while at the cobbler's, at the junk dealer's, at the plumber's, rolls one paper after another, and smokes, seated on those shop stools, his long, smooth, thief's hands on his knees, his gaze dull, listening like a spy to everyone, hardly ever contributing a word to the talk except for brief remarks and unexpected smiles, crooked and yellow. In the evening, when the last shop has closed, he goes to the wine counter and drains a bottle, burning up the cigarettes he has left, until they also pull down the shutters. He comes out; his wife is still on her beat along the Corso, in her short dress, her swollen feet in her tight shoes. Lilin appears around a corner, gives her a low whistle, mutters a few words to tell her it's late now, she should come to bed. Without looking at him, on the curb as if on a stage, her bosom compressed in the armature of wire and elastic, her old-woman's body in her young-girl's dress, nervously twitching her purse in her hands, drawing circles on the pavement with her heels, suddenly humming, she tells him no, people are still around, he must go off and wait. They woo each other like this every night.

"Well, then, Gim?" Armanda says, widening her eyes.

He has already found some cigarettes on the night table and lights one.

"I have to spend the night here. Tonight."

And he is already taking off his jacket, undoing his tie.

"Sure, Gim, get into bed. You go onto the sofa, Lilin; go on, Lilin honey, clear out now, let Gim get to bed."

Lilin lies there a bit, like a stone, then he pulls himself up, emitting a complaint without distinct words; he gets down from the bed, takes his pillow, a blanket, the tobacco from the table, the cigarette papers, matches, ashtray. "Go on, Lilin honey, go on." Tiny and hunched, he goes off under his load toward the sofa in the corridor.

Gim smokes as he undresses, folds his trousers neatly and hangs them up, arranges his jacket around a chair by the head of the bed, brings the cigarettes from the dresser to the night table, matches, an ashtray, and climbs into bed. Armanda turns off the lamp and sighs. Gim smokes. Lilin sleeps in the corridor. Armanda rolls over. Gim stubs out his cigarette. There is a knocking at the door.

With one hand Gim is already touching the revolver in the pocket of his jacket; with the other he has taken Armanda by the elbow, warning her to be careful. Armanda's arm is fat and soft; they stay like that for a while.

"Ask who it is, Lilin," Armanda says in a low voice.

Lilin, in the hall, huffs impatiently. "Who is it?" he asks rudely.

"Hey, Armanda, it's me. Angelo."

"Angelo who?" she says.

"Angelo the sergeant, Armanda. I happened to be going by, and I thought I'd come up. . . . Can you open the door a minute?"

Gim has got out of the bed and is signaling her to be quiet He opens a door, looks into the bathroom, takes the chair with his clothes, and carries it inside.

"Nobody's seen me. Get rid of him fast," he says softly and locks himself in the bathroom.

"Come on, Lilin honey, get back into bed; come on, Lilin." From the bed, Armanda directs the rearrangement.

"Armanda, you're keeping me waiting," the other man says, beyond the door.

Calmly, Lilin collects blanket, pillow, tobacco, matches, papers, ashtray, and comes back to bed, gets in, and pulls the sheet to his eyes. Armanda grabs the cord and clicks open the door.

Sergeant Soddu comes in; he has the rumpled look of an

old policeman in civilian clothes, his mustache gray against his fat face.

"You're out late, Sergeant," Armanda says.

"Oh, I was just taking a walk," Soddu says, "and I thought I'd pay you a call."

"What was it you wanted?'

Soddu was at the head of the bed, wiping his sweaty face with his handkerchief.

"Nothing, just a little visit. What's new?"

"New how?"

"Have you seen Albanesi, by any chance?"

"Gim? What's he done now?"

"Nothing. Kid stuff . . . We wanted to ask him something. Have you seen him?"

"Three days ago."

"I mean now "

"I've been asleep for two hours, Sarge. Why are you asking me? Go ask his girls: Rosy, Nilde, Lola. . . ."

"No use. When he's in trouble, he stays away from them."

"He hasn't shown up here. Next time, Sarge."

"Well, Armanda, I was just asking. Anyway, I'm glad to pay you a visit."

"Good night, Sarge."

"Good night."

Soddu turned, but didn't leave.

"I was thinking . . . it's practically morning, and I don't have any other rounds to make. I don't feel like going back to that cot. As long as I'm here, I've got half a mind to stay. What about it, Armanda?"

"Sergeant, you're always great, but to tell you the truth, at this time of night I'm not receiving. That's how it is, Sarge. We all have our schedule."

"Armanda . . . an old friend like me." Soddu was already removing his jacket, his undershirt.

"You're a nice man, Sergeant. Why don't we get together tomorrow night?"

Soddu went on undressing. "It's to pass the night, you understand, Armanda? Well, make some room for me."

"Lilin will go on the sofa, then. Go on, Lilin honey, go on out now."

Lilin groped with his long hands, found the tobacco on the table, pulled himself up, grumbling, climbed from the bed almost without opening his eyes, collected pillow, blanket, papers, matches. "Go on, Lilin honey." He went off, dragging the blanket along the hall. Soddu turned over between the sheets.

Next door, Gim looked through the panes of the little window at the sky, turning green. He had left his cigarettes on the table, that was the trouble. And now the other man was getting into bed and Gim had to stay shut up until daylight between that bidet and those boxes of talcum powder, unable to smoke. He had dressed again in silence, had combed his hair neatly, looking at himself in the washstand mirror, above the fence of perfumes and eyedrops and syringes and medicines and insecticides that adorned the shelf. He read some labels in the light from the window, stole a box of pills, then continued his tour of the bathroom. There weren't many discoveries to be made: some clothes in a tub, others on a line. He tested the taps of the bidet; the water spurted noisily. What if Soddu had heard? To hell with Soddu and with jail. Gim was bored; he went back to the basin, sprinkled some cologne on his jacket, spread brilliantine on his hair. The fact was, if they didn't arrest him today, they would tomorrow, but they hadn't caught him red-handed, and if all went well they'd turn him loose right away. To wait there another two or three hours, without cigarettes, in that cubbyhole . . . why did he bother? Of course they'd let him out right away. He opened a closet; it creaked. To hell with the closet and everything else. Inside it, Armanda's clothes were hanging. Gim stuck his revolver into the pocket of a fur coat. I'll come back and get it, he thought; she won't be wearing this till winter anyhow. He drew out his hand, white with naphthalene. All the better: the gun won't get moth-eaten. He laughed. He went to wash his hands again, but Armanda's towels turned his stomach and he dried himself on a topcoat in the closet.

Lying in bed, Soddu had heard noises next door. He put one hand on Armanda. "Who's there?" She turned, pressed to him, and put her big, soft arm around his neck. "It's nothing. . . . Who could it be? . . ." Soddu didn't want to free himself, but he still heard movements in there, and he asked, as if playing: "What is it? What's that?"

Gim opened the door. "Come on, Sarge, don't play dumb. Arrest me."

Soddu reached out one hand to the revolver in his jacket, hung on a peg; but he didn't let go of Armanda. "Who's that?"

"Gim Bolero."

"Hands up."

"I'm not armed, Sarge, don't be silly. I'm turning myself in."

He was standing at the head of the bed, his jacket around his shoulders, his hands half raised.

"Oh, Gim," Armanda said.

"I'll come back to see you in a few days, 'Anda," Gim said.

Soddu got up, mumbling, and slipped on his trousers. "What a lousy job . . . Never a moment's peace . . ."

Gim took his cigarettes from the table, lighted one, slipped the pack into his pocket.

"Give me a smoke, Gim," Armanda said, and she leaned out, lifting her flabby bosom.

Gim put a cigarette in her mouth, lighted it for her, helped Soddu on with his jacket. "Let's go, Sarge."

"Another time, Armanda," Soddu said.

"So long, Angelo," she said.

"So long, Armanda," Soddu said again.

" 'Bye, Gim."

They went out. In the corridor Lilin was sleeping, perched on the edge of the broken-down sofa; he didn't even move.

Armanda was smoking, seated on the big bed; she turned off the lamp, because a gray light was already coming into the room.

"Lilin," she called. "Come on, Lilin, come to bed, come on, Lilin honey, come."

Lilin was already gathering up the pillow, the ashtray.

STORIES OF LOVE AND LONELINESS

THE ADVENTURE OF A SOLDIER

IN THE compartment, a lady came and sat down, tall and buxom, next to Private Tomagra. She must have been a widow from the provinces, to judge by her dress and her veil: the dress was black silk, appropriate for prolonged mourning, but with useless frills and furbelows; and the veil went all around her face, falling from the brim of a massive, old-fashioned hat. Other places were free, there in the compartment, Private Tomagra noticed, and he had assumed the widow would surely choose one of them. But, on the contrary, despite the vicinity of a coarse soldier like himself, she came and sat right there—no doubt for some reason connected with travel, the soldier quickly decided, a draft, or the direction of the train.

Her body was in full bloom, solid, indeed a bit square. If its upper curves had not been tempered by a matronly softness, you would have said she was no more than thirty; but when you looked at her face, at the complexion both marmoreal and relaxed, the unattainable gaze beneath the heavy eyelids and the thick black brows, at the sternly sealed lips, hastily colored with a jarring red, she seemed, instead, past forty.

Tomagra, a young infantryman on his first leave (it was

Easter), huddled down in his seat for fear that the lady, so ample and shapely, might not fit; immediately he found himself in the aura of her perfume, a popular and perhaps cheap scent, but now, out of long wear, blended with natural human odors.

The lady sat down with a composed demeanor, revealing, there beside him, less majestic proportions than he had imagined when he had seen her standing. Her hands were plump, with tight, dark rings; she kept them folded in her lap, over a shiny purse and a jacket she had taken off to expose round, white arms. At her first movement Tomagra had shifted to make space for a broad maneuvering of her arms; but she had remained almost motionless, slipping out of the sleeves with a few brief twitches of her shoulders and torso.

The railroad seat was therefore fairly comfortable for two, and Tomagra could feel the lady's extreme closeness, though without any fear of offending her by his contact. All the same, Tomagra reasoned, lady though she was, she had surely not shown any sign of repugnance toward him, toward his rough uniform; otherwise she would have sat farther away. And at these thoughts his muscles, till now contracted and tensed, relaxed freely, serenely; indeed, without his moving, they tried to expand to their greatest extension, and his leg—its tendons taut, at first detached even from the cloth of his trousers—settled more broadly, tightening the material that covered it, and the wool grazed the widow's black silk. And now, through this wool and that silk, the soldier's leg was adhering to her leg with a soft, fleeting motion, like one shark grazing another, and sending waves through its veins to those other veins.

It was still a very light contact, which every jolt of the train could break off and re-create; the lady had strong, fat knees, and Tomagra's bones could sense at every jerk the lazy bump of the kneecap. The calf had raised a silken cheek that, with an imperceptible thrust, had to be made to coincide with his own This meeting of calves was precious, but it came at a price, a loss: in fact, the body's weight was shifted and the reciprocal support of the hips no longer occurred with the same docile abandon. In order to achieve a natural and satisfied position, it was necessary to move slightly on the seat, with the aid of a curve in the track and also of the comprehensible need to shift position every so often.

The lady was impassive beneath her matronly hat, her gaze fixed, lidded, and her hands steady on the purse in her lap. And yet her body, for a very long stretch, rested against that stretch of man: hadn't she realized this yet? Or was she preparing to flee? To rebel?

Tomagra decided to transmit, somehow, a message to her: he contracted the muscle of his calf into a kind of hard, square fist, and then with this calf-fist, as if a hand inside it wanted to open, he quickly knocked at the calf of the widow. To be sure, this was a very rapid movement, barely long enough for a flicker of the tendons; but in any case, she didn't draw back —at least not so far as he could tell, because immediately, needing to justify that covert movement, Tomagra extended his leg as if to get a kink out of it.

Now he had to begin all over again; that patient and prudently established contact had been lost. Tomagra decided to be more courageous; as if looking for something, he stuck his hand in his pocket, the pocket toward the woman and then, as if absently, he left it there. It had been a rapid action, Tomagra didn't know whether he had touched her or not, an inconsequential gesture; yet he now realized what an important step forward he had made, and in what a risky game he was now involved. Against the back of his hand, the hip of the lady in black was now pressing; he felt it weighing on every finger, ever knuckle; now any movement of his hand would have been an act of incredible intimacy toward the widow. Holding his breath, Tomagra turned his hand inside his pocket; in other words, he set the palm toward the lady, open against her, though still in that pocket. It was an impossible position, the wrist twisted. And yet at this point he might just as well attempt a decisive action: and so he ventured to move the fingers of that contorted hand. There could no longer be any possible doubt: the widow couldn't have helped noticing his maneuvering, and if she didn't draw back, but pretended to be impassive and absent, it meant that she wasn't rejecting his advances. When Tomagra thought about it, however, her paying no attention to his mobile right hand might mean that she really believed he was hunting for something in that pocket: a railroad ticket, a match. . . . There: and if now the soldier's fingertips, the pads, seemingly endowed with a sudden clairvoyance, could sense through those different stuffs the hems of subterranean garments and even the very minute roughness of skin, pores and moles—if, as I said, his fingertips arrived at this, perhaps her flesh, marmoreal and lazy, was hardly aware that these were, in fact, fingertips, and not, for example, nails or knuckles.

Then, with furtive steps, the hand emerged from the pocket, paused there undecided, and, with sudden haste to adjust the trouser along the side seam, proceeded all the way down to the knee. More precisely, it cleared a path: to go forward, it had to dig in between himself and the woman, a route that, even in its speed, was rich in anxieties and sweet emotions.

It must be said that Tomagra had thrown his head back against the seat, so one might also have thought he was sleeping: this was not so much an alibi for himself as it was a way of offering the lady, in the event that his insistence didn't irritate her, a reason to feel at ease, knowing that his actions were divorced from his consciousness, barely surfacing from the depths of sleep. And there, from this alert semblance of sleep, Tomagra's hand, clutching his knee, detached one finger, and sent it out to reconnoiter. The finger slid along her knee, which remained still and docile; Tomagra could perform diligent figures with the little finger on the silk of the stocking, which, through his half-closed eyes, he could barely glimpse, light and curving. But he realized that the risk of this game was without reward, because the little finger, scant of surface and awkward in movement, transmitted only partial hints of sensations and was incapable of conceiving the form and substance of what it was touching.

Then he reattached the little finger to the rest of the hand, not withdrawing it, but adding to it the ring finger, the middle finger, the forefinger: now his whole hand rested inert on that female knee, and the train cradled it in a rocking caress.

It was then that Tomagra thought of the others: if the lady, whether out of compliance or out of a mysterious intangibility, didn't react to his boldness, facing them were still seated otner persons who might be scandalized by that nonsoldierly behavior of his, and by that possible silent complicity on the woman's part. Chiefly to spare the lady such suspicion, Tomagra withdrew his hand, or rather, he hid it, as if it were the only guilty party. But hiding it, he later thought, was only a hypocritical pretext: in abandoning it there on the seat he intended simply to move it closer to the lady, who occupied, in fact, such a large part of the space.

Indeed, the hand groped around. There: like a butterfly's lighting, the fingers already sensed her presence; and there: it was enough merely to thrust the whole palm forward gently, and the widow's gaze beneath the veil was impenetrable, the bosom only faintly stirred by her respiration. But no! Tomagra had already withdrawn his hand, like a mouse scurrying off.

She didn't move; he thought: Maybe she wants this. But he also thought: Another moment and it will be too late. Or maybe she's sitting there studying me, preparing to make a scene.

Then, for no reason except prudent verification, Tomagra slid his hand along the back of the seat and waited until the train's jolts, imperceptibly, made the lady slide over his fingers. To say he waited is not correct: actually, with the tips of his fingers wedgelike between the seat and her, he made an invisible push, which could also have been the effect of the train's speeding. If he stopped at a certain point, it wasn't because the lady had given any indication of disapproval, but, on the contrary, because Tomagra thought that if she did accept, it would be easy for her, with a half rotation of the muscles, to meet him halfway, to fall, as it were, on that expectant hand. To suggest to her the friendly nature of his attention, Tomagra, in that position beneath the lady, attempted a discreet wiggle of the fingers; the lady was looking out of the window, and her hand was idly toying with the purse clasp, opening and closing it. Was this a signal to him to stop? Was it a final concession she was granting him, a warning that her patience could be tried no longer? Was it this?—Tomagra asked himself—Was it this?

He noticed that his hand, like a stubby octopus, was clasping her flesh. Now all was decided: he could no longer draw back, not Tomagra. But what about her? She was a sphinx.

With a crab's oblique scuttle, the soldier's hand now descended her thigh. Was it out in the open, before the eyes of the others? No, now the lady was adjusting the jacket she held folded on her lap, allowing it to spill to one side. To offer him cover, or to block his path? There: now the hand moved freely and unseen, it clasped her, it opened in fleeting caresses like brief puffs of wind. But the widow's face was still turned away, distant; Tomagra stared at a part of her, a zone of naked skin between the ear and the curve of her full chignon. And in that dimple beneath the ear a vein throbbed: this was the answer she was giving him, clear, heart-rending, and fleeting. She turned her face all of a sudden, proud and marmoreal; the veil hanging below the hat stirred like a curtain; the gaze was lost beneath the heavy lids. But that gaze had gone past him, Tomagra, perhaps had not even grazed him; she was looking beyond him, at something, or nothing, the pretext of some thought, but anyway something more important than he. This he decided later, because earlier, when he had barely seen that movement of hers, he had immediately thrown himself back and shut his eyes tight, as if he were asleep, trying to quell the flush spreading over his face, and thus perhaps losing the opportunity to catch in the first glint of her eyes an answer to his own extreme doubts.

His hand, hidden under the black jacket, had remained as if detached from him, numb, the fingers drawn back toward the wrist: no longer a real hand, now without sensitivity beyond that arboreal sensitivity of the bones. But as the truce the widow had granted to her own impassivity with that vague glance around soon ended, blood and courage flowed back into the hand. And it was then that, resuming contact with that soft saddle of leg, he realized he had reached a limit: the fingers were running along the hem of the skirt, beyond which there was the leap to the knee, and the void.

It was the end, Private Tomagra thought, of this secret spree. Thinking back, he found it truly a poor thing in his memory, though he had greedily blown it up while experiencing it: a clumsy feel of a silk dress, something that could in no way have been denied him simply because of his miserable position as a soldier, and something that the lady had discreetly condescended, without any show, to concede.

He was interrupted, however, in his desolate intention of withdrawing his hand when he noticed the way she was holding her jacket on her knees: no longer folded (though it had seemed so to him before), but flung carelessly, so that one edge fell in front of her legs. His hand was thus in a sealed den—perhaps a final proof of the trust the lady was giving him, confident that the disparity between her station and the soldier's was so great that he surely wouldn't take advantage of the opportunity. And the soldier recalled, with effort, what had happened so far between the widow and himself as he tried to discover something in her behavior that hinted at further condescension; now he considered whether his own actions had been insignificant and trivial, casual grazings and strokings, or, on the other hand, of a decisive intimacy, committing him not to withdraw again.

His hand surely agreed with this second consideration, because before he could reflect on the irreparable nature of the act, he was already passing the frontier. And the lady? She was asleep. She had rested her head, with the pompous hat, against a corner of the seat, and she was keeping her eyes closed. Should he, Tomagra, respect this sleep, genuine or false as it might be, and retire? Or was it a consenting woman's device, which he should already know, for which he should somehow indicate gratitude? The point he had now reached admitted no hesitation: he could only advance.

Private Tomagra's hand was small and plump, and its hard parts and calluses had become so blended with the muscle that it was uniform, flexible; the bones could not be felt, and its movement was made more with nerves, though gently, than with joints. And this little hand had constant and general and minuscule movements, to maintain the completeness of the contact alive and burning. But when, finally, a first stirring ran through the widow's softness, like the motion of distant marine currents through secret underwater channels, the soldier was so surprised by it that, as if he really supposed the widow had noticed nothing till then, had really been asleep, he drew his hand away in fright.

Now he sat there with his hands on his own knees, huddled in his seat as he had been when she came in. He was behaving absurdly; he realized that. With a scraping of heels, a stretching of hips, he seemed eager to re-establish the contacts, but this prudence of his was absurd, too, as if he wanted to start his extremely patient operation again from the beginning, as if he were not sure now of the deep goals already gained. But had he really gained them? Or had it been only a dream?

A tunnel fell upon them. The darkness became denser and denser, and Tomagra, first with timid gestures, occasionally drawing back as if he were really at the first advances and amazed at his own temerity, then trying more and more to convince himself of the profound intimacy he had already reached with that woman, extended one hand, shy as a pullet, toward her bosom, large and somewhat abandoned to its own gravity, and with an eager groping he tried to explain to her the misery and the unbearable happiness of his condition, and his need of nothing else but for her to emerge from her reserve.

The widow did react, but with a sudden gesture of shielding herself and rejecting him. It was enough to send Tomagra crouching in his corner, wringing his hands. But it was, probably, a false alarm caused by a passing light in the corridor, which had made the widow fear the tunnel was suddenly going to end. Perhaps; or had he gone too far, had he committed some horrible rudeness toward her, who had already been so generous toward him? No, by now there could be nothing forbidden between them; and her action, on the contrary, was a sign that this was all real, that she accepted, participated. Tomagra approached again. To be sure, in these reflections a great deal of time had been wasted; the tunnel wouldn't last much longer, and it wasn't wise to allow oneself to be caught by the sudden light. Tomagra was already expecting the first grayness there on the wall; the more he expected it, the riskier it was to attempt anything. Of course, this was a long tunnel; he remembered it from other journeys as very, very long. And if he took advantage immediately, he would have a lot of time ahead of him. Now it was best to wait for the end, but it never ended, and so this had perhaps been his last chance. There: now the darkness was being dispelled, it was ending.

They were at the last stations of a provincial line. The train was emptying; some passengers in the compartment had already got out, and now the last ones were taking down their bags, leaving. Finally they were alone in the compartment, the soldier and the widow, very close and detached, their arms folded, silent, eyes staring into space. Tomagra still had to think: Now that all the seats are free, if she wanted to be nice and comfortable, if she were fed up with me, she would move. . . .

Something restrained him and frightened him still, perhaps the presence of a group of smokers in the passage, or a light that had come on because it was evening. Then he thought to draw the curtains on the passage, like somebody wanting to get some sleep. He stood up with elephantine steps; with slow, meticulous care be began to unfasten the curtains, draw them, fasten them again. When he turned, he found her stretched out. As if she wanted to sleep: even though she had her eyes open and staring, she had slipped down, maintaining her matronly composure intact, with the majestic hat still on her head, which was resting on the seat arm.

Tomagra was standing over her. Still, to protect this image of sleep, he chose also to darken the outside window; and he stretched over her, to undo the curtain. But it was only a way of shifting his clumsy actions above the impassive widow. Then he stopped tormenting that curtain's snap and understood he had to do something else; show her all his own, compelling condition of desire, if only to explain to her the misunderstanding into which she had certainly fallen, as if to say to her: You see, you were kind to me because you believe we have a remote need for affection, we poor lonely soldiers, but here is what I really am, this is how I received your courtesy, this is the degree of impossible ambition I have reached, you see, here.

And since it was now evident that nothing could manage

to surprise the lady, and indeed everything seemed somehow to have been foreseen by her, Private Tomagra could only make sure that no further doubts were possible; and finally the urgency of his madness managed also to grasp its mute object: her

When Tomagra stood up and, beneath him, the widow remained with her clear, stern gaze (she had blue eyes), with her hat and veil still squarely on her head, and the train never stopped its shrill whistling through the fields, and outside those endless rows of grapevines went on, and the rain that throughout the journey had tirelessly streaked the panes now resumed with new violence, he had again a brief spurt of fear, thinking how he, Private Tomagra, had been so daring.

THE ADVENTURE OF A BATHER

WHILE ENJOYING a swim at the beach at ———, Signora Isotta Barbarino had an unfortunate mishap. She was swimming far out in the water, and when it seemed time to go back in and she turned toward the shore, she realized that an irreparable event had occurred. She had lost her bathing suit.

She couldn't tell whether it had slipped off just then, or whether she had already been swimming without it for some time, but of the new two-piece suit she had been wearing, only the halter was left. At some twist of her hip, some buttons must have popped, and the bottom part, reduced to a shapeless rag, had slipped down her leg. Perhaps it was still sinking a few feet below her; she tried dropping down underwater to look for it, but she immediately lost her breath, and only vague green shadows flashed before her eyes.

Stifling the anxiety rising inside her, she tried to think in a calm, orderly fashion. It was noon; there were people around in the sea, in kayaks and in rowboats, or swimming. She didn't know anyone; she had arrived the day before with her husband, who had had to go back to the city at once. Now there was no other course, the signora thought (and she was the first to be surprised at her clear, serene reasoning), but to find among these people a beach attendant's boat, which there had to be, or the boat of some other person who inspired trust, hail it, or, rather, approach it, and manage to ask for both help and tact.

This is what Signora Isotta was thinking as she kept afloat, huddled almost into a ball, pawing the water, not daring to look around. Only her head emerged and, unconsciously, she lowered her face toward the surface, not to delve into its secrecy, now held inviolable, but like someone rubbing eyelids and temples against the sheet or the pillow to stem tears provoked by some night-thought. And it was a genuine pressure of tears that she felt at the corners of her eyes, and perhaps that instinctive movement of her head was really meant to dry those tears in the sea: this is how distraught she was, this is what a gap there was in her between reason and feeling. She wasn't calm, then: she was desperate. Inside that motionless sea, wrinkled only at long intervals by the barely indicated hump of a wave, she also kept herself motionless, no longer with slow strokes, but only by a pleading movement of the hands, half in the water; and the most alarming sign of her condition, though perhaps not even she realized it, was this usury of strength she was observing, as if she had a very long and exhausting time ahead of her.

She had put on her two-piece suit that morning for the first time; and at the beach, in the midst of all those strangers, she realized it made her feel a bit ill at ease. But the moment she was in the water, she had felt content, freer in her movements, with a greater desire to swim. She liked to take long swims, well away from the shore, but her pleasure was not an athlete's, for she was actually rather plump and lazy; what meant most to her was the intimacy with the water, feeling herself a part of that peaceful sea. Her new suit gave her that very impression; indeed, the first thing she had thought as she swam was: It's like being naked. The only irksome thing was the recollection of that crowded beach. It was not unreasonable that her future beach acquaintances would perhaps form an idea of her that they would have to some extent to modify later: not so much an opinion about her behavior, since at the seaside all the women dressed like this, but a belief, for example, that she was athletic, or fashionable, whereas she was really a very simple, domestic person. It was perhaps because she was already feeling this sensation of herself as different from usual that she had noticed nothing when the mishap took place. Now that uneasiness she had felt on the beach, and that novelty of the water on her bare skin, and her vague concern at having to return among the other bathers: all had been enlarged and engulfed by her new and far more serious dismay.

What she would have preferred never to look at was the beach. And she looked at it. Bells were ringing noon; and on the beach the great umbrellas with black and yellow concentric circles were casting black shadows in which the bodies be came flat, and the teeming of the bathers spilled into the sea; and none of the boats was on the shore now, and as soon as one returned it was seized even before it could touch bottom; and the black rim of the blue expanse was disturbed by constant explosions of white splashing, especially behind the ropes, where the horde of children was roiling; and at every bland wave a shouting arose, its notes immediately swallowed up by the blast. Just off that beach, she was naked.

Nobody would have suspected it, seeing only her head rising from the water, and occasionally her arms and her bosom, as she swam cautiously, never lifting her body to the surface. She could, then, carry out her search for help without exposing herself too much. And to check how much of her could be glimpsed by alien eyes, Signora Isotta now and then stopped and tried to look at herself, floating almost vertically. With anxiety she saw the sun's beams sway in the water in limpid, underwater glints, and illuminate drifting seaweed and rapid schools of little striped fish, on the bottom the corrugated sand, and on top, her body. In vain, twisting it with clenched legs, she tried to hide it from her own gaze: the skin of the pale belly gleamed revealingly, between the tan of the bosom and the thighs, and neither the motion of a wave nor the half-sunken drift of seaweed could merge the darkness and the pallor of her abdomen. The signora resumed swimming in that mongrel way of hers, keeping her body as low as she could, but, never stopping, she would turn to look over her shoulder, out of the corner of her eye: at every stroke, all the white breadth of her person appeared in the light of day, in its most identifiable and secret forms. She did everything possible to change the style and direction of her swimming—she turned in the water, she observed herself at every angle and in every light, she writhed upon herself—and always this offensive, naked body pursued her. It was a flight from her own body that she was attempting, as if from another person whom she, Signora Isotta, was unable to save at a difficult juncture, and could only abandon to her fate. Yet this body, so rich and so impossible to conceal, had indeed been a glory of hers, a source of self-satisfaction; only a contradictory chain of circumstances, apparently sensible, could make it now a cause for shame. Or perhaps not; perhaps her life always consisted only of the clothed lady she had been all of her days, and her nakedness hardly belonged to her, was a rash state of nature revealed only every now and then, arousing wonder in human beings, foremost in her. Now

Signora Isotta recalled that even when she was alone or in private with her husband she had always surrounded her being naked with an air of complicity, of irony, part embarrassed and part feline, as if she were temporarily putting on joyous but outrageous disguises, for a kind of secret carnival between husband and wife. She had become accustomed with some reluctance to owning a body, after the first disappointed, romantic years, and she had taken it on like someone who learns he can command a long-yearned-for property. Now the awareness of this right of hers disappeared again among the old fears, as that yelling beach loomed ahead.

When noon had passed, among the bathers scattered through the sea a reflux toward the shore began; it was the hour of lunch at the *pensioni*, of picnics outside the cabins, and also the hour in which the sand was to be enjoyed at its most searing, under the vertical sun. As the keels of boats and the pontoons of catamarans passed close to the signora, she studied the faces of the men on board, and sometimes she almost decided to move toward them; but each time a flash, a glance beneath their lashes, or the hint of an abrupt jerk of shoulder or elbow put her to flight, with false-casual strokes, whose calm masked an already burdensome weariness. The men in the boats, alone or in groups, boys all excited by the physical exercise, or gentlemen with shrewd demands or insistent gaze, on encountering her—lost in the sea, her prim face unable to conceal a shy, pleading anxiety, with a cap that gave her a slightly peevish, doll-like expression, and with her soft shoulders heaving around, uncertain—immediately emerged from their self-centered or bustling nirvana. Those who were not alone pointed her out to their companions with a snap of the chin or a wink; and those who were alone, braking with one oar, swerved their prow deliberately to cross her path. Her need for trust was met by these rising barriers of slyness and *double-entendre*, a hedge of piercing pupils, of incisors bared in ambiguous laughter, of oars pausing, suddenly interrogatory, on the surface of the water; and the only thing she could do was flee. An occasional swimmer passed by, ducking his head blindly and puffing out spurts of water without raising his eyes; but the signora distrusted these men and evaded them. In fact, even though they passed at some distance from her, the swimmers, overcome by sudden fatigue, let themselves float and stretched their legs in a senseless splashing until she displayed her disdain by moving away. Thus this net of insistent hints was already spread around her, as if lying in ambush for her, as if each of those men had been daydreaming for years of a woman to whom what had happened to her would happen, and these men spent their summers at the sea hoping to be present at the right moment. There was no way out: the front of preordained male insinuations extended to all men, with no possible breach, and that savior she had stubbornly dreamed of as the most anonymous possible creature, almost angelic, a beach boy, a sailor, could not exist: she was now sure of that. The beach guard she did see pass by, certainly the only one who would be out in a boat to prevent possible accidents, given this calm sea, had such fleshy lips and such tense muscles that she would never have had the courage to entrust herself to his hands, even if—she actually thought in the emotion of the omment—it were to have him unlock a cabin or set up an umbrella.

In her disappointed fantasies, the people to whom she had hoped to turn had always been men. She hadn't thought of women, and yet with them everything should have been more simple; a kind of female solidarity would certainly have gone into action in this serious crisis, in this anxiety that only a fellow woman could completely understand. But possibilities of communication with members of her own sex were rarer and more uncertain, unlike the perilous ease of encounters with men; and a distrust—reciprocal this time—blocked such communication. Most of the women went by in catamarans accompanied by men, and they were jealous, inaccessible, seeking the open sea, where the body, whose shame she suffered passively, would for them be the weapon of an aggressive and calculable strategy. Now and then a boat came out packed with chirping, overheated young girls, and the signora thought of the distance between the profound vulgarity of her suffering and their volatile heedlessness; she thought of how she would have to repeat her appeal to them, because they surely wouldn't understand her the first time; she thought of how their expression would change at the news, and she couldn't bring herself to call out to them. A blonde also went by in a catamaran, alone, tanned, full of smugness and egoism; surely she was going far out to take the sun completely naked, and it would never remotely occur to her that nakedness could be a misfortune or a torment. Signora Isotta realized then how alone a woman is, and how rare, among her own kind, is solidarity, spontaneous and good (destroyed perhaps by the pact made with man), which would have foreseen her appeals and come to her side at the merest hint in the moment of a secret misfortune no man would understand. Women would never save her; and her own man was away. She felt her strength abandoning her.

A little rust-colored buoy, till then fought over by a cluster of diving kids, was suddenly, at a general plunge, deserted. A seagull lighted on it, flapped its wings, then flew off as Signora Isotta grasped the buoy's rim. She would have drowned if she hadn't grabbed it in time. But not even death was possible, not even that indefensible, excessive remedy was left her: when she was about to faint and couldn't manage to keep her chin up, drawn down toward the water, she saw a rapid, tensed alertness among the men on the surrounding boats, all ready to dive in and come to her rescue. They were there only to save her, to carry her naked and unconscious among the questions and stares of a curious public; and her risk of death would have achieved only the ridiculous and vulgar result that she was trying in vain to evade.

From the buoy, looking at the swimmers and rowers, who seemed to be gradually reabsorbed by the shore, she remembered the marvelous weariness of those returns, and the cries from one boat to another—"See you on shore!" or "I'll race you there!"—filled her with a boundless envy. But then, when she noticed a thin man in long pants, the only person still out in the water, standing erect in a motionless motorboat, looking at something or other in the water, immediately her longing to go ashore burrowed down, hid within her fear of being seen, her anxious effort to conceal herself behind the buoy.

She no longer remembered how long she had been there: already the beach crowd was thinning out, boats were again lined up on the sand, the umbrellas, furled one after the other, were now only a cemetery of short poles, the gulls skimmed the water, and on the motionless motorboat the thin man had disappeared and in his place a dumbfounded boy's curly head peered from the side; and over the sun a cloud passed, driven by a just-wakened wind against a cumulus collected above the hills. The signora thought of that hour as seen from the land, the polite afternoons, the destiny of unassuming correctness and respectful joys she had thought was guaranteed her and of the contemptible incongruity that had occurred to contradict it, like the chastisement for a sin not committed. Not committed? But that abandonment of hers in bathing, that desire to swim all alone, that joy in her own body in the two-piece suit recklessly chosen: weren't these perhaps signs of a flight begun some time past, the defiance of an inclination to sin, the progressive stages of a mad race toward this state of nakedness that now appeared to her in all its wretched pallor? And the society of men, among whom she had thought to pass intact like a big butterfly, pretending a compliant, doll-like nonchalance, now revealed its basic cruelties, its doubly diabolical essence, the presence of an evil against which she had not sufficiently armed herself and, at once, the agent, the instrument of her sentence.

Clinging to the studs of the buoy with bloodless fingertips now with accentuated wrinkles from the prolonged stay in the water, the signora felt herself cast out by the whole world, and she couldn't understand why this nakedness that all people carry with themselves forever should banish her alone, as if she were the only one who was naked, the only being who could remain naked under heaven. And as she raised her eyes, she saw now the man and boy together on the motorboat, both standing, making signs to her as if to say she should remain there, that she shouldn't distress herself pointlessly. They were serious, the two of them, composed, unlike any of the other, earlier, ones, as if they were announcing a verdict to her: she was to resign herself, she alone had been chosen to pay for all. If, as they gesticulated, they tried to muster a kind of smile, it was without any hint of maliciousness: perhaps an invitation to accept her sentence good-naturedly, willingly.

Immediately the boat sped off, faster than one would have

thought possible, and the two paid attention to the motor and the course and didn't turn again toward the signora, who tried to smile back at them, as if to show that if she were accused only of being made in this way so dear and prized by all, if she had only to expiate our somewhat clumsy tenderness of forms, well, she would take the whole burden on herself, content.

The boat, with its mysterious movements, and her own tangled reasoning had kept her in a state of such timorous bewilderment that it was a while before she became aware of the cold. A sweet plumpness allowed Signora Isotta to take long and icy swims that amazed her husband and family, all thin people. But now she had been in the water too long, and the sun was covered, and her smooth skin rose in grainy bumps, and ice was slowly taking possession of her blood. There, in this shivering that ran through her, Isotta realized she was alive, and in danger of death, and innocent. Because the nakedness that had suddenly seemed to grow on her body was something she had always accepted not as a guilt but as her anxious innocence, as her secret fraternity with others as flesh and root of her being in the world. And they, or the contrary, the smart men in the boats and the fearless women under the umbrellas, who did not accept it, who in sinuated it was a crime, an accusation—only they were guilty She didn't want to pay for them; and she wriggled, clinging to the buoy, her teeth chattering, tears on her cheeks. . . Over there, from the harbor, the motorboat was returning even faster than before, and at the prow the boy was holding up a narrow green sail: a skirt!

When the boat stopped near her, and the thin man stretched out one hand to help her on board and covered his eyes with the other, smiling, the signora was already so far from any hope of being saved, and the train of her thoughts had traveled so far afield, that for a moment she couldn't connect her senses with her reasoning and action, and she raised her hand toward the man's outstretched hand even before realizing that it wasn't her imagination, that the boat was really there, and had really come to her rescue. She understood, and all of a sudden everything became perfect and unfailing, and her thoughts, the cold, her fear were forgotten. From pale, she turned red as fire; and standing on the deck, she slipped on that garment while the man and the boy, facing the horizon, looked at the gulls.

They started the motor, and, seated at the prow in a green skirt with orange flowers, she saw on the bottom of the boat a mask for underwater fishing; and she knew how the pair had learned her secret. The boy, swimming below the surface with mask and harpoon, had seen her and had alerted the man, who had also dived in to see. Then, without being understood, they had motioned her to wait for them, and had sped to the port to procure a dress from some fisherman's wife.

The two were sitting at the poop, hands on their knees, and smiling: the boy, an urchin of about eight, was all eyes, with a dazed, coltish smile; the man had a gray, shaggy head, a brick-red body with long muscles, and a slightly sad smile, with a dead cigarette stuck to his lip. It occurred to Signora Isotta that perhaps the two of them, looking at her dressed, were trying to remember her as they had seen her underwater; but this didn't make her feel ill at ease. After all, since someone had perforce to see her, she was glad it had been these two, and also that they had felt curiosity and pleasure. To get to the beach, the man took the boat past the docks and the harbor and the vegetable gardens along the sea; anyone who saw them from the shore no doubt believed that the three were a little family coming home in their boat as they did every evening during the fishing season. The gray fishermen's houses overlooked the dock; red nets were stretched across short stakes; and from the boats, already tied up, some youths lifted lead-colored fish and passed them to girls standing with square baskets, the low rims propped against their hips. Men with tiny gold earrings, seated on the ground with spread legs, were sewing endless nets; and in some tubs they were boiling tannin to dye the nets again. Little stone walls marked off tiny vegetable gardens on the sea, where the boats lay beside the canes of the seedbeds. Women with their mouths full of nails helped their husbands, lying under the keel, to patch holes. Every pink house had a low roof covered with tomatoes split in two and set out to dry with salt on a grill; and under the asparagus plants the kids were hunting for worms; and some old men with bellows were spraying insecticide on their loquats; and the yellow melons were growing under creeping leaves; and in flat pans the old women were frying squid and polyps or else pumpkin flowers dredged in flour; and the prows of fishing boats rose in the yards redolent of wood fresh from the plane; and a brawl among the boys caulking the hulls had broken out, with threats of brushes black with tar; and then the beach began, with the little sand castles and volcanoes abandoned by the children.

Signora Isotta, seated in the boat with that pair, in that excessive green-and-orange dress, would even have liked the trip to continue. But the boat was aiming its prow at the shore, and the beach attendants were carrying away the deck chairs, and the man had bent over the motor, turning his back: that brick-red back divided by the knobs of the spine, on which the hard, salty skin rippled as if moved by a sigh.

THE ADVENTURE OF A CLERK

It so happened that Enrico Gnei, a clerk, spent a night with a beautiful lady Coming out of her house, early, he felt the air and the colors of the spring morning open before him, cool and bracing and new, and it was as if he were walking to the sound of music.

It must be said that only a lucky conjunction of circum stances had rewarded Enrico Gnei with this adventure: a party at some friends' house a special, fleeting mood of the lady's—a woman otherwise controlled and hardly prone to obeying whims—a slight alcoholic stimulation, whether real or feigned, and in addition a rather favorable logistic combination at the moment of good-byes. All this, and not any personal charm of Gnei's—or, rather, none but his discreet and somewhat anonymous looks, which would mark him as an undemanding, unobtrusive companion—had produced the unexpected result of that night. He was well aware of all this and, modest by nature, he considered his good luck all the more precious. He also knew that the event would have no sequel; nor did he complain of that, because a steady relationship would have created problems too awkward for his usual way of living. The perfection of the adventure lay in its having begun and ended in the space of a night. Therefore Enrico Gnei that morning was a man who has received what he could most desire in the world.

The lady's house was in the hill district. Gnei came down a green and fragrant boulevard. It was not yet the hour when he was accustomed to leave home for the office. The lady had made him slip out now, so the servants wouldn't see. The fact that he hadn't slept didn't bother him; in fact, it gave him a kind of unnatural lucidity, an arousal no longer of the senses but of the intellect. A gust of wind, a buzzing, an odor of trees seemed to him things he should somehow grasp and enjoy; he couldn't become accustomed again to humbler ways of savoring beauty.

Because he was a methodical sort of man, getting up in a strange house and dressing in haste without shaving left in him an impression of disturbed habits; for a moment he thought of dashing home to shave and tidy himself up before going to the office. He would have had the time, but Gnei immediately dismissed the idea; he preferred to convince himself it was too late, because he was seized by the fear that his house, the repetition of daily acts, would dispel the rich and extraordinary atmosphere in which he now moved.

He decided that his day would follow a calm and generous curve, to retain as far as possible the inheritance of that night. His memory, if he could patiently reconstruct the hours he had passed, second by second, promised him boundless Edens. And thus, letting his thoughts stray, Enrico Gnei went without haste to the beginning of the tramline.

The tram, almost empty, was waiting for the time when its schedule began. Some drivers were there, smoking. Gnei whistled as he climbed aboard, his overcoat open, flapping; he sat down, sprawling slightly, then immediately assumed a more citified position, pleased that he had thought to correct himself promptly but not displeased by the carefree attitude that had come to him naturally.

The neighborhood was sparsely inhabited, and the inhabitants were not early risers. On the tram there was an elderly housewife, two workmen having an argument, and himself, the contented man. Solid, morning people. He found them likable; he, Enrico Gnei, was for them a mysterious gentleman, mysterious and content, never seen before on this tram at this hour. Where could he come from? they were perhaps asking themselves now. And he gave them no clue: he was looking at the wistaria. He was a man who looks at the wistaria like a man who knows how wistaria should be looked at: he was aware of this, Enrico Gnei was. He was a passenger who hands the money for his ticket to the conductor, and between him and the conductor there is a perfect passenger-conductor relationship; it couldn't be better. The tram moved down toward the river; it was a great life.

Enrico Gnei got off downtown and went to a café. Not the usual one. A café with mosaic walls. It had just opened; the cashier hadn't arrived yet; the counterman was starting up the coffee machine. Gnei strode like a master right to the center of the place, went to the counter, ordered a coffee, chose a cake from the glass pastry case, and bit into it, first with hunger, then with the expression of a man with a bad taste in his mouth after a wild night.

A newspaper lay open on the counter; Gnei glanced at it. He hadn't bought the paper this morning—and to think that that was always the first thing he did on leaving his house. He was a habitual reader, meticulous; he kept up with the most trivial events and there wasn't a page he skipped without reading. But that day his gaze ran over the headlines and his thoughts remained unconnected. Gnei couldn't manage to read: perhaps—who knows?—stirred by the food, by the hot coffee, or by the dulling of the morning air's effect, a wave of sensations from the night came over him. He shut his eyes, raised his chin, and smiled.

Attributing this pleased expression to the sports news in the paper, the counterman said to him, "Ah, you're glad Boccadasse will be playing again on Sunday?" and he pointed to the headline that announced the return of a center-half. Gnei read, recovered himself, and instead of exclaiming, as he would have liked to, "Oh, I've got something a lot better than Boccadasse to think about, my friend!" he confined himself to saying, "Hmm . . . right . . ." And, unwilling to let a conversation about the forthcoming match disrupt the flow of his feelings, he turned toward the cashier's desk, where, in the meantime, a young girl with a disenchanted look had installed herself.

"So," Gnei said, in a tone of intimacy, "I owe you for a coffee and a cake." The cashier yawned. "Sleepy? Too early for you?" Gnei asked. Without smiling, the cashier nodded. Gnei assumed an air of complicity: "Aha! Didn't get enough sleep last night, did you?" He thought for a moment, then, persuading himself he was with a person who would understand, added, "I still haven't gone to bed." Then he was silent, enigmatic, discreet. He paid, said good morning to all, and left. He went to the barber's.

"Good morning, sir. Have a seat, sir," the barber said in a professional falsetto that to Enrico Gnei was like a wink of the eye.

"Um hum, give me a shave!" he replied with skeptical condescension, looking at himself in the mirror. His face, with the towel knotted around his neck, had the appearance of an independent object, and some trace of weariness, no longer corrected by the general bearing of his person, was beginning to show. It was still quite a normal face, like that of a traveler who had got off the train at dawn, or a gambler who has spent the night over his cards; except there was a certain look that marked the special nature of his weariness—Gnei observed smugly—a certain relaxed, indulgent expression, that of a man who has had his share of things and is prepared to take the bad with the good.

Far different caresses—Gnei's cheeks seemed to say to the brush that encased them in warm foam—far different caresses from yours are what we're used to!

Scrape, razor—his skin seemed to say—you won't scrape off what I have felt and know!

It was, for Gnei, as if a conversation filled with allusions were taking place between him and the barber, who, however, was also silent, devoting himself to handling his implements. He was a young barber, somewhat taciturn more from lack of imagination than from a reserved character; and in fact, attempting to start a conversation, he said, "Some year, eh? The good weather's already here. Spring . . ."

The remark reached Gnei right in the middle of his imaginary conversation, and the word "spring" became charged with meanings and hidden references. "Aaah! Spring . . ." he said, a knowing smile on his foamy lips. And here the conversation died.

But Gnei felt the need to talk, to express, to communicate, and the barber didn't say anything further. Two or three times Gnei started to open his mouth when the young man lifted the razor, but he couldn't find any words, and the razor descended again over his lip and chin.

"What did you say?" the barber asked, having seen Gnei's lips move without producing any sound.

And Gnei, with all his warmth, said, "Sunday, Boccadasse'll be back with the team!"

He had almost shouted; the other customers turned toward him their half-lathered faces; the barber had remained with his razor suspended in air.

"Ah, you're a ——— fan?" he said, a bit mortified. "I'm a follower of ———," and he named the city's other team.

"Oh, ——— has an easy game Sunday; they can't lose. . . " But his warmth was already extinguished.

Shaven, he came outside. The city was loud and bustling; there were glints of gold on the windows, water flew over the fountains, the trams' poles struck sparks from the overhead wires. Enrico Gnei proceeded as if on the crest of a wave, bursts of vigor alternating in his heart with fits of lassitude.

"Why, it's Gnei!"

"Why, it's Bardetta!"

He ran into an old schoolmate he hadn't seen for ten years. They traded the usual remarks, how time had gone by, how they hadn't changed. Actually, Bardetta had somewhat faded, and the vulpine, slightly crafty expression of his face had become accentuated. Gnei knew that Bardetta was in business, but had a rather murky record and had been living abroad for some time.

"Still in Paris?"

"Venezuela. I'm about to go back. What about you?"

"Still here," and, in spite of himself, he smiled in embarrassment, as if he were ashamed of his sedentary life, and at the same time irked because he couldn't make it clear, at first sight, that his existence in reality was fuller and more satisfied than might be imagined.

"Are you married?" Bardetta asked.

To Gnei this seemed an opportunity to rectify the first impression. "Bachelor!" he said. "Still a bachelor, ha ha! We're a vanishing race!" Yes, Bardetta, a man without scruples, about to leave again for America, with no ties now to the city and its gossip, was the ideal person; with him Gnei could give free rein to his euphoria, to him alone Gnei could confide his secret. Indeed, he could even exaggerate a little, talk of last night's adventure as if it were, for him, something habitual. "That's right," he insisted. "The old guard of bachelorhood, us two, eh?"—meaning to refer to Bardetta's onetime reputation as a successful chaser of chorus girls. And he was already studying the remark he would make to arrive at the subject, something on the order of "Why, only last night, for example . . ."

"To tell the truth," Bardetta said, with a somewhat shy smile, "I'm married and have four children. . . ."

Gnei heard this as he was re-creating around himself the atmosphere of a completely heedless, epicurean world; and he was thrown a bit off balance by it. He stared at Bardetta; only then did he notice the man's shabby, downtrodden look, his worried, tired manner. "Ah, four children . . ." he said, in a dull voice. "Congratulations! And how are things going over there?"

"Hmph . . . not much doing . . . It's the same all over. . . . Scraping by . . . feeding the family . . ." and he stretched out his arms in a gesture of defeat.

Gnei, with his instinctive humility, felt compassion and

remorse: how could he have thought of trumpeting his own good luck to impress a wreck of a man like this? "Oh, here, too, I can tell you," he said quickly, changing his tone again, "we barely manage, living from day to day. . . ."

"Well, let's hope things will get better. . . ."

"Yes, we have to keep hoping. . . ."

They exchanged all best wishes, said good-bye, and went off in different directions. Immediately, Gnei felt overwhelmed with regret: the possibility of confiding in Bardetta, that Bardetta he had first imagined, seemed to him an immense boon, now lost forever. Between the two of them—Gnei thought—a man-to-man conversation could have taken place, good-natured, a shade ironic, without any showing off, without boasting; his friend would have left for America bearing a memory that would remain unchangeable; and Gnei vaguely saw himself preserved in the thoughts of that imaginary Bardetta, there in his Venezuela, remembering old Europe—poor, but always faithful to the cult of beauty and pleasure—and thinking instinctively of his friend, the schoolmate seen again after so many years, always with that prudent appearance and yet completely sure of himself: the man who hadn't abandoned Europe and virtually symbolized its ancient wisdom of life, its wary passions. . . . Gnei grew excited: thus the adventure of the previous night could have left a mark, taken on a definitive meaning, instead of vanishing like sand in a sea of empty days, all alike.

Perhaps he should have talked about it to Bardetta anyway, even if Bardetta was a poor wretch with other things on his mind, even at the cost of humiliating him. Besides, how could he be sure that Bardetta really was a failure? Perhaps he just said that and he was still the old fox he had been in the past. . . . I'll overtake him—Gnei thought—I'll start a conversation, and I'll tell him.

He ran ahead along the sidewalk, turned into the square, proceeded under the arcade. Bardetta had disappeared. Gnei looked at the time; he was late; he hurried toward his job. To calm himself, he decided that this telling others about his affairs, like a schoolboy, was too alien to his character, his ways; this was why he had refrained from doing it. Thus reconciled with himself, his pride restored, he punched the time clock at the office.

For his job, Gnei harbored that amorous passion that, though unconfessed, makes clerks' hearts warm, once they come to know the secret sweetness and the furious fanaticism that can charge the most habitual bureaucratic routine, the answering of indifferent correspondence, the precise keeping of a ledger. Perhaps this morning his unconscious hope was that amorous stimulation and clerkish passion would become a single thing, merge one with the other, to go on burning and never be extinguished. But the sight of his desk, the familiar look of a pale-green folder with "Pending" written on it, sufficed to make him feel the sharp contrast between the dizzying beauty from which he had just parted and his usual days.

He walked around the desk several times, without sitting down. He had been overwhelmed by a sudden, urgent love for the beautiful lady, and he could find no rest. He went into the next office, where the accountants, careful and dissatisfied, were tapping on their adding machines.

He began walking past each of them, saying hello, nervously cheery, sly, basking in the memory, without hopes for the present, mad with love among the accountants. As I move now in your midst, in your office—he was thinking—so I was turning in her blankets, not long ago. "Yes, that's right, Marinotti!" he said, banging his fist on a fellow clerk's papers.

Marinotti raised his eyeglasses and asked slowly, "Say, did they take an extra four thousand lire out of your salary this month, too, Gnei?"

"No, my friend, in February," Gnei began, and at the same time he recalled a movement the lady had made, late, in the morning hours, that to him had seemed a new revelation and opened immense, unknown possibilities of love—"no, they already deducted mine then," he went on, in a mild voice, and he moved his hand gently before him, in mid-air, pursing his lips. "They took the whole amount from my February pay, Marinotti." He would have liked to add further details and explanations, just to keep talking, but he wasn't able to.

This is the secret—he decided, going back to his office—at every moment, in everything I do or say, everything I have experienced must be implicit. But he was consumed by an anxiety that he could never live up to what he had been, could never succeed in expressing, with hints, or still less with explicit words, and perhaps not even with his thoughts, the fullness he knew he had reached.

The telephone rang. It was the general manager. He was asking for the background on the Giuseppieri complaint.

"It's like this, sir," Gnei explained over the telephone. "Giuseppieri and Company, on the sixth of March . . ." and he wanted to say: You see, when she slowly said, "Are you going?" I realized I shouldn't let go of her hand. . . .

"Yes, sir, the complaint was in reference to goods previously billed . . ." and he thought to say: Until the door closed behind us, I still wasn't sure. . . .

"No," he explained, "the claim wasn't made through the local office . . ." and he meant: But only then did I realize that she was entirely different from the way I had imagined her, so cold and haughty. . . .

He hung up. His brow was beaded with sweat. He felt tired now, burdened with sleep. It had been a mistake not to go by the house and freshen up, change: even the clothes he was wearing irked him.

He went to the window. There was a large courtyard surrounded by high walls full of balconies, but it was like being in a desert. The sky could be seen above the roofs, no longer limpid, but bleached, covered by an opaque patina, as in Gnei's memory an opaque whiteness was wiping out every memory of sensations, and the presence of the sun was marked by a vague, still patch of light, like a secret pang of grief.

THE ADVENTURE OF A PHOTOGRAPHER

When spring comes, the city's inhabitants, by the hundreds of thousands, go out on Sundays with leather cases over their shoulders. And they photograph one another. They come back as happy as hunters with bulging game bags; they spend days waiting, with sweet anxiety, to see the developed pictures (anxiety to which some add the subtle pleasure of alchemistic manipulations in the darkroom, forbidding any intrusion by members of the family, relishing the acid smell that is harsh to the nostrils). It is only when they have the photos before their eyes that they seem to take tangible possession of the day they spent, only then that the mountain stream, the movement of the child with his pail, the glint of the sun on the wife's legs take on the irrevocability of what has been and can no longer be doubted. Everything else can drown in the unreliable shadow of memory.

Seeing a good deal of his friends and colleagues, Antonio Paraggi, a nonphotographer, sensed a growing isolation. Every week he discovered that the conversations of those who praise the sensitivity of a filter or discourse on the number of DINs were swelled by the voice of yet another to whom he had confided until yesterday, convinced that they were shared, his sarcastic remarks about an activity that to him seemed so unexciting, so lacking in surprises.

Professionally, Antonino Paraggi occupied an executive position in the distribution department of a production firm, but his real passion was commenting to his friends on current events large and small, unraveling the thread of general causes from the tangle of details; in short, by mental attitude he was a philosopher, and he devoted all his thoroughness to grasping the significance of even the events most remote from his own experience. Now he felt that something in the essence of photographic man was eluding him, the secret appeal that made new adepts continue to join the ranks of the amateurs of the lens, some boasting of the progress of their technical and artistic skill, others, on the contrary, giving all the credit to the efficiency of the camera they had purchased, which was capable (according to them) of producing masterpieces even when operated by inept hands (as they declared their own to be, because wherever pride aimed at magnifying the virtues of mechanical devices, subjective talent accepted a proportionate humiliation). Antonino Paraggi understood that neither the one nor the other motive of satisfaction was decisive: the secret lay elsewhere.

It must be said that his examination of photography to discover the causes of a private dissatisfaction—as of someone who feels excluded from something—was to a certain extent a trick Antonino played on himself, to avoid having to consider another, more evident, process that was separating him from his friends. What was happening was this: his acquaintances, of his age, were all getting married, one after another, and starting families, while Antonino remained a bachelor.

Yet between the two phenomena there was undoubtedly a connection, inasmuch as the passion for the lens often develops in a natural, virtually physiological way as a secondary effect of fatherhood. One of the first instincts of parents, after they have brought a child into the world, is to photograph it. Given the speed of growth, it becomes necessary to photograph the child often, because nothing is more fleeting and unmemorable than a six-month-old infant, soon deleted and replaced by one of eight months, and then one of a year; and all the perfection that, to the eyes of parents, a child of three may have reached cannot prevent its being destroyed by that of the four-year-old. The photograph album remains the only place where all these fleeting perfections are saved and juxtaposed, each aspiring to an incomparable absoluteness of its own. In the passion of new parents for framing their offspring in the sights to reduce them to the immobility of black-and-white or a full-color slide, the nonphotographer and non-procreator Antonino saw chiefly a phase in the race toward madness lurking in that black instrument. But his reflections on the iconography-family-madness nexus were summary and reticent: otherwise he would have realized that the person actually running the greatest risk was himself, the bachelor.

In the circle of Antonino's friends, it was customary to spend the weekend out of town, in a group, following a tradition that for many of them dated back to their student days and that had been extended to include their girl friends, then their wives and their children, as well as wet nurses and governesses, and in some cases in-laws and new acquaintances of both sexes. But since the continuity of their habits, their getting together, had never lapsed, Antonino could pretend that nothing had changed with the passage of the years and that they were still the band of young men and women of the old days, rather than a conglomerate of families in which he remained the only surviving bachelor.

More and more often, on these excursions to the sea or the mountains, when it came time for the family group or the multi-family picture, an outsider was asked to lend a hand, a passer-by perhaps, willing to press the button of the camera already focused and aimed in the desired direction. In these cases, Antonino couldn't refuse his services: he would take the camera from the hands of a father or a mother, who would then run to assume his or her place in the second row, sticking his head forward between two other heads, or crouching among the little ones; and Antonino, concentrating all his strength in the finger destined for this use, would press. The first times, an awkward stiffening of his arm would make the lens veer to capture the masts of ships or the spires of steeples, or to decapitate grandparents, uncles, and aunts. He was accused of doing this on purpose, reproached for making a joke in poor taste. It wasn't true: his intention was to lend the use of his finger as docile instrument of the collective wish, but also to exploit his temporary position of privilege to admonish both photographers and their subjects as to the significance of their actions. As soon as the pad of his finger reached the desired condition of detachment from the rest of his person and personality, he was free to communicate his theories in well-reasoned discourse, framing at the same time well-composed little groups. (A few accidental successes had sufficed to give him nonchalance and assurance with viewfinders and light meters.)

". . . Because once you've begun," he would preach, "there is no reason why you should stop. The line between the reality that is photographed because it seems beautiful to us and the reality that seems beautiful because it has been photographed is very narrow. If you take a picture of Pierluca because he's building a sand castle, there is no reason not to take his picture while he's crying because the castle has collapsed, and then while the nurse consoles him by helping him find a sea shell in the sand. The minute you start saying something, 'Ah, how beautiful! We must photograph it!' you are already close to the view of the person who thinks that everything that is not photographed is lost, as if it had never existed, and that therefore, in order really to live, you must photograph as much as you can, and to photograph as much as you can you must either live in the most photographable way possible, or else consider photographable every moment of your life. The first course leads to stupidity; the second to madness."

"You're the one who's mad and stupid," his friends would say to him, "and a pain in the ass, into the bargain."

"For the person who wants to capture everything that passes before his eyes," Antonino would explain, even if nobody was listening to him any more, "the only coherent way to act is to snap at least one picture a minute, from the instant he opens his eyes in the morning to when he goes to sleep. This is the only way that the rolls of exposed film will represent a faithful diary of our days, with nothing left out. If I were to start taking pictures, I'd see this thing through, even if it meant losing my mind. But the rest of you still insist on making a choice. What sort of choice? A choice in the idyllic sense, apologetic, consolatory, at peace with nature, the fatherland, the family. Your choice isn't only photographic; it is a choice of life, which leads you to exclude dramatic conflicts, the knots of contradiction, the great tensions of will, passion, aversion. So you think you are saving yourselves from madness, but you are falling into mediocrity, into hebetude."

A girl named Bice, someone's ex–sister-in-law, and another named Lydia, someone else's ex-secretary, asked him please to take a snapshot of them while they were playing ball among the waves. He consented, but since in the meanwhile he had worked out a theory in opposition to snapshots, he dutifully expressed it to the two friends:

"What drives you two girls to cut from the mobile continuum of your day these temporal slices, the thickness of a second? Tossing the ball back and forth, you are living in the present, but the moment the scansion of the frames is insinuated between your acts it is no longer the pleasure of the game that motivates you but, rather, that of seeing yourselves again in the future, of rediscovering yourselves in twenty years' time, on a piece of yellowed cardboard (yellowed emotionally, even if modern printing procedures will preserve it unchanged). The taste for the spontaneous, natural, lifelike snapshot kills spontaneity, drives away the present. Photographed reality immediately takes on a nostalgic character, of joy fled on the wings of time, a commemorative quality, even if the picture was taken the day before yesterday. And the life that you live in order to photograph it is already, at the outset, a commemoration of itself. To believe that the snapshot is more *true* than the posed portrait is a prejudice. . . ."

So saying, Antonino darted around the two girls in the water, to focus on the movements of their game and cut out of the picture the dazzling glints of the sun on the water. In a scuffle for the ball, Bice, flinging herself on the other girl, who was submerged, was snapped with her behind in close-up, flying over the waves. Antonino, so as not to lose this angle, had flung himself back in the water while holding up the camera, nearly drowning.

"They all came out well, and this one's stupendous," they commented a few days later, snatching the proofs from each other. They had arranged to meet at the photography shop. "You're good; you must take some more of us."

Antonino had reached the conclusion that it was necessary to return to posed subjects, in attitudes denoting their social position and their character, as in the nineteenth century. His antiphotographic polemic could be fought only from within the black box, setting one kind of photography against another.

"I'd like to have one of those old box cameras," he said to his girl friends, "the kind you put on a tripod. Do you think it's still possible to find one?"

"Hmm, maybe at some junk shop . . ."

"Let's go see."

The girls found it amusing to hunt for this curious object; together they ransacked flea markets, interrogated old street photographers, followed them to their lairs. In those cemeteries of objects no longer serviceable lay wooden columns, screens, backdrops with faded landscapes; everything that suggested an old photographer's studio, Antonino bought. In the end he managed to get hold of a box camera, with a bulb to squeeze. It seemed in perfect working order. Antonino also bought an assortment of plates. With the girls helping him, he set up the studio in a room of his apartment, all fitted out with old-fashioned equipment, except for two modern spotlights.

Now he was content. "This is where to start," he explained

to the girls. "In the way our grandparents assumed a pose, in the convention that decided how groups were to be arranged, there was a social meaning, a custom, a taste, a culture. An official photograph, or one of a marriage or a family or a school group, conveyed how serious and important each role or institution was, but also how far they were all false or forced, authoritarian, hierarchical. This is the point: to make explicit the relationship with the world that each of us bears within himself, and which today we tend to hide, to make unconscious, believing that in this way it disappears, whereas . . ."

"Who do you want to have pose for you?"

"You two come tomorrow, and I'll begin by taking some pictures of you in the way I mean."

"Say, what's in the back of your mind?" Lydia asked, suddenly suspicious. Only now, as the studio was all set up, did she see that everything about it had a sinister, threatening air. "If you think we're going to come and be your models, you're dreaming!"

Bice giggled with her, but the next day she came back to Antonino's apartment, alone.

She was wearing a white linen dress with colored embroidery on the edges of the sleeves and pockets. Her hair was parted and gathered over her temples. She laughed, a bit slyly, bending her head to one side. As he let her in, Antonino studied her manner—a bit coy, a bit ironic—to discover what were the traits that defined her true character.

He made her sit in a big armchair, and stuck his head under the black cloth that came with his camera. It was one of those boxes whose rear wall was of glass, where the image is reflected as if already on the plate, ghostly, a bit milky, deprived of every link with space and time. To Antonino it was as if he had never seen Bice before. She had a docility in her somewhat heavy way of lowering her eyelids, of stretching her neck forward, that promised something hidden, as her smile seemed to hide behind the very act of smiling.

"There. Like that. No, head a bit farther; raise your eyes. No, lower them." Antonino was pursuing, within that box, something of Bice that all at once seemed most precious to him, absolute.

"Now you're casting a shadow; move into the light. No, it was better before."

There were many possible photographs of Bice and many Bices impossible to photograph, but what he was seeking was the unique photograph that would contain both the former and the latter.

"I can't get you," his voice emerged, stifled and complaining from beneath the black hood, "I can't get you any more; I can't manage to get you."

He freed himself from the cloth and straightened up again. He was going about it all wrong. That expression, that accent, that secret he seemed on the very point of capturing in her face, was something that drew him into the quicksands of moods, humors, psychology: he, too, was one of those who pursue life as it flees, a hunter of the unattainable, like the takers of snapshots.

He had to follow the opposite path: aim at a portrait completely on the surface, evident, unequivocal, that did not elude conventional appearance, the stereotype, the mask. The mask, being first of all a social, historical product, contains more truth than any image claiming to be "true"; it bears a quantity of meanings that will gradually be revealed. Wasn't this precisely Antonino's intention in setting up this fair booth of a studio?

He observed Bice. He should start with the exterior elements of her appearance. In Bice's way of dressing and fixing herself up—he thought—you could recognize the somewhat nostalgic, somewhat ironic intention, widespread in the mode of those years, to hark back to the fashions of thirty years earlier. The photograph should underline this intention: why hadn't he thought of that?

Antonino went to find a tennis racket; Bice should stand up in a three-quarter turn, the racket under her arm, her face in the pose of a sentimental postcard. To Antonino, from under the black drape, Bice's image—in its slimness and suitability to the pose, and in the unsuitable and almost incongruous aspects that the pose accentuated—seemed very interesting. He made her change position several times, studying the geometry of legs and arms in relation to the racket and to some element in the background. (In the ideal postcard in his mind there would have been the net of the tennis court, but you couldn't demand too much, and Antonino made do with a Ping-Pong table.)

But he still didn't feel on safe ground: wasn't he perhaps trying to photograph memories—or, rather, vague echoes of recollection surfacing in the memory? Wasn't his refusal to live the present as a future memory, as the Sunday photographers did, leading him to attempt an equally unreal operation, namely to give a body to recollection, to substitute it for the present before his very eyes?

"Move! Don't stand there like a stick! Raise the racket, damn it! Pretend you're playing tennis!" All of a sudden he was furious. He had realized that only by exaggerating the poses could he achieve an objective alienness; only by feigning a movement arrested halfway could he give the impression of the unmoving, the nonliving.

Bice obediently followed his orders even when they became vague and contradictory, with a passivity that was also a way of declaring herself out of the game, and yet somehow insinuating, in this game that was not hers, the unpredictable moves of a mysterious match of her own. What Antonino now was expecting of Bice, telling her to put her legs and arms this way and that way, was not so much the simple performance of a plan as her response to the violence he was doing her with his demands, an unforeseeable aggressive reply to this violence that he was being driven more and more to wreak on her.

It was like a dream, Antonino thought, contemplating, from the darkness in which he was buried, that improbable tennis player filtered into the glass rectangle: like a dream when a presence coming from the depth of memory advances, is recognized, and then suddenly is transformed into something unexpected, something that even before the transformation is already frightening because there's no telling what it might be transformed into.

Did he want to photograph dreams? This suspicion struck him dumb, hidden in that ostrich refuge of his with the bulb in his hand, like an idiot; and meanwhile Bice, left to herself, continued a kind of grotesque dance, freezing in exaggerated tennis poses, backhand, drive, raising the racket high or lowering it to the ground as if the gaze coming from that glass eye were the ball she continued to slam back.

"Stop, what's this nonsense? This isn't what I had in mind."

Antonino covered the camera with the cloth and began pacing up and down the room.

It was all the fault of that dress, with its tennis, prewar connotations. . . . It had to be admitted that if she wore a street dress the kind of photograph he described couldn't be taken. A certain solemnity was needed, a certain pomp, like the official photos of queens. Only in evening dress would Bice become a photographic subject, with the décolleté that marks a distinct line between the white of the skin and the darkness of the fabric, accentuated by the glitter of jewels, a boundary between an essence of woman, almost atemporal and almost impersonal in her nakedness, and the other abstraction, social this time, the dress, symbol of an equally impersonal role, like the drapery of an allegorical statue.

He approached Bice, began to unbutton the dress at the neck and over the bosom, and slip it down over her shoulders. He had thought of certain nineteenth-century photographs of women in which from the white of the cardboard emerge the face, the neck, the line of the bared shoulders, while all the rest disappears into the whiteness.

This was the portrait outside of time and space that he now wanted; he wasn't quite sure how it was achieved, but he was determined to succeed. He set the spotlight on Bice, moved the camera closer, fiddled around under the cloth adjusting the aperture of the lens. He looked into it. Bice was naked.

She had made the dress slip down to her feet; she wasn't wearing anything underneath it; she had taken a step forward—no, a step backward, which was as if her whole body were advancing in the picture; she stood erect, tall before the camera, calm, looking straight ahead, as if she were alone.

Antonino felt the sight of her enter his eyes and occupy the whole visual field, removing it from the flux of casual and fragmentary images, concentrating time and space in a finite form. And as if this visual surprise and the impression of the plate were two reflexes connected among themselves, he immediately pressed the bulb, loaded the camera again, snapped, put in another plate, snapped, and went on changing plates and snapping, mumbling, stifled by the cloth, "There, that's right now, yes, again, I'm getting you fine now, another."

He had run out of plates. He emerged from the cloth. He was pleased. Bice was before him, naked, as if waiting.

"Now you can dress," he said, euphoric, but already in a hurry. "Let's go out."

She looked at him, bewildered.

"I've got you now," he said.

Bice burst into tears.

Antonino realized that he had fallen in love with her that same day. They started living together, and he bought the most modern cameras, telescopic lens, the most advanced equipment; he installed a darkroom. He even had a set-up for photographing her when she was asleep at night. Bice would wake at the flash, annoyed; Antonino went on taking snapshots of her disentangling herself from sleep, of her becoming furious with him, of her trying in vain to find sleep again by plunging her face into the pillow, of her making up with him, of her recognizing as acts of love these photographic rapes.

In Antonino's darkroom, strung with films and proofs, Bice peered from every frame, as thousands of bees peer out from the honeycomb of a hive, but always the same bee: Bice in every attitude, at every angle, in every guise, Bice posed or caught unaware, an identity fragmented into a powder of images.

"But what's this obsession with Bice? Can't you photograph anything else?" was the question he heard constantly from his friends, and also from her.

"It isn't just a matter of Bice," he answered. "It's a question of method. Whatever person you decide to photograph, or whatever thing, you must go on photographing it always, exclusively, at every hour of the day and night. Photography has a meaning only if it exhausts all possible images."

But he didn't say what meant most to him: to catch Bice in the street when she didn't know he was watching her, to keep her in the range of hidden lenses, to photograph her not only without letting himself be seen but without seeing her, to surprise her as she was in the absence of his gaze, of any gaze. Not that he wanted to discover any particular thing; he wasn't a jealous man in the usual sense of the word. It was an invisible Bice that he wanted to possess, a Bice absolutely alone, a Bice whose presence presupposed the absence of him and everyone else.

Whether or not it could be defined as jealousy, it was, in any case, a passion difficult to put up with. And soon Bice left him.

Antonino sank into deep depression. He began to keep a diary—a photographic diary, of course. With the camera slung around his neck, shut up in the house, slumped in an armchair, he compulsively snapped pictures as he stared into the void. He was photographing the absence of Bice.

He collected the photographs in an album: you could see ashtrays brimming with cigarette butts, an unmade bed, a damp stain on the wall. He got the idea of composing a catalogue of everything in the world that resists photography, that is systematically omitted from the visual field not only by cameras but also by human beings. On every subject he spent days, using up whole rolls at intervals of hours, so as to follow the changes of light and shadow. One day he became obsessed with a completely empty corner of the room, containing a radiator pipe and nothing else: he was tempted to go on photographing that spot and only that till the end of his days.

The apartment was completely neglected; old newspapers, letters lay crumpled on the floor, and he photographed them. The photographs in the papers were photographed as well, and an indirect bond was established between his lens and that of distant news photographers. To produce those black spots the lenses of other cameras had been aimed at police assaults, charred automobiles, running athletes, ministers, defendants.

Antonino now felt a special pleasure in portraying domestic objects framed by a mosaic of telephotos, violent patches of ink on white sheets. From his immobility he was surprised to find he envied the life of the news photographer, who moves following the movements of crowds, bloodshed, tears, feasts, crime, the conventions of fashion, the falsity of official ceremonies; the news photographer, who documents the extremes of society, the richest and the poorest, the exceptional moments that are nevertheless produced at every moment and in every place.

Does this mean that only the exceptional condition has a meaning? Antonino asked himself. Is the news photographer the true antagonist of the Sunday photographer? Are their worlds mutually exclusive? Or does the one give meaning to the other?

Reflecting like this, he began to tear up the photographs with Bice or without Bice that had accumulated during the months of his passion, ripping to pieces the strips of proofs hung on the walls, snipping up the celluloid of the negatives, jabbing the slides, and piling the remains of this methodical destruction on newspapers spread out on the floor.

Perhaps true, total photography, he thought, is a pile of fragments of private images, against the creased background of massacres and coronations.

He folded the corners of the newspapers into a huge bundle to be thrown into the trash, but first he wanted to photograph it. He arranged the edges so that you could clearly see two halves of photographs from different newspapers that in the bundle happened, by chance, to fit together. In fact he reopened the package a little so that a bit of shiny pasteboard would stick out, the fragment of a torn enlargement. He turned on a spotlight; he wanted it to be possible to recognize in his photograph the half-crumpled and torn images, and at the same time to feel their unreality as casual, inky shadows, and also at the same time their concreteness as objects charged with meaning, the strength with which they clung to the attention that tried to drive them away.

To get all this into one photograph he had to acquire an extraordinary technical skill, but only then would Antonino quit taking pictures. Having exhausted every possibility, at the moment when he was coming full circle Antonino realized that photographing photographs was the only course that he had left—or, rather, the true course he had obscurely been seeking all this time.

THE ADVENTURE OF A TRAVELER

Federico V., who lived in a northern Italian city, was in love with Cinzia U., a resident of Rome. Whenever his work permitted, he would take the train to the capital. Accustomed to budgeting his time strictly, at the job and in his pleasures, he always traveled at night: there was one train, the last, that was not crowded—except in the holiday season—and Federico could stretch out and sleep.

Federico's days in his own city went by nervously, like the hours of someone between trains who, as he goes about his business, cannot stop thinking of the schedule. But when the evening of his departure finally came and his tasks were done and he was walking with his suitcase toward the station, then, even in his haste to avoid missing his train, he began to feel a sense of inner calm pervade him. It was as if all the bustle around the station—now at its last gasp, given the late hour—were part of a natural movement, and he also belonged to it. Everything seemed to be there to encourage him, to give a spring to his steps like the rubberized pavement of the station, and even the obstacles—the wait, his minutes numbered, at the last ticket window still open, the difficulty of breaking a large bill, the lack of small change at the newsstand—seemed to exist for his pleasure in confronting and overcoming them.

Not that he betrayed any sign of this mood: a staid man, he liked being undistinguishable from the many travelers arriving and leaving, all in overcoats like him, a case in hand; and yet he felt as if he were borne on the crest of a wave, because he was rushing toward Cinzia.

The hand in his overcoat pocket toyed with a telephone token. Tomorrow morning, as soon as he landed at the Stazione Termini in Rome, he would run, token in hand, to the nearest public telephone, dial the number, and say, "Hello, darling, I'm here. . . ." And he clutched the token as if it were a most precious object, the only one in the world, the sole tangible proof of what awaited him on his arrival.

The trip was expensive and Federico wasn't rich. If he saw a second-class coach with padded seats and empty compartments, Federico would buy a second-class ticket. Or, rather, he always bought a second-class ticket, with the idea that, if he found too many people there, he would move into first, paying the difference to the conductor. In this operation, he enjoyed the pleasure of economy (besides, when the cost of first-class was paid in two installments, and through necessity, it upset him less), the satisfaction of profiting by his own experience, and a sense of freedom and expansiveness in his actions and in his thoughts.

As sometimes happens with men whose lives are more conditioned by others, exterior, poured out, Federico tended constantly to defend his own inner concentration, and actually it took very little, a hotel room, a train compartment all to himself, for him to adjust the world into harmony with his life; the world seemed created specially for him, as if the railroads that swathed the peninsula had been built deliberately to bear him triumphantly toward Cinzia. That evening, again, second-class was almost empty. Every sign was favorable.

Federico V. chose an empty compartment, not over the wheels but not too far into the coach, either, because he knew that as a rule people who board a train in haste tend to reject the first few compartments. The defense of the space necessary to stretch out and travel lying down is made up of tiny psychological devices; Federico knew them and employed them all. For example, he drew the curtains over the door, an act that, performed at this point, might even seem excessive; but it aimed, in fact, at a psychological effect. Seeing those drawn curtains, the traveler who arrives later is almost always overcome by an instinctive scruple and prefers, if he can find it, a compartment with perhaps two or three people in it already but with the curtains open. Federico strewed his bag, overcoat, newspapers on the seats opposite and beside him. Another elementary move, abused and apparently futile but actually of use. Not that he wanted to make people believe those places were occupied: such a subterfuge would have been contrary to his civic conscience and to his sincere nature. He wanted only to create a rapid impression of a cluttered, not very inviting compartment, a simple, rapid impression.

He sat down and heaved a sigh of relief. He had learned that being in a setting where everything can only be in its place, the same as always, anonymous, without possible surprises, filled him with calm, with self-awareness, freedom of thought. His whole life rushed along in disorder, but now he found the perfect balance between interior stimulus and the impassive neutrality of material things.

It lasted an instant (if he was in second; a minute if he

was in first); then he was immediately seized by a pang: the squalor of the compartment, the plush threadbare in places, the suspicion of dust all about, the faded texture of the curtains in the old-style coaches, gave him a sensation of sadness, the uneasy prospect of sleeping in his clothes, on a bunk not his, with no possible intimacy between him and what he touched. But he immediately recalled the reason he was traveling, and he felt caught up again in that natural rhythm, as of the sea or the wind, that festive, light impulse; he had only to seek it within himself, closing his eyes or clasping the telephone token in his hand, and that sense of squalor was defeated; only he existed, alone, facing the adventure of his journey.

But something was still missing: what? Ah: he heard the bass voice approaching under the marquee: "Pillows!" He had already stood up, was lowering the window, extending his hand with the two hundred-lire pieces, shouting, "I'll take one!" It was the pillow man who, every time, gave the journey its starting signal. He passed by the window a minute before departure, pushing in front of him the wheeled rack with pillows hanging from it. He was a tall old man, thin, with white mustache and large hands, long, thick fingers: hands that inspire trust. He was dressed all in black: military cap, uniform, overcoat, a scarf wound tight around his neck. A character from the times of King Umberto; perhaps an old colonel, or only a faithful quartermaster sergeant. Or a postman, an old rural messenger: with those big hands, when he extended the thin pillow to Federico, holding it with his fingertips, he seemed to be delivering a letter, or perhaps to be posting it through the window. The pillow now was in Federico's arms, square, flat, just like an envelope, and, what's more, covered with postmarks: it was the daily letter to Cinzia, also departing this evening, and instead of the page of eager scrawl there was Federico in person to take the invisible path of the night mail, through the hand of the old winter messenger, the last incarnation of the rational, disciplined North before the incursion among the unruly passions of the Center-South.

But still, and above all, it was a pillow; namely, a soft object (though pressed and compact) and white (though covered with postmarks) from the steam laundry. It contained in itself, as a concept is enclosed within an ideographic sign, the idea of the bed, the twisting and turning, the privacy; and Federico was already anticipating with pleasure the island of freshness it would be for him, that night, amid that rough and treacherous plush. And further: that slender rectangle of comfort prefigured later comforts, later intimacy, later sweetnesses, whose enjoyment was the reason he was setting out on this journey; indeed, the very fact of departing, the hiring of the cushion, was a form of enjoying them, a way of entering the dimension where Cinzia reigned, the circle enclosed by her soft arms.

And it was with an amorous, caressing motion that the train began to glide among the columns of the marquees, snaking through the iron-clad fields of the switches, hurling itself into the darkness, and becoming one with the impulse that till then Federico had felt within himself. And as if the release of his tension in the speeding of the train had made him lighter, he began to accompany its race, humming the tune of a song that this speed brought to his mind: "*J'ai deux amours. . . . Mon pays et Paris . . . Paris toujours . . .*"

A man entered; Federico fell silent. "Is this place free?" He sat down. Federico had already made a quick mental calculation: strictly speaking, if you want to make your journey lying down, it's best to have someone else in the compartment, one person stretched out on one side and the other on the other, for then nobody dares disturb you; but if, on the other hand, half the compartment remains free, when you least expect it a family of six boards the train, complete with children, all bound for Siracusa, and you're forced to sit up. Federico was quite aware, then, that the wisest thing to do, on entering an uncrowded train, was to take a seat not in an empty compartment but in a compartment where there was already one traveler. But he never did this: he preferred to aim at total solitude, and when, through no choice of his, he acquired a traveling companion, he could always console himself with the advantages of the new situation.

And so he did now. "Are you going to Rome?" he asked the newcomer, so that he could then add: Fine, let's draw the curtains, turn off the light, and nobody else will come in. But instead the man answered, "No, Genoa." It would be fine for him to get off at Genoa and leave Federico alone again, but for a few hours' journey he wouldn't want to stretch out, would probably remain awake, wouldn't allow the light to be turned off; and other people could come in at the stations along the way. Thus Federico had the disadvantages of traveling in company, with none of the corresponding advantages.

But he didn't dwell on this. His forte had always been his ability to dismiss from the area of his thoughts any aspect of reality that upset him or was of no use to him. He erased the man seated in the corner opposite his, reduced him to a shadow, a gray patch. The newspapers that both held open before their faces assisted the reciprocal impermeability.

Federico could go on soaring in his amorous flight. "*Paris toujours . . .*" No one could imagine that in that sordid setting of people coming and going, driven by necessity and by forbearance, he was flying to the arms of a woman the like of Cinzia U. And to feed this sense of pride, Federico felt impelled to consider his traveling companion (at whom he had not even glanced so far) to compare—with the cruelty of the *nouveau riche*—his own fortunate state with the grayness of other existences.

The stranger, however, didn't look the least downcast. He was still a young man, sturdy, hefty; his manner was satisfied, active; he was reading a sports magazine and had a large suitcase at his side. He looked, in other words, like the agent for some firm, a commercial traveler. For a moment, Federico V. was gripped by the feeling of envy always inspired in him by people who seemed more practical and vital than he; but it was the impression of a moment, which he immediately dismissed, thinking: He's a man who travels in corrugated iron, or paints, whereas I . . . And he was seized again by that desire to sing, in a release of euphoria, clearing his mind. "*Je voyage en amour!*" he warbled in his mind, to the earlier rhythm that he felt harmonized with the race of the train, adapting words specially invented to enrage the salesman, if he could have heard them. "*Je voyage en volupté!*," underlining as much as he could the lilt and the languor of the tune, "*Je voyage toujours . . . l'hiver et l'été. . . .*" He was thus becoming more and more worked up—"*l'hiver et . . . l'été!*"—to such a degree that a smile of complete mental beatitude must have appeared on his lips. At that moment he realized the salesman was staring at him.

He promptly resumed his staid mien and concentrated on

reading his paper, denying even to himself that he had been caught a moment before in such a childish mood. Childish? Why? Nothing childish about it: his journey put him in a propitious condition of spirit, a condition characteristic, in fact, of the mature man, of the man who knows the good and the evil of life and is now preparing himself to enjoy, deservedly, the good. Serene, his conscience perfectly at peace, he leafed through the illustrated weeklies, shattered images of a fast, frantic life, in which he sought some of the same things that moved him. Soon he discovered that the magazines didn't interest him in the least, mere scribbles of immediacy, of the life that flows on the surface. His impatience was voyaging through loftier heavens. "*L'hiver et . . . l'été!*" Now it was time to settle down to sleep.

He received an unexpected satisfaction: the salesman had fallen asleep sitting up, without changing position, the newspaper on his lap. Federico considered people who were capable of sleeping in a seated position with a sense of estrangement that didn't even manage to be envy: for him, sleeping on the train involved an elaborate procedure, a detailed ritual, but this, too, was precisely the arduous pleasure of his journeys.

First, he had to take off his good trousers and put on an old pair, so he wouldn't arrive all rumpled. The operation would take place in the W.C.; but before—to have greater freedom of movement—it was best to change his shoes for slippers. From his bag Federico took out his old trousers and the slipper bag, took off his shoes, put on the slippers, hid the shoes under the seat, went to the W.C. to change his trousers. "*Je voyage toujours!*" He came back, arranged his good trousers on the rack so they would keep their crease. "*Trallala-la-la!*" He placed the pillow at the end of the seat toward the corridor, because it was better to hear the sudden opening of the door above your head than to be struck by it visually as you suddenly opened your eyes. "*Du voyage, je sais tout!*" At the other end of the seat he put a newspaper, because he didn't lie down barefoot, but kept his slippers on. He hung his jacket from a hook over the pillow, and in one pocket he put his change purse and his money clip, which would have pressed against his leg if left in his trouser pocket. But he kept his ticket in the little pocket below his belt. "*Je sais bien voyager. . . .*" He replaced his good sweater, so as not to wrinkle it, with an old one; he would change his shirt in the morning.

The salesman, waking when Federico came back into the compartment, had followed his maneuvering as if not completely understanding what was going on. "*Jusqu'à mon amour . . .*" He took off his tie and hung it up, took the celluloid stiffeners from his shirt collar and put them in a pocket of his jacket, along with his money. "*. . . j'arrive avec le train!*" He took off his suspenders (like all men devoted to an elegance not merely external, he wore suspenders) and his garters; he undid the top button of his trousers so they wouldn't be too tight over the belly. "*Trallala-la-la!*" He didn't put the jacket on again over his old pullover, but his overcoat instead, after having taken his house keys from the pocket; he left the precious token, though, with the heart-rending fetishism of a child who puts his favorite toy under the pillow. He buttoned up the overcoat completely, turned up the collar; if he was careful, he could sleep in it without leaving a wrinkle. "*Maintenant voilà!*" Sleeping on the train meant waking with your hair all disheveled and maybe finding yourself in the station without even the time to comb it; so he pulled a beret all the way down on his head. "*Je suits prêt, alors!*" He swayed across the compartment in the overcoat, which, worn without a jacket, hung on him like a priestly vestment; he drew the curtains across the door, pulling them until the metallic buttons reached the leather buttonholes. With a gesture toward his companion, he asked permission to turn off the light; the salesman was sleeping. He turned the light off; in the bluish penumbra of the little safety light, he moved just enough to close the curtains at the window, or, rather, to draw them almost closed: here he always left a crack open: in the morning he liked to have a day of sunshine in his bedroom. One more operation: wind his watch. There, now he could go to bed. With one bound, he had flung himself horizontally on the seat, on his side, the overcoat smooth, his legs bent, hands in his pockets, token in his hand, his feet—still in his slippers—on the newspaper, nose against the pillow, beret over his eyes. Now, with a deliberate relaxation of all his feverish inner activity, a vague anticipation of tomorrow, he would fall asleep.

The conductor's curt intrusion (he opened the door with a yank, with confident hand unbuttoned both curtains in a single movement as he raised his other hand to turn on the light) was foreseen. Federico, however, preferred not to wait for it: if the man arrived before he had fallen asleep, fine; if his first sleep had already begun, a habitual and anonymous appearance like the conductor's interrupted it only for a few seconds, just as a sleeper in the country wakes at the cry of a nocturnal bird but then rolls over as if he hadn't waked at all. Federico had the ticket ready in his pocket and held it out, not getting up, almost not opening his eyes, his hand remaining open until he felt the ticket again between his fingers; he pocketed it and would immediately have fallen back to sleep if he hadn't been obliged to perform an operation that nullified all his earlier effort at immobility: namely, to get up and fasten the curtains again. On this trip he was still awake, and the ticket check lasted a bit longer than usual, because the salesman, caught in his sleep, took a while to get his bearings and find his ticket. He doesn't have prompt reflexes like mine, Federico thought, and took the opportunity to overwhelm him with new variations of his imaginary song. "*Je voyage l'amour . . .*" he crooned. The idea of using the verb *voyager* transitively gave him the sense of fullness that poetic inspiration, even the slightest, gives, and the satisfaction of having finally found an expression adequate to his spiritual state. "*Je voyage amour! Je voyage liberté! Jour et nuit je cours . . . par les chemins-de-fer. . . .*"

The compartment was again in darkness. The train devoured its invisible road. Could Federico ask more of life? From such bliss to sleep, the transition is brief. Federico dozed off as if sinking into a pit of feathers. Five or six minutes only: then he woke. He was hot, all in a sweat. The coaches were already heated, since it was well into autumn, but he, recalling the cold he had felt on his previous trip, had thought to lie down in his overcoat. He rose, took it off, flung it over himself like a blanket, leaving his shoulders and chest free but still trying to spread it out so as not to make ugly wrinkles. He turned onto his other side. The sweat had spread over his body a network of itching. He unbuttoned his shirt, scratched his chest, scratched one leg. The constricted condition of his body that he now felt evoked thoughts of physical freedom, the sea, nakedness, swimming, running, and all this culminated in the embracing of Cinzia, the sum of the good of existence. And there, half asleep, he could no longer distinguish present discomforts from the yearned-for good; he had everything at once; he writhed in an uneasiness that presupposed and almost contained every possible well-being. He fell asleep again.

The loudspeakers of the stations that woke him every so often are not as disagreeable as many people suppose. Waking and knowing at once where you are offers two different possibilities of satisfaction: you can think, if the station is farther along than you imagined: How much I've slept! How far I've gone without realizing it! Or, if the station is way behind: Good, now I have plenty of time to fall asleep again and con tinue sleeping without any concern.

Now he was in the second of these situations. The salesman was there, now also stretched out asleep, softly snoring. Federico was still warm. He rose, half-sleeping, groped for the regulator of the electric heating system, found it on the wall opposite his, just above the head of his traveling companion, extended his hands, balancing on one foot because one of his slippers had come off, and angrily turned the dial to "Low." The salesman had to open his eyes at that moment and see that clawing hand over his head: he gulped, swallowed saliva, then sank back into his haze. Federico flung himself down. The electric regulator let out a hum, a red light came on, as if it were trying to explain, to start a dialogue. Federico impatiently waited for the heat to be dispelled; he rose to lower the window a crack, but since the train was now moving very fast, he felt cold and closed it again. He shifted the regulator toward "Automatic." His face on the amorous pillow, he lay for a while listening to the buzzes of the regulator like mysterious messages from ultraterrestrial worlds. The train was traveling over the earth, surmounted by endless spaces, and in all the universe he and he alone was the man who was speeding toward Cinzia U.

The next awakening was at the cry of a coffee vendor in the Stazione Principe, Genoa. The salesman had vanished. Carefully, Federico stopped up the gaps in the wall of curtains, and listened with apprehension to every footstep approaching along the passage, to every opening of a door. No, nobody came in. But at Genoa-Brignole, a hand opened a breach, groped, tried to part the curtains, failed; a human form appeared, crouching, and cried in dialect toward the corridor, "Come on! It's empty here!" A heavy shuffling of boots replied, with scattered voices, and four Alpine soldiers entered the darkness of the compartment and almost sat down on top of Federico. As they bent over him, as if over an unknown animal—"Oh! Who's this here?"—he pulled himself up abruptly on his arms and confronted them: "Aren't there any other compartments?" "No. All full," they answered, "but never mind. We'll all sit over on this side. Stay comfortable." They seemed intimidated, but actually they were simply accustomed to curt manners and paid no attention to anything; brawling, they flung themselves on the other seat. "Are you going far?" Federico asked, meeker now, from his pillow. No, they were getting off at one of the first stations. "And where are you going?" "To Rome." "Madonna! All the way to Rome!" Their tone of amazed compassion was transformed, in Federico's heart, into a heroic, melting pride.

And so the journey continued. "Could you turn off the light?" They turned it off, and remained faceless in the dark, noisy, cumbersome, shoulder to shoulder. One raised a curtain at the window and peered out: it was a moonlit night. Lying down, Federico saw only the sky and now and then the row of lights of a little station that dazzled his eyes and cast a rake of shadows on the ceiling. These *alpini* were rough country boys, going home on leave; they never stopped talking loud and hailing one another, and at times in the darkness they punched and slapped one another, except one of them who was sleeping and another who coughed. They spoke a murky dialect. Federico could grasp words now and then—talk about the barracks, the brothel. For some reason, he felt he didn't hate them. Now he was with them, almost one of them, and he identified with them for the pleasure of then imagining himself tomorrow at the side of Cinzia U., feeling the dizzying, sudden shift of fate. But this was not to belittle them, as with the stranger earlier; now he remained obscurely on their side; their unaware blessing accompanied him toward Cinzia; in everything that was most remote from her lay the value of having her, the sense of his being the one who had her.

Now Federico's arm was numb. He lifted it, shook it; the numbness wouldn't go away, turned into pain; the pain turned into slow well-being as he flapped his bent arm in the air. The *alpini*, all four of them, sat there staring at him, mouths agape. "What's come over him? . . . He's dreaming. . . . Hey, what are you doing? . . ." Then, with youthful fickleness, they went back to teasing one another. Federico now tried to revive the circulation in one leg, putting his foot on the floor and stamping hard.

Between dozing and clowning, an hour went by. And he didn't feel he was their enemy; perhaps he was no one's enemy; perhaps he had become a good man. He didn't hate them even when, a little before their station, they went out, leaving the door and the curtains wide open. He got up, barricaded himself again, savored once more the pleasure of solitude, but with no bitterness toward anyone.

Now his legs were cold. He pushed the cuffs of his trousers inside his socks, but he was still cold. He wrapped the folds of his overcoat around his legs. Now his stomach and shoulders were cold. He turned the regulator up almost to "High," tucked himself in again, pretended not to notice that the overcoat was getting ugly creases though he felt them under him. Now he was ready to renounce everything for his immediate comfort; the awareness of being good to his neighbor drove him to be good to himself and, in this general indulgence, to find once more the road to sleep.

From now on the awakenings were intermittent and mechanical. The entrances of the conductor, with his practiced movement in opening the curtains, were easily distinguishable from the uncertain attempts of the night travelers who had got on at an intermediate station and were bewildered at finding a series of compartments with the curtains drawn. Equally professional but more brusque and grim was the appearance of the policeman, who abruptly turned on the light in the sleeper's face, examined him, turned it off, and went out in silence, leaving behind him a prison chill.

Then a man came in, at some station buried in the night. Federico became aware of him when he was already huddled in one corner, and from the damp odor of his coat realized that outside it was raining. When he woke again the man had vanished, at God knows what other invisible station, and for Federico he had been only a shadow smelling of rain, with heavy respiration.

He was cold; he turned the regulator all the way to "High," then stuck his hand under the seat to feel the warmth rise.

He felt nothing; he groped there; everything must have been cut off. He put his overcoat on again, then removed it; he hunted for his good sweater, took off the old one, put on the good one, put the old one on over it, put the overcoat on again, huddled down, and tried to achieve once more the sensation of fullness that earlier had led him to sleep; but he couldn't manage to recall anything, and when he remembered the song he was already sleeping, and that rhythm continued cradling him triumphantly in his sleep.

The first morning light came through the cracks like the cries of "Hot coffee!" and "Newspapers!" at a station perhaps still in Tuscany, or at the very beginning of Latium. It wasn't raining; beyond the damp windows the sky already displayed a southern indifference to autumn. The desire for something hot, and also the automatic reaction of the city man who begins all his mornings by glancing at the newspapers, acted on Federico's reflexes; and he felt that he should rush to the window and buy coffee or the paper or both. But he succeeded so well in convincing himself that he was still asleep and hadn't heard anything that this persuasion still held when the compartment was invaded by the usual people from Civitavecchia who take the early-morning trains into Rome. And the best part of his sleep, that of the first hours of daylight, had almost no breaks.

When he really did wake up, he was dazzled by the light that came in through the panes, now without curtains. On the seat opposite him a row of people were lined up, including even a little boy on a fat woman's lap, and a man was seated on Federico's own seat, in the space left free by his bent legs. The men had various faces but all had something vaguely bureaucratic about them, with the one possible variant of an air-force officer in a uniform laden with ribbons; it was also obvious that the women were going to call on relatives who worked in some government office. In any case, these were people going to Rome to deal with red tape for themselves or for others. And all of them, some looking up from the conservative newspaper *Il Tempo*, observed Federico stretched out there at the level of their knees, shapeless, bundled into that overcoat, without feet, like a seal; as he was detaching himself from the saliva-stained pillow, disheveled, the beret on the back of his head, one cheek marked by the wrinkles in the pillowcase; as he got up, stretched with awkward, seal-like movements, gradually rediscovering the use of his legs, slipping the slippers on the wrong feet, and now unbuttoning and scratching himself between the double sweaters and the rumpled shirt, while running his still-sticky eyes over them and smiling.

At the window, the broad Roman *campagna* spread out. Federico sat there for a moment, his hands on his knees, still smiling; then, with a gesture, he asked permission to take the newspaper from the knees of the man facing him. He glanced at the headlines, felt as always the sense of finding himself in a remote country, looked olympically at the arches of the aqueducts that sped past outside the window, returned the newspaper, and got up to look for his toilet kit in his suitcase.

At the Stazione Termini the first to jump down from the car, fresh as a daisy, was Federico. He was clasping the token in his hand. In the niches between the columns and the newsstands, the gray telephones were waiting only for him. He put the token in the slot, dialed the number, listened with beating heart to the distant ring, heard Cinzia's "Hello . . ." still suffused with sleep and soft warmth, and he was already in the tension of their days together, in the desperate battle against the hours; and he realized he would never manage to tell her anything of the significance of that night, which he now sensed was fading, like every perfect night of love, at the cruel explosion of day.

THE ADVENTURE OF A READER

The coast road ran high above the cape; the sea was below, a sheer drop, and on all sides, as far as the hazy mountainous horizon. The sun was on all sides, too, as if the sky and the sea were two glasses magnifying it. Down below, against the jagged, irregular rocks of the cape, the calm water slapped without making foam. Amedeo Oliva climbed down a steep flight of steps, shouldering his bicycle, which he then left in a shady place, after closing the padlock. He continued down the steps amid spills of dry yellow earth and agaves jutting into the void, and he was already looking around for the most comfortable stretch of rock to lie down. Under his arm he had a rolled-up towel and, inside the towel, his bathing trunks and a book.

The cape was a solitary place: only a few groups of bathers dived into the water or took the sun, hidden from one another by the irregular conformation of the place. Between two boulders that shielded him from view, Amedeo undressed, put on his trunks, and began jumping from the top of one rock to the next. Leaping in this way on his skinny legs, he crossed half the rocky shore, sometimes almost grazing the faces of half-hidden pairs of bathers stretched out on beach towels. Having gone past an outcrop of sandy rock, its surface porous and irregular, he came upon smooth stones, with rounded corners; Amedeo took off his sandals, held them in his hand, and continued running barefoot, with the confidence of someone who can judge distances between rocks and whose soles nothing can hurt. He reached a spot directly above the sea; there was a kind of shelf running around the cliff at the halfway point. There Amedeo stopped. On a flat ledge he arranged his clothes, carefully folded, and set the sandals on them, soles up, so no gust of wind would carry everything off (in reality, only the faintest breath of air was stirring, from the sea; but this precaution was obviously a habit with him). A little bag he was carrying turned into a rubber cushion; he blew into it until it had filled out, then set it down; and below it, at a point slightly sloping from that rocky ledge, he spread out his towel. He flung himself on it supine, and already his hands were opening his book at the marked page. So he lay stretched out on the ledge, in that sun glaring on all sides, his skin dry (his tan was opaque, irregular, as of one who takes the sun without any method but doesn't burn); on the rubber cushion he set his head sheathed in a white canvas cap, moistened (yes, he had also climbed down to a low rock, to dip his cap in the water), immobile except for his eyes (invisible behind his dark glasses), which followed along the black and white lines the horse of Fabrizio del Dongo. Below him opened a little cove of greenish-blue water, transparent almost to the bottom. The rocks, according to their exposure, were bleached white or covered with algae. A little pebble beach was at their foot. Every now and then Amedeo raised his eyes to that broad view, lingered on a glinting of the surface, on the oblique dash of a crab; then he went back, gripped, to the page where Raskolnikov counted the steps that separated him from the old woman's door, or where Lucien de Rubempré, before sticking his head into the noose, gazed at the towers and roofs of the Conciergerie.

For some time Amedeo had tended to reduce his participation in active life to the minimum. Not that he didn't like action: on the contrary, love of action nourished his whole character, all his tastes; and yet, from one year to the next, the yearning to be someone who did things declined, declined, until he wondered if he had ever really harbored that yearning. His interest in action survived, however, in his pleasure in reading; his passion was always the narration of events, the stories, the tangle of human situations—nineteenth-century novels especially, but also memoirs and biographies, and so on down to thrillers and science fiction, which he didn't disdain but which gave him less satisfaction because they were short. Amedeo loved thick tomes, and in tackling them he felt the physical pleasure of undertaking a great task. Weighing them in his hand, thick, closely printed, squat, he would consider with some apprehension the number of pages, the length of the chapters, then venture into them, a bit reluctant at the beginning, without any desire to perform the initial chore of remembering the names, catching the drift of the story; then he would entrust himself to it, running along the lines, crossing the grid of the uniform page, and beyond the leaden print the flame and fire of battle appeared, the cannonball that, whistling through the sky, fell at the feet of Prince Andrei, and the shop filled with engravings and statues where Frédéric Moreau, his heart in his mouth, was to meet the Arnoux family. Beyond the surface of the page you entered a world where life was more alive than here on this side: like the surface of the water that separates us from that blue-and-green world, rifts as far as the eye can see, expanses of fine, ribbed sand, creatures half animal and half vegetable.

The sun beat down hard, the rock was burning, and after a while Amedeo felt he was one with the rock. He reached the end of the chapter, closed the book, inserted an advertising coupon to mark his place, took off his canvas cap and his glasses, stood up half dazed, and with broad leaps went down to the far end of the rock, where a group of kids were constantly, at all hours, diving in and climbing out. Amedeo stood erect on a shelf over the sea, not too high, a couple of yards above the water; his eyes, still dazzled, contemplated the luminous transparence below him, and all of a sudden he plunged. His dive was always the same: headlong, fairly correct, but with a certain stiffness. The passage from the sunny air to the tepid water would have been almost unnoticeable if it hadn't been abrupt. He didn't surface immediately: he liked to swim underwater, down, down, his belly almost scraping bottom, as long as his breath held out. He very much enjoyed physical effort, setting himself difficult assignments (for this he came to read his book at the cape, making the climb on his bicycle, pedaling up furiously under the noonday sun). Every time, swimming underwater, he tried to reach a wall of rocks that rose at a certain point from the sandy bed and was covered by a thick patch of sea grasses. He surfaced among those rocks and swam around a bit; he began to do "the Australian crawl" methodically, but expending more energy than necessary; soon, tired of swimming with his face in the water, as if blind, he took to a freer side stroke; sight gave him more satisfaction than movement, and in a little while he gave up the side stroke to drift on his back, moving less and less regularly and steadily, until he stopped altogether, in a dead-man's-float. And so he turned and twisted in that sea as in a bed without sides; he would set himself the goal of a sandbar to be reached, or limit the number of strokes, and he couldn't rest until he had carried out that task. For a while he would dawdle lazily, then he would head out to sea, taken by the desire to have nothing around him but sky and water; for a while he would move close to the rocks scattered along the cape, not to overlook any of the possible itineraries of that little archipelago. But as he swam, he realized that the curiosity occupying more and more of his mind was to know the outcome—for example—of the story of Albertine. Would Marcel find her again, or not? He swam furiously or floated idly, but his heart was between the pages of the book left behind on shore. And so, with rapid strokes, he would regain his rock, seek the place for climbing up, and, almost without realizing it, he would be up there again, rubbing the Turkish towel on his back. Sticking the canvas cap on his head once more, he would lie in the sun again, to begin the next chapter.

He was not, however, a hasty, voracious reader. He had reached the age when rereading a book—for the second, third, or fourth time—affords more pleasure than a first reading. And yet he still had many continents to discover. Every summer, the most laborious packing before his departure for the sea involved the heavy suitcase to be filled with books. Following the whims and dictates of the months of city life, each year Amedeo would choose certain famous books to reread and certain authors to essay for the first time. And there, on the rock, he went through them, lingering over sentences, often raising his eyes from the page to ponder, to collect his thoughts.

At a certain point, raising his eyes in this way, he saw that on the little pebble beach below, in the cove, a woman had appeared and was lying there.

She was deeply tanned, thin, not very young or particularly beautiful, but nakedness became her (she wore a very tiny "two-piece," rolled up at the edges to get as much sun as she could), and Amedeo's eye was drawn to her. He realized that as he read he was raising his eyes more and more often from the book to gaze into the air; and this air was the air that lay between that woman and himself. Her face (she was stretched out on the sloping shore, on a rubber mattress, and at every flicker of his pupils Amedeo saw her legs, not shapely but harmonious, the excellently smooth belly, the bosom slim in a perhaps not unpleasant way but probably sagging a bit, the shoulders a bit too bony, and then the neck and the arms, and the face masked by the sunglasses and by the brim of the straw hat) was slightly lined, lively, aware, and ironic. Amedeo classified the type: the independent woman, on holiday by herself, who dislikes crowded beaches and prefers the more deserted rocks, and likes to lie there and become black as coal; he evaluated the amount of lazy sensuality and of chronic frustration there was in her; he thought fleetingly of the likelihood of a rapidly consummated fling, measured it against the prospect of a trite conversation, a program for the evening, probable logistic difficulties, the effort of concentration always required to become acquainted, even superficially, with a person; and he went on reading, convinced that this woman couldn't interest him at all.

But he had been lying on that stretch of rock for too long, or else those fleeting thoughts had left a wake of restlessness in him; anyway, he felt an ache, the harshness of the rock under the towel that was his only pallet began to chafe him. He got up to look for another spot where he could stretch out. For a moment, he hesitated between two places that seemed equally comfortable to him: one more distant from the little beach where the tanned lady was lying (actually behind an outcrop of rock that blocked the sight of her), the other closer. The thought of approaching, and of then perhaps being led by some unforeseeable circumstance to start a conversation, and thus perforce to interrupt his reading, made him immediately prefer the farther spot; but when he thought it over, it really would look as if, the moment that lady had arrived, he wanted to run off, and this might seem a bit rude; so he picked the closer spot, since his reading absorbed him so much anyway that the view of the lady—not specially beautiful, for that matter—could hardly distract him. He lay on one side, holding the book so that it blocked the sight of her, but it was awkward to keep his arm at that height, and in the end he lowered it. Now, every time he had to start a new line, the same gaze that ran along the lines encountered, just beyond the edge of the page, the legs of the solitary vacationer. She, too, had shifted slightly, looking for a more comfortable position, and the fact that she had raised her knees and crossed her legs precisely in Amedeo's direction allowed him to observe better her proportions, not at all unattractive. In short, Amedeo (though a shaft of rock was sawing at his hip) couldn't have found a finer position: the pleasure he could derive from the sight of the tanned lady—a marginal pleasure, something extra, but not for that reason to be discarded, since it could be enjoyed with no effort—did not mar the pleasure of reading, but was inserted into its normal process, so that now he was sure he could go on reading without being tempted to look away.

Everything was calm; only the course of his reading flowed on, with the motionless landscape serving as frame; the tanned lady had become a necessary part of this landscape. Amedeo was naturally relying on his own ability to remain absolutely still for a long time, but he hadn't taken into account the woman's restlessness: now she rose, was standing, making her way among the stones toward the water. She had moved—Amedeo understood immediately—to get a closer look at a great medusa that a group of boys were bringing ashore, poking at it with lengths of reed. The tanned lady bent toward the overturned body of the medusa and was questioning the boys; her legs rose from wooden clogs with very high heels, unsuited to those rocks; her body, seen from behind as Amedeo now saw it, was that of a more attractive younger woman than she had first seemed to him. He thought that, for a man seeking a romance, that dialogue between her and the fisher-boys would have been a "classic" opening: approach, also remark on the capture of the medusa, and in that way engage her in conversation. The very thing he wouldn't have done for all the gold in the world! he added to himself, plunging again into his reading.

To be sure, this rule of conduct of his also prevented him from satisfying a natural curiosity concerning the medusa, which seemed, as he saw it there, of unusual dimensions, and also of a strange hue between pink and violet. This curiosity about marine animals was in no way a sidetrack, either; it was coherent with the nature of his passion for reading. At that moment, in any case, his concentration on the page he was reading—a long descriptive passage—had been relaxing; in short, it was absurd that to protect himself against the danger of starting a conversation with that woman he should also deny himself spontaneous and quite legitimate impulses such as that of amusing himself for a few minutes by taking a close look at a medusa. He shut his book at the marked page and stood up. His decision couldn't have been more timely: at that same moment the lady moved away from the little group of boys, preparing to return to her mattress. Amedeo realized this as he was approaching and felt the need of immediately saying something in a loud voice. He shouted to the kids, "Watch out! It could be dangerous!"

The boys, crouched around the animal, didn't even look up: they continued, with the lengths of reed they held in their hands, to try to raise it and turn it over; but the lady turned abruptly and went back to the shore, with a half-questioning, half-fearful air "Oh, how frightening! Does it bite?"

"If you touch it, it stings," he explained and realized he was heading not toward the medusa but toward the lady, who, for some reason, covered her bosom with her arms in a useless shudder and cast almost furtive glances, first at the supine animal, then at Amedeo. He reassured her, and so, predictably, they started conversing; but it didn't matter, because Amedeo would soon be going back to the book awaiting him: he only wanted to take a glance at the medusa. He led the tanned lady over, to lean into the center of the circle of boys. The lady was now observing with revulsion, her knuckles against her teeth, and at a certain point, as she and he were side by side, their arms came into contact and they delayed a moment before separating them. Amedeo then started talking about medusas. His direct experience wasn't great, but he had read some books by famous fishermen and underwater explorers, so—skipping the smaller fauna—he began promptly talking about the famous manta. The lady listened to him, displaying great interest and interjecting something from time to time, always irrelevantly, the way women will. "You see this red spot on my arm? That wasn't a medusa, was it?" Amedeo touched the spot, just above the elbow, and said no. It was a bit red because she had been leaning on it while lying down.

With that, it was all over. They said good-bye; she went back to her place, and he to his, where he resumed reading. It had been an interval lasting the right amount of time, neither more nor less, a human encounter, not unpleasant (the lady was polite, discreet, unassuming) precisely because it was barely adumbrated. In the book he now found a far fuller and more concrete attachment to reality, where everything had a meaning, an importance, a rhythm. Amedeo felt himself in a perfect situation: the printed page opened true life to him, profound and exciting, and, raising his eyes, he found a pleasant but casual juxtaposition of colors and sensations, an accessory and decorative world that couldn't commit him to anything. The tanned lady, from her mattress, gave him a smile and a wave; he replied also with a smile and a vague gesture, and immediately lowered his eyes. But the lady had said something.

"Eh?"

"You're reading. Do you read all the time?"

"Mmm . . ."

"Interesting?"

"Yes."

"Enjoy yourself!"

"Thank you."

He mustn't raise his eyes again. At least not until the end of the chapter. He read it in a flash. The lady now had a cigarette in her mouth and motioned to him, as she pointed to it. Amedeo had the impression that for some time she had been trying to attract his attention. "I beg your pardon?"

". . . match. Forgive me. . . ."

"Oh, I'm very sorry. I don't smoke. . . ."

The chapter was finished. Amedeo rapidly read the first lines of the next one, which he found surprisingly attractive, but to begin the next chapter without anxiety he had to resolve as quickly as possible the matter of the match. "Wait!" He stood up, began leaping among the rocks, half dazed by the sun, until he found a little group of people smoking. He borrowed a box of matches, ran to the lady, lighted her cigarette, ran back to return the matches; and they said to him, "Keep them, you can keep them." He ran again to the lady to leave the matches with her, and she thanked him; he waited a moment before leaving her, but realized that after this delay he had to say something, and so he said, "You aren't swimming?"

"In a little while," the lady said. "What about you?"

"I've already had my swim."

"And you're not going to take another dip?"

"Yes, I'll read one more chapter, then have a swim again."

"Me, too, when I finish my cigarette, I'll dive in."

"See you later then."

"Later . . ."

This kind of appointment restored to Amedeo a calm such as he—now he realized—had not known since the moment he became aware of the solitary lady: now his conscience was no longer oppressed by the thought of having to have any sort of relationship with that lady; everything was postponed to the moment of their swim—a swim he would have taken anyway, even if the lady hadn't been there—and for now he could abandon himself without remorse to the pleasure of reading. So thoroughly that he didn't notice when, at a certain point—before he had reached the end of the chapter—the lady finished her cigarette, stood up, and approached him to invite him to go swimming. He saw the clogs and the straight legs just beyond the book; his eyes moved up; he lowered them again to the page—the sun was dazzling—and read a few lines in haste, looked up again, and heard her say, "Isn't your head about to explode? I'm going to have a dip!" It was nice to stay there, to go on reading and look up every now and then. But since he could no longer put it off, Amedeo did something he never did: he skipped almost half a page, to the conclusion of the chapter, which he read, on the other hand, with great attention, and then he stood up. "Let's go. Shall we dive from the point there?"

After all the talk of diving, the lady cautiously slipped into the water from a ledge on a level with it. Amedeo plunged headlong from a higher rock than usual. It was the hour of the still slow inclining of the sun. The sea was golden. They swam in that gold, somewhat separated: Amedeo at times sank for a few strokes underwater and amused himself by frightening the lady, swimming beneath her. Amused himself, after a fashion: it was kid stuff, of course, but for that matter, what else was there to do, anyway? Swimming with another person was slightly more tiresome than swimming alone, but the difference was minimal. Beyond the gold glints, the water's blue deepened, as if from down below rose an inky darkness. It was useless: nothing equaled the savor of life found in books. Skimming over some bearded rocks in mid-water and leading her, frightened (to help her onto a sandbar, he also clasped her hips and bosom, but his hands, from the immersion, had become almost insensitive, with white, wrinkled pads), Amedeo turned his gaze more and more often toward land, where the colored jacket of his book stood out. There was no other story, no other possible expectation beyond what he had left suspended, between the pages where his bookmark was; all the rest was an empty interval.

However, returning to shore, giving her a hand, drying himself, then each rubbing the other's back, finally created a kind of intimacy, so that Amedeo felt it would have been impolite to go off on his own once more. "Well," he said, "I'll stretch out and read here; I'll go get my book and pillow." And *read*: he had taken care to warn her. She said, "Yes, fine. I'll smoke a cigarette and read *Annabella* a bit myself." She had one of those women's magazines with her, and so both of them could lie and read, each on his own. Her voice struck him like a drop of cold water on the nape of the neck, but she was only saying, "Why do you want to lie there on that hard rock? Come onto the mattress: I'll make room for you." The invitation was polite, the mattress was comfortable, and Amedeo gladly accepted. They lay there, he facing in one direction and she in the other. She didn't say another word, she leafed through those illustrated pages, and Amedeo managed to sink completely into his reading. It was a lingering sunset, when the heat and light hardly decline but remain only barely, sweetly attenuated. The novel Amedeo was reading had reached the point where the darkest secrets of characters and plot are revealed, and you move in a familiar world, and you achieve a kind of parity, an ease between author and reader: you proceed together, and you would like to go on forever.

On the rubber mattress it was possible to make those slight movements necessary to keep the limbs from going to sleep, and one of his legs, in one direction, came to graze a leg of hers, in the other. He didn't mind this, and kept his leg there; and obviously she didn't mind, either, because she also refrained from moving. The sweetness of the contact mingled with the reading and, as far as Amedeo was concerned, made it the more complete; but for the lady it must have been different, because she rose, sat up, and said, "Really . . ."

Amedeo was forced to raise his head from the book. The woman was looking at him, and her eyes were bitter.

"Something wrong?" he asked.

"Don't you ever get tired of reading?" she asked. "You could hardly be called good company! Don't you know that, with women, you're supposed to make conversation?" she added; her half smile was perhaps meant only to be ironic, though to Amedeo, who at that moment would have paid anything rather than give up his novel, it seemed downright threatening. What have I got myself into, moving down here? he thought. Now it was clear that with this woman beside him he wouldn't read a line.

I must make her realize she's made a mistake, he thought, that I'm not at all the type for a beach courtship, that I'm the sort it's best not to pay too much attention to. "Conversation," he said, aloud, "what kind of conversation?" and he extended his hand toward her. There, now: if I lay a hand on her, she will surely be insulted by such an unsuitable action, maybe she'll give me a slap and go away. But whether it was his own natural reserve, or there was a different, sweeter yearning that in reality he was pursuing, the caress, instead of being brutal and provocatory, was shy, melancholy, almost entreating: he grazed her throat with his fingers, lifted a little necklace she was wearing, and let it fall. The woman's reply consisted of a movement, first slow, as if resigned and a bit ironic—she lowered her chin to one side, to trap his hand—then rapid, as if in a calculated, aggressive spring: she bit the back of his hand. "Ow!" Amedeo cried. They moved apart.

"Is this how you make conversation?" the lady said.

There, Amedeo quickly reasoned, my way of making conversation doesn't suit her, so there won't be any conversing, and now I can read; he had already started a new paragraph. But he was trying to deceive himself: he understood clearly that by now they had gone too far, that between him and the tanned lady a tension had been created that could no longer be interrupted; he also understood that he was the first to wish not to interrupt it, since in any case he wouldn't be able to return to the single tension of his reading, all intimate and interior. He could, on the contrary, try to make this exterior tension follow, so to speak, a course parallel to the other, so that he would not be obliged to renounce either the lady or the book.

Since she had sat up, with her back propped against a rock, he sat beside her, put his arm around her shoulders, keeping his book on his knees. He turned toward her and kissed her. They moved apart, then kissed again. Then he lowered his head toward the book and resumed reading.

As long as he could, he wanted to continue reading. His fear was that he wouldn't be able to finish the novel: the beginning of a summer affair could be considered the end of his calm hours of solitude, for a completely different rhythm would dominate his days of vacation; and obviously, when you are completely lost in reading a book, if you have to interrupt it, then pick it up again some time later, most of the pleasure is lost: you forget so many details, you never manage to become immersed in it as before.

The sun was gradually setting behind the next promontory, and then the next, and the one after that, leaving remnants of color against the light. From the little coves of the cape, all the bathers had gone. Now the two of them were alone. Amedeo had his arm around the woman's shoulders, he was reading, he gave her kisses on the neck and on the ears—which it seemed to him she liked—and every now and then, when she turned, on the mouth; then he resumed reading. Perhaps this time he had found the ideal equilibrium: he could go on like this for a hundred pages or so. But once again it was she who wanted to change the situation. She began to stiffen, almost to reject him, and then said, "It's late. Let's go. I'm going to dress."

This abrupt decision opened up quite different prospects. Amedeo was a bit disoriented, but he didn't stop to weigh the pros and cons. He had reached a climax in the book, and her dimly heard words, "I'm going to dress," had, in his mind, immediately been translated into these others: While she dresses, I'll have time to read a few pages without being disturbed.

But she said, "Hold up the towel, please," addressing him as *tu* for perhaps the first time. "I don't want anyone to see me." The precaution was useless because the shore by now was deserted, but Amedeo consented amiably, since he could hold up the towel while remaining seated and so continue to read the book on his knees.

On the other side of the towel, the lady had undone her

halter, paying no attention to whether he was looking at her or not. Amedeo didn't know whether to look at her, pretending to read, or to read, pretending to look at her. He was interested in the one thing and the other, but looking at her seemed too indiscreet, while going on reading seemed too indifferent. The lady did not follow the usual method used by bathers who dress outdoors, first putting on clothes and then removing the bathing suit underneath them. No: now that her bosom was bared, she also took off the bottom of her suit. This was when, for the first time, she turned her face toward him; and it was a sad face, with a bitter curl to the mouth, and she shook her head, shook her head and looked at him.

Since it has to happen, it might as well happen immediately, Amedeo thought, diving forward, book in hand, one finger between the pages; but what he read in that gaze—reproach, commiseration, dejection, as if to say: Stupid, all right, we'll do it if it has to be done like this, but you don't understand a thing, any more than the others—or, rather, what he did *not* read, since he didn't know how to read gazes, but only vaguely sensed, roused in him a moment of such transport toward the woman that, embracing her and falling onto the mattress with her, he only slightly turned his head toward the book to make sure it didn't fall into the sea.

It had fallen, instead, right beside the mattress, open, but a few pages had flipped over; and Amedeo, even in the ecstasy of his embraces, tried to free one hand to put the bookmark at the right page. Nothing is more irritating when you're eager to resume reading than to have to search through the book, unable to find your place.

Their lovemaking was a perfect match. It could perhaps have been extended a bit longer: but, then, hadn't everything been lightning-fast in their encounter?

Dusk was falling. Below, the rocks opened out, sloping, into a little harbor. Now she had gone down there and was halfway into the water. "Come down; we'll have a last swim. . . ." Amedeo, biting his lip, was counting how many pages were left till the end.

THE ADVENTURE OF A NEARSIGHTED MAN

Amilcare Carruga was still young, not lacking resources, without exaggerated material or spiritual ambitions: nothing, therefore, prevented him from enjoying life. And yet he came to realize that for a while now this life, for him, had imperceptibly been losing its savor. Trifles, like, for example, looking at women in the street: there had been a time when he would cast his eyes on them greedily; now perhaps he would instinctively start to look at them, but it would immediately seem to him that they were speeding past like a wind, stirring no sensation, so he would lower his eyelids, indifferent. Once new cities had excited him—he traveled often, since he was a merchant—but now he felt only irritation, confusion, loss of bearings. Before, since he lived alone, he used to go to the movies every evening; he enjoyed himself, no matter what the picture was. Anyone who goes all the time sees, as it were, one huge film, in endless installments: he knows all the actors, even the character players and the walk-ons, and this recognition of them every time is amusing in itself. Well: now even at the movies, all those faces seemed to have become colorless to him, flat, anonymous; he was bored.

He caught on, finally. The fact was that he was nearsighted. The oculist prescribed eyeglasses for him. After that moment his life changed, became a hundred times richer in interest than before.

Just slipping on the glasses was, every time, a thrill for him. He might be, for instance, at a tram stop, and he would be overcome by sadness because everything, people and objects around him, was so vague, banal, worn from being as it was; and him there, groping in the midst of a flabby world of nearly decayed forms and colors. He would put on his glasses to read the number of the arriving tram, and all would change: the most ordinary things, even lampposts, were etched with countless tiny details, with sharp lines, and the faces, the faces of strangers, each filled up with little marks, dots of beard, pimples, nuances of expression that there had been no hint of before; and he could understand what material clothes were made of, could guess the weave, could spot the fraying at the hem. Looking became an amusement, a spectacle; not looking at this thing or that—just looking. And so Amilcare Carruga forgot to note the tram number, missed one car after another or else climbed onto the wrong one. He saw such a quantity of things that it was as if he no longer saw anything. Little by little, he had to become accustomed, learn all over again from the beginning what was pointless to look at and what was necessary.

The women he encountered in the street, who before had been reduced for him to impalpable, blurred shadows, he could now see in all the precise interplay of voids and solids that their bodies make as they move inside their dresses, and could judge the freshness of the skin and the warmth contained in their gaze, and it seemed to him he was not only seeing them but already actually possessing them. He might be walking along without his glasses (he didn't wear them all the time, to avoid tiring his eyes unnecessarily; only if he had to look into the distance) and there, ahead of him on the sidewalk, a bright-colored dress would be outlined. With a now automatic movement, Amilcare would promptly take his glasses from his pocket and slip them onto his nose. This indiscriminate covetousness of sensations was often punished: maybe the woman proved a hag. Amilcare Carruga became more cautious. And at times an approaching woman might seem to him, from her colors, her walk, too humble, insignificant, not worth taking into consideration, and he wouldn't put on his glasses; but then, when they passed each other close, he realized that, on the contrary, there was something about her that attracted him strongly, God knows what, and at that moment he seemed to catch a look of hers, as if of expectation, perhaps a look that she had trained on him at his first appearance and he hadn't been aware of it. But by now it was too late: she had vanished at the intersection, climbed into the bus, was far away beyond the traffic light, and he wouldn't be able to recognize her another time. And so, through his need for eyeglasses, he was slowly learning how to live.

But the newest world his glasses opened up to him was that of the night. The night city, formerly shrouded in shapeless clouds of darkness and colored glows, now revealed precise divisions, prominences, perspectives; the lights had specific borders, the neon signs once immersed in a vague halo now could be read letter by letter. The beautiful thing about night was, however, that the margin of haziness his lenses dispelled in daylight, here remained: Amilcare Carruga would feel impelled to put his glasses on, then realized he was already wearing them. The sense of fullness never equaled the drive of insatisfaction; darkness was a bottomless humus in which he never tired of digging. In the streets, above the houses spotted with yellow windows, square at last, he raised his eyes toward the starry sky: and he discovered that the stars were not splattered against the ground of the sky like broken eggs, but were very sharp jabs of light that opened up infinite distances around themselves.

This new concern with the reality of the external world was connected with his worries about what he himself was, also inspired by the use of eyeglasses. Amilcare Carruga didn't attach much importance to himself; however, as sometimes happens with the most unassuming of people, he was greatly attached to his way of being. Now, to pass from the category of men without glasses to that of men with glasses seems nothing, but it is a very big leap. For example: when someone who doesn't know you is trying to describe you, the first thing he says is "He wears glasses"; so that accessory detail, which two weeks earlier was completely unknown to you, becomes your prime attribute, is identified with your very existence. To Amilcare—foolishly, if you like—becoming all at once someone who "wears glasses" was a bit irritating. But that wasn't the real trouble: it was that once you begin to suspect that everything concerning you is purely casual, subject to transformation, and that you could be completely different and it wouldn't matter at all, then, following this line of reasoning, you come to think it's all the same whether you exist or don't exist, and from this notion to despair is only a brief step. Therefore Amilcare, when he had to select a kind of frame, instinctively chose some fine, very understated earpieces, just a pair of thin silver hooks, to hold the naked lenses and connect them over the nose with a little bridge. But after a while, he realized he wasn't happy: if he inadvertently caught sight of himself in the mirror with his glasses on, he felt a keen dislike for his face, as if it were the typical face of a category of persons alien to him. It was precisely those glasses, so discreet, light, almost feminine, that made him look more than ever like "a man who wears glasses," one who had never done anything in his whole life but wear glasses, so that you now no longer even notice he wears them. They were becoming part of his physiognomy, those glasses, blending with his features, and so they were diminishing every natural contrast between what was his face—an ordinary face, but still a face—and what was an extraneous object, an industrial product.

He didn't love them, and so it wasn't long before they fell and broke. He bought another pair. This time his choice took the opposite direction: he selected a pair of black plastic frames an inch thick, with hinged corners that stuck out from the cheekbones like a horse's blinders, side pieces heavy enough to bend the ear. They were a kind of mask that hid half his face, but behind them he felt like himself: there was no doubt that he was one thing and the glasses another, completely separate; it was clear he was wearing glasses only incidentally and, without glasses, he was an entirely different man. Once again—insofar as his nature allowed it—he was happy.

In that period he happened to go to V. on business. The city of V. was Amilcare Carruga's birthplace, and there he had spent all his youth. He had left it, however, ten years before, and his trips back had become more and more brief and sporadic; several years had gone by now since he last set foot there. You know how it is when you move away from a place where you've lived a long time: returning at long intervals, you feel disoriented; it seems that those sidewalks, those friends, those conversations in the café either must be everything or can no longer be anything; either you follow them day by day or else you are no longer able to participate in them, and the thought of reappearing after too long a time inspires a kind of remorse, and you dismiss it. And so Amilcare had gradually stopped seeking occasions for going back to V.; then, if occasions did arise, he let them pass; and in the end he actually avoided them. But in recent times, in this negative attitude toward his native city, there had been, beyond the motive just defined, also that sense of general disaffection that had come over him, which he had subsequently identified with the worsening of his nearsightedness. So now, finding himself in a new frame of mind thanks to the glasses, the first time a chance to go to V. presented itself, he seized it promptly, and went.

V. appeared to him in a totally different light from the last few times he had been there. But not because of its changes: true, the city had changed a great deal, new buildings everywhere, shops and cafés and movie theaters all different from before, the younger generation all strangers, and the traffic twice what it had been. All this newness, however, only underlined and made more recognizable what was old; in short, Amilcare Carruga managed for the first time to see the city again with the eyes of his boyhood, as if he had left it the day before. Thanks to his glasses he saw a host of insignificant details, a certain window, for example, a certain railing; or, rather, he was conscious of seeing them, of distinguishing them from all the rest, whereas in the past he had merely seen them. To say nothing of the faces: a news vendor, a lawyer, some having aged, others still the same. Amilcare Carruga no longer had any real relatives in V., and his group of close friends had also dispersed long since. He did, however, have endless acquaintances: nothing else would have been possible in a city so small—as it had been in the days when he lived there—that, practically speaking, everybody knew everybody else, at least by sight. Now the population had grown a lot, here too—as everywhere in the well-to-do cities of the North—there had been a certain influx of Southerners, and the majority of the faces Amilcare encountered belonged to strangers. But for this very reason he enjoyed the satisfaction of recognizing at first glance the old inhabitants, and he recalled episodes, connections, nicknames.

V. was one of those provincial cities where the tradition of an evening stroll along the main street still obtained; and in that, nothing had changed from Amilcare's day to the present. As always happens in these cases, one of the sidewalks was crammed with a steady flow of people; the other sidewalk less so. In their day, Amilcare and his friends, out of a kind of anticonformism, had always walked on the less popular sidewalk, from there casting glances and greetings and quips at the girls going by on the other. Now he felt as he had then, indeed even more excited, and he set off along his old sidewalk, looking at all the people who passed. Encountering familiar people this time didn't make him uneasy: it amused him, and he hastened to greet them. With some of them he would also have liked to stop and exchange a few words, but the main street of V. had sidewalks so narrow that the crowd of people kept shoving you forward, and, what's more, the traffic of vehicles was now so much increased that you could no longer, as in the past, walk a bit in the middle of the street and cross it whenever you chose. In short, the stroll proceeded either too rushed or too slow, with no freedom of movement. Amilcare had to follow the current or struggle against it; and when he saw a familiar face he barely had time to wave a greeting before it vanished, and he could never be sure whether he had been seen or not.

Thus he ran into Corrado Strazza, his classmate and billiards companion for many years. Amilcare smiled at him and waved broadly. Corrado Strazza came forward, his gaze on him, but it was as if that gaze went right through him, and Corrado continued on his way. Was it possible he hadn't recognized Amilcare? Time had gone by, but Amilcare Carruga knew very well he hadn't changed much; so far he had warded off a paunch, as he had baldness, and his features had not been greatly altered. Here came Professor Cavanna. Amilcare gave him a deferential greeting, a little bow. At first the professor started to respond to it, instinctively, but then he stopped and looked around, as if seeking someone else. Professor Cavanna, who was famous for his visual memory! Because of all his many classes, he remembered faces and first and last names and even semester grades. Finally Ciccio Corba, the coach of the football team, returned Amilcare's greeting. But immediately afterward he blinked and began to whistle, as if realizing he had intercepted by mistake the greeting of a stranger, addressed to God knows what other person.

Amilcare became aware that nobody would recognize him. The eyeglasses that made the rest of the world visible to him, those eyeglasses in their enormous black frames, made him invisible. Who would ever think that behind that sort of mask there was actually Amilcare Carruga, so long absent from V., whom no one was expecting to run into at any moment? He had barely managed to formulate these conclusions in his mind when Isa Maria Bietti appeared. She was with a girl friend, strolling and looking in shopwindows; Amilcare blocked her way and was about to cry "Isa Maria!" but his voice was paralyzed in his throat; Isa Maria Bietti pushed him aside with her elbow, said to her friend, "The way people behave nowadays . . . ," and went on.

Not even Isa Maria Bietti had recognized him. He understood all of a sudden that it was only because of Isa Maria Bietti that he had come back, just as it was only because of Isa Maria Bietti that he had decided to leave V. and had stayed away so many years; everything, everything in his life and everything in the world, was only because of Isa Maria Bietti; and now finally he saw her again, their eyes met and Isa Maria Bietti didn't recognize him. In his great emotion, he hadn't noticed if she had changed, grown fat, aged, if she was attractive as ever, or less or more—he had seen nothing except that she was Isa Maria Bietti and that Isa Maria Bietti hadn't seen him.

He had reached the end of the stretch of the street frequented in the evening stroll. Here, at the corner with the ice-cream parlor, or a block farther on, at the newsstand, the people turned around and headed back along the sidewalk in the opposite direction. Amilcare Carruga also turned. He had taken off his glasses. Now the world had become once more that insipid cloud and he groped, groped with his eyes widened, and could bring nothing to the surface. Not that he didn't succeed in recognizing anyone: in the better-lighted places he was always within a hair's breadth of identifying a face or two, but a shadow of doubt that perhaps this wasn't the person he thought always remained, and anyway, who it was or wasn't mattered little to him after all. Someone nodded, waved; this greeting might actually have been for him, but Amilcare couldn't quite tell who the person was. Another pair, too, greeted him as they went by; he was about to respond, but had no idea who they were. From the opposite sidewalk, one shouted a "*Ciao, Carrù!*" to him. To judge by the voice, it might have been a man named Stelvi. To his satisfaction, Amilcare realized they recognized him, they remembered him. The satisfaction was relative, because he couldn't even see them, or else couldn't manage to recognize them; they were persons who became confused in his memory, one with another, persons who basically were of little importance to him. "Good evening!" he said every so often, when he noticed a wave, a movement of the head. There, the one who had just greeted him must have been Bellintusi or Carretti, or Strazza. If it was Strazza, Amilcare would have liked perhaps to stop a moment with him and talk. But by now he had returned the greeting rather hastily; and, when he thought about it, it seemed natural that their relations should be like this, conventional and hurried greetings.

His looking around, however, clearly had one purpose: to track down Isa Maria Bietti. She was wearing a red coat, so she could be sighted at a distance. For a while Amilcare followed a red coat, but when he managed to pass it he saw that it wasn't she, and meanwhile those other two red coats had gone past in the other direction. That year medium-weight red coats were all the fashion. Earlier, for example, in the same coat, he had seen Gigina, the one from the tobacco shop. Now he began to suspect that it hadn't been Gigina from the tobacco shop but had really been Isa Maria Bietti! But how was it possible to mistake Isa Maria for Gigina? Amilcare retraced his steps to make sure. He came upon Gigina; this was she, no doubt about it. But if she was now coming this way, she couldn't have covered the whole distance; or had she made a shorter circuit? He was completely at sea. If Isa Maria had greeted him and he had responded coldly, his whole journey, all his waiting, all those years had gone by in vain. Amilcare went back and forth along those sidewalks, sometimes putting on his glasses, sometimes taking them off, sometimes greeting everyone and sometimes receiving the greetings of foggy, anonymous ghosts.

Beyond the other extreme of the stroll, the street continued and was soon beyond the city limits. There was a row of trees, a ditch, a hedge and the fields. In his day, you came out here in the evening with your girl on your arm, if you had a girl; or else, if you were alone, you came here to be even more alone, to sit on a bench and listen to the crickets sing. Amilcare Carruga went on in that direction; now the city extended a bit farther, but not much. There was the bench, the ditch, the crickets, as before. Amilcare Carruga sat down. Of that whole landscape the night left only some great swaths of shadow. Whether he put on or took off his eyeglasses here, it was really all the same. Amilcare Carruga realized that perhaps the thrill of his new glasses had been the last of his life, and now it was over.

THE ADVENTURE OF A POET

The little island had a high, rocky shoreline. On it grew the thick, low scrub, the vegetation that survives by the sea. Gulls flew in the sky. It was a small island near the coast, deserted, uncultivated: in half an hour you could circle it in a rowboat, or in a rubber dinghy like the one the approaching couple had, the man calmly paddling, the woman stretched out, taking the sun. As they came nearer, the man listened intently.

"What do you hear?" she asked.

"Silence," he said. "Islands have a silence you can hear."

In fact, every silence consists of the network of minuscule sounds that enfolds it: the silence of the island was distinct from that of the calm sea surrounding it because it was pervaded by a vegetable rustling, the calls of birds, or a sudden whirr of wings.

Down below the rock, the water, without a ripple these days, was a sharp, limpid blue, penetrated to its depths by the sun's rays. In the cliff faces the mouths of grottoes opened, and the couple in the rubber boat were going lazily to explore them.

It was a coast in the South, still hardly affected by tourism, and these two were bathers who came from elsewhere. He was one Usnelli, a fairly well known poet; she, Delia H., a very beautiful woman.

Delia was an admirer of the South, passionate, even fanatical, and, lying in the boat, she talked with constant ecstasy about everything she was seeing, and perhaps also with a hint of hostility toward Usnelli, who was new to those places and, it seemed to her, did not share her enthusiasm as much as he should have.

"Wait," Usnelli said, "wait."

"Wait for what?" she said. "What could be more beautiful than this?"

He, distrustful (by nature and through his literary education) of emotions and words already the property of others, accustomed more to discovering hidden and spurious beauties than those that were evident and indisputable, was still nervous and tense. Happiness, for Usnelli, was a suspended condition, to be lived holding your breath. Ever since he began loving Delia, he had seen his cautious, sparing relationship with the world endangered; but he wished to renounce nothing, either of himself or of the happiness that opened before him. Now he was on guard, as if every degree of perfection that nature achieved around him—a decanting of the blue of the water, a languishing of the coast's green into gray, the glint of a fish's fin at the very spot where the sea's expanse was smoothest—were only heralding another, higher, degree, and so on to the point where the invisible line of the horizon would part like an oyster revealing all of a sudden a different planet or a new word.

They entered a grotto. It began spaciously, like an interior lake of pale green, under a broad vault of rock. Farther on, it narrowed to a dark passage. The man with the paddle turned the dinghy around to enjoy the various effects of the light. The light from outside, through the jagged aperture, dazzled with colors made more vivid by the contrast. The water there sparkled, and the shafts of light ricocheted upward, in conflict with the soft shadows that spread from the rear. Reflections and flashes communicated to the rock walls and the vault the instability of the water.

"Here you understand the gods," the woman said.

"Hum," Usnelli said. He was nervous. His mind, accustomed to translating sensations into words, was now helpless, unable to formulate a single one.

They went farther in. The dinghy passed a shoal, a hump of rock at the level of the water; now the dinghy floated among rare glints that appeared and disappeared at every stroke of the paddle, the rest was dense shadow; the paddle now and then struck a wall. Delia, looking back, saw the blue orb of the open sky constantly change outline.

"A crab! Huge! Over there!" she cried, sitting up.

". . . ab! . . . ere!" the echo sounded.

"The echo!" she said, pleased, and started shouting words under those grim vaults: invocations, lines of verse.

"You, too! You shout, too! Make a wish!" she said to Usnelli.

"Hoooo . . ." Usnelli shouted. "Heeey . . . Echoooo . . ."

Now and then the boat scraped. The darkness was deeper.

"I'm afraid. God knows what animals . . ."

"We can still get through."

Usnelli realized that he was heading for the darkness like a fish of the depths who flees sunlit water.

"I'm afraid; let's go back," she insisted.

To him, too, basically, any taste for the horrid was alien. He paddled backward. As they returned to where the cavern broadened, the sea became cobalt.

"Are there any octopuses?" Delia asked.

"You'd see them. The water's so clear."

"I'll have a swim, then."

She slipped over the side of the dinghy, let go, swam in that underground lake, and her body at times seemed white (as if that light stripped it of any color of its own) and at times as blue as that screen of water.

Usnelli had stopped rowing; he was still holding his breath. For him, being in love with Delia had always been like this, as in the mirror of this cavern: in a world beyond words. For that matter, in all his poems he had never written a verse of love: not one.

"Come closer," Delia said. As she swam, she had taken off the scrap of clothing covering her bosom; she threw it into the dinghy. "Just a minute." She also undid the piece of cloth tied at her hips and handed it to Usnelli.

Now she was naked. The whiter skin of her bosom and hips was hardly distinct, because her whole person gave off that pale-blue glow, like a medusa. She was swimming on one side, with a lazy movement, her head (the expression firm, almost ironic, a statue's) just out of the water, and at times the curve of a shoulder and the soft line of an extended arm. The other arm, in caressing strokes, covered and revealed the high bosom, taut at its tips. Her legs barely struck the water, supporting the smooth belly, marked by the navel like a faint print on the sand, and the star as of some mollusk. The sun's rays, reflected underwater, grazed her, making a kind of garment for her, or stripping her all over again.